To Suzanne and Mace,

BATTLES ON
LORD'S CREEK

Shannon O'Barr Sausville

Shannon

Many thanks to Mary Beth McGee for her commentary on the draft text.

Cover Photographs Copyright © 2019 Edward Sausville
The back cover photograph was taken with
a classic medium format twin lens Rolleiflex.
All rights reserved.

Cover Design Shannon O'Barr Sausville
All rights reserved.

LARKINGTON COVE BOOKS

ISBN-13: 978-0-578-53284-4
ISBN-10: 0-578-53284-0

For every parent of a veteran

PROLOGUE

CRITICAL JUNCTURE

MARCH 2015

"This thief is clever, very clever," Siobhan thought to herself as she took off her drugstore reading glasses, pushed an errant lock of her auburn hair back behind her ear, and looked up from her laptop on the cafeteria table in the break room at the nursing home and rehab center where she was conducting a pharmacy audit.

Siobhan, a part-time pharmacist, rotates through all the facilities of a health care system consisting of surgery and orthopedic rehab centers, nursing homes and assisted living facilities dotted around the Western Shore of the Chesapeake Bay. Based on her seniority and experience, she not only performs the routine tasks of all pharmacists as needed, but also is often called upon to audit other pharmacists' records at the facilities.

Siobhan thinks back fondly to the departed world where internal audits were no more than doing inventory and assuring compliance with controlled substances regulations. Now, however, she can't open her work e-mail without seeing a news item about how employee theft and diversion of opioids are responsible for the loss of hundreds of millions of dollars and hundreds of thousands of doses per year from health care facilities. Siobhan used to believe that with all of their professional pride and knowledge of the dangers of opioid overdoses that her colleagues would be above theft. Unfortunately, as audit after audit showed, the nurses, doctors, pharmacists and techs with whom she worked were just as vulnerable to opioid diversion, overprescribing and misuse as the rest of the country.

And Siobhan had just uncovered a cleverly disguised series of thefts. Siobhan had been working as a pharmacist for more than twenty-five years and performing audits for at least half of that time. She had learned over those years that most employee thefts were absurdly obvious. For instance, an employee would outright steal pills from a dispensary at a time when that employee was the only one whose pass key accessed the dispensary. Or even more obviously, an employee would steal medicine off the patient's over-bed table, only to be turned in by the patient who was not quite as unconscious as the employee had believed.

This thief, however, was smart. This thief knew the failings and weaknesses of the facility's paperwork and electronic records trails, and the thief had exploited several of them to hide the thefts. A less experienced auditor probably would have missed the discrepancies or chalked them up to honest mistakes or patient noncompliance.

Siobhan was not convinced that the government's and therefore her upper management's push to switch to all electronic health records was as much a panacea as they made it out to be, and she was cynical enough to see that the financial incentives offered by the federal government were the real driver behind her management's push to computerize. But despite their headlong push to convert to a fully electronic system, the management had not invested in a full-time on-site information technology specialist at this small facility; therefore every time the network connection had a problem, the staff reverted to the backup paper system while they waited for IT central to fix the issue. In the case of these thefts, if this facility hadn't had to revert to its backup paper system so often, the pilferer would not have been able to exploit the inherent opportunity for mistakes caused by switching back and forth between paper and electronic records.

Computer issues aside, several months ago, Siobhan had had an inkling that an employee was exploiting the facility's failure to inventory the pills patients brought with them when they transferred from the hospital. She had made a strong suggestion to the management at that time to implement controls to close that loophole, and they had followed her advice. This thief, however, had been clever or lucky enough not to get caught in that snare and had merely discovered other avenues.

When Siobhan had first started working as a pharmacist, a larcenous employee would have been summarily fired. Now, an employee caught purloining pills was granted the opportunity to confidentially enter a therapy program as long as the employee admitted to having a problem prior to being drug tested.

And since this particular thief was Siobhan's friend, neighbor and dog sitter Linda, Siobhan sincerely hoped Linda could get herself clean. Siobhan lives in a tightknit waterfront community on the Western Shore of the Chesapeake Bay. She had grown up in the neighborhood, moved away for college, and returned permanently when her mother became ill. Since her mother's death, Siobhan had developed cherished friendships with her neighbors, many of whom Siobhan had met walking her dogs in the community park or along the waterline. Linda was one such friend, and Siobhan had been friends with Linda long enough to have seen her wearing a brace, limping before and after knee replacement surgery. Siobhan was well aware that most middle-class working professionals did not set out to become opioid addicts. They started out by receiving valid prescriptions for legitimate medical conditions, but then found that they couldn't back off the pills as easily as they had started them; Linda likely fell into this category.

However, friend or no, Siobhan would not shirk her professional responsibility to inform the management of what she had found, as well as the limitations of the evidence. Although Siobhan was personally sure that only Linda in that small facility was capable of pulling off all of these thefts, Siobhan knew that the evidence wasn't enough to prove the identity of the thief or even to definitively prove that a single person was responsible for all the thefts; she would not take the professional risk of accusing someone of a series of infractions of this magnitude without irrefutable proof. Siobhan would simply present the management with the evidence she found, make recommendations as to how to prevent future thefts through better inventory control and recordkeeping practices, and leave it to the management to intervene with its staff. Siobhan was therefore certain that Linda would at least be interviewed by management and hopefully would be forced to come face to face with her opioid problem.

Siobhan finished up the day going back through older records now that she knew what to look for, well aware that when she met with the facility director first thing the next morning, she would need hard data on when the problem started.

Siobhan went home to her cottage on an estuary of the Chesapeake Bay with a heavy heart. Siobhan did not pass moral judgments on people who developed pill problems, having had a mother who formed a lifelong relationship with Valium after Siobhan's brother died in a boating accident. However, Siobhan's mother had not been a nurse like Linda, making medical judgments that could affect other people's health while under the influence. Siobhan had butterflies in her stomach as she leashed up her two chocolate labs for their daily visit to the community waterfront park, where she often ran into Linda with her golden retriever, uncertain whether she could keep a poker face if she did.

No sooner had Siobhan unleashed her two labs to chase geese than Linda appeared at the far end of the park with her dog. Linda had been watching Siobhan's dogs for her whenever she was out of town since Siobhan first got her dogs as pups. No way could she pretend not to see Linda or even act as if she was just about done as she was sure Linda had seen her unhooking the dogs. Instead she waved cheerily and bent down to retie her shoelaces, giving herself extra time.

As the two women walked toward each other across the field, Linda tripped on a rough patch and took the last few steps toward Siobhan with a slight limp.

"Are you OK?" Siobhan asked with real concern.

"Sorta kinda," Linda replied. "Remember how I had my right knee replaced not that long ago, as a legacy of my high school field hockey career." Siobhan nodded and Linda continued, "Well, I'm afraid I'm heading the same way with my left knee now. I was hoping I'd never have to go through that again, but I took the day off to see my orthopedist."

Having completed her audit, Siobhan was fairly certain that Linda's pill problems had started with her first knee replacement, as Siobhan had found no evidence of the widespread patterns of thefts before. Siobhan could not bring herself to believe that someone intelligent enough to disguise her thefts as cleverly as Linda would have started out popping pain pills for the weekend fun of it. Saying none of this, Siobhan merely responded, "Oh, no fun. I didn't notice you around today when I was auditing."

The women watched the dogs running around the field for a few minutes in silence. Siobhan whistled at her two, whistled again, and when her two labs finally came over to her after the third whistle, she hooked the leashes back on. Resolving her inner conflict between her professional responsibility and her friend, Siobhan looked Linda straight in the face before they both headed off. Calmly but resolutely, Siobhan said, "Linda, I found the thefts." She continued to stare meaningfully at Linda.

Linda started to respond, but when Siobhan kept staring at her, Linda stopped whatever she had been planning to say, mouth still open. The color drained a bit from her face.

"I can't prove who the thief is, even though I myself am certain, but I can prove that there have been thefts. I have to give my report of everything I can prove to management in the morning. Just thought you should know."

Siobhan started to head home with her labs. As she stepped onto the asphalt, she heard Linda weakly croak, "Thanks." Siobhan decided she had committed no major breach. She would still meet with the facility director first thing in the morning and would hold nothing back from the findings she could prove. If Linda could salvage anything from hearing that the thefts had been discovered between now and opening of business tomorrow, God bless her.

* * * * *

Linda hurried Goldy home as quickly as she could once Siobhan headed across the field. She perfunctorily wiped off Goldy's feet and let the dog in the house. She entered the house, shut the front door and leaned her back against it. A sob escaped her throat. Thank God her son Matt wasn't home. Once that single sob got out, Linda couldn't stop. She stood with her back against the front door and the tears poured. She had been denying for months that she had a problem with pills, and she had steadfastly refused to consider that she might be physically dependent or addicted or both. Self-delusion is an amazing phenomenon. She had truly convinced herself that she wasn't stealing pills from her patients or from her work. Where had this all started? How could she have reached this point? Was it the knee surgery? Or was it further back, when Matt had come home from the Army? But she hadn't had the pills until the surgery. Was she using the stress of dealing with a son with post-traumatic stress disorder as an excuse for allowing herself to lose control of the pain pills following the surgery? Dammit, she hadn't even wanted the pain pills, had sworn she would recover from the surgery with nothing more than ibuprofen. Actually, she hadn't wanted the surgery itself; she had tried to get by with only physical therapy and cortisone shots. She was only a handful of years away from an early retirement, had a solid job that paid all her bills, a twin sister who was her best friend, a great house on Lord's Creek only a few miles from the Chesapeake Bay. And now, she was going to have to go to war not to lose it all because of the damned pain pills.

As she leaned against the door and was honest with herself for the first time in years, she saw that the elements of her fall had been assembling themselves for several years before she took that first pain pill.

PART ONE

MOUNTING PRESSURES

CHAPTER ONE

Linda went to visit her son Matt in North Carolina not long after his discharge from the Army. He had moved in with his girlfriend Casey, whom he had been dating since before his deployments to Iraq and Afghanistan. When Linda got into town Friday afternoon she drove first to her basic but spotlessly clean chain hotel to get settled for her weekend stay. On her visit to their apartment later that afternoon, Matt and Casey showed her their small living quarters over Casey's parents' garage. They then descended to the living room of her parents' house to chat because the apartment was too cramped to hold even an extra chair.

Casey was the energetic, athletic type to whom Matt had always gravitated. Casey's father, however, reclined lifelessly on the couch the entire time that Linda was there. He perfunctorily shook Linda's hand when Casey introduced them, but he continued to watch ESPN while Matt, Casey and Linda tried to make conversation. After about twenty minutes of this, Linda suggested that they go out for an early dinner somewhere. She politely offered to include Casey's parents, but her father waved them off. Casey's mother never appeared while Linda was in the house.

Casey drove them to a sports pub in the parking lot of a local mall. As she was driving, Casey apologized, "Sorry about my Dad, Mrs. MacDermott, he was in a car accident a few months ago and he isn't moving around too well. But Matt here keeps him company watching ESPN."

Linda wondered why Casey had decided to lamely disguise a dig at Matt under an apology about her father. And from the edema Linda had seen on Casey's father's ankles where his sweatpants had crept up, the whiskers that were far more than one day's worth of growth, and the prescription bottles on the end table behind his head, Linda suspected there was more to Casey's father's indolence than a recent car accident. Her son's girlfriend's father was not her problem though.

The sports pub was noisy with twenty-somethings, many of whom had military haircuts, standing or sitting at the bar watching eight or nine college football games at once. While waiting for the hostess, Matt leaned against the door jamb and shifted uneasily from foot to foot. When the hostess arrived to seat them, Linda said, "Three, please."

The hostess pulled three menus out from the podium and led them to a table in the middle of the main dining room.

Matt immediately barked, "Not here. Not in the middle of the room. We need to sit against a wall."

The hostess raised her eyebrows at Matt, but then shrugged and led them to a booth at the far corner of the dining room.

Casey snorted as the hostess walked off, "Ah yes, we can't let anyone sneak up behind us at a sports bar."

Since Linda wasn't sure what Casey's remark was about, she decided to reset the conversation, "This looks like a popular hangout. Do y'all come here a lot?"

"I wish," answered Casey. "I keep trying to get Matt out here with some of the guys from his company, but he'd rather eat leftover spaghetti."

Linda thought Casey's remark was yet another odd comment to make to her boyfriend's mother.

Matt was obviously displeased and snapped, "I spent months eating MREs and crappy Army food with those guys, I don't have to eat with them now that I'm home. Besides, I talk to them all the time."

Casey quickly retorted, "Posting comments about how awful it was in Iran on Facebook is not talking to the guys."

Linda could see from the flush on his face that Matt was pissed. "We were in Iraq. At least get the country right." Linda was relieved that the waitress came up to the table with their drinks at that exact moment.

On the following morning, Matt and Casey weren't ready to go until almost lunch time, leaving Linda to amuse herself in her hotel all morning. Linda was relieved to see some signs of enthusiasm from Matt as he pointed out deer poop and bird nests while they walked along a nature trail around a lake at a local park in the afternoon, but at dinner at another noisy restaurant of Casey's choice Matt clammed up while Casey babbled.

The forecast for Sunday was heavy rain all day. All three of them were relieved when Linda suggested that in lieu of a morning visit she would instead start driving early to avoid the inevitably bad traffic and get home in time to rest up before an early shift Monday morning.

Linda stewed the whole drive home about how changed Matt was. She felt as if the Matt she visited in North Carolina when he returned home from his second deployment in 2007 was a completely different human being.

* * * * *

When Linda arrived to visit Matt in the spring of 2007, he was playing basketball at a court outside his base housing with a group of men as she pulled up. Matt jogged over and grabbed her in a bear hug as she got out of the car, "I'm glad you came down, Mom. I've missed you."

A fireplug of a young Latino interjected, "See, we knew he was a Momma's boy."

Matt put Linda down, "Mom, this is our grenadier Ricardo, but we all call him Rico. Best teammate anyone could ever have." Linda shook Rico's hand.

Another man, a tall muscular African-American, stuck his hand out toward Linda, "Mrs. MacDermott, I'm Sergeant Wilson, Matt's squad leader. Your son is the finest marksman I've ever been deployed with. What did you and your husband feed this boy to make his eyesight so good?"

"I'm afraid Matt's father probably deserves most of the credit for Matt's shooting skills," Linda demurred.

"Well, whatever you all did, it worked. I'd have him in the field with me any day."

"As a mother, I'm hoping that another deployment won't be necessary for any of you," Linda rejoined.

"Not for me anyway. My wife just had our third. She threatened to kill me if I re-upped my contract and left her at home with three kids." The sergeant shook Linda's hand again and then politely excused himself.

"So Matt, I'm starving after the drive. Where can we get something to eat?" Linda inquired.

Matt asked, "Can we bring Rico? And also, I promised Casey we'd pick her up. You remember Casey, right?"

At a local pizza joint where one could make endless trips to a buffet counter with a wide variety of pies, Linda was stunned by the amount of pizza that Matt and Rico were able to put away. The place was obviously a favorite for the local military, and Linda was astonished that the place could stay in business if all the soldiers had the appetite that Matt and Rico did. Each time Matt got up to grab another slice of pizza or refill his drink from the soda fountain, at least three soldiers intercepted him on the way with comments like: "Looks like eagle eyes has spotted another piece of pizza" or "Getting more carrots from the salad bar to keep those eyes sharp." Matt smiled modestly at their comments.

While Matt and Rico continued to gorge, Linda listened as Casey described the Pilates and yoga classes that she was teaching at the local gym, "Of course, I have to do classes or work out almost all day long to make up for all the food I eat around these two." Linda thought this an exaggeration as she had only seen Casey take down two slices of pizza, but she could appreciate the difficulty of being around two young men who could apparently consume as many calories as they wanted with no consequences. "The other guys call them the Mattrico duo and say that no food is safe anywhere near the two of them," Casey continued. "The local burger joint had some eat-'til-you-drop contest, and whoever ate the most didn't have to pay. Matt and Rico were the last two at the table. The restaurant finally agreed to give them both their meals free to stop losing all their food. Now these two insist on trying to outdo each other at every single meal."

Matt paused his consumption briefly to comment, "We drill hard. I need my strength. And besides, the food we got in Afghanistan was kinda weird. I missed pizza." Matt went back to the current slice of meatlover's on his plate.

"I think he missed pizza more than me," Casey joked.

"Well, I know he missed pizza more than his mother," Linda joined in. "Any suggestions on what we should do tomorrow?" Linda inquired of the table.

Casey piped in, "I have to teach three Pilates sessions tomorrow, so I'm out. I knew you were coming down, so I didn't ask for time off so you and Matt could spend time together."

"Rico and I should take you on the Cape Fear River Trail if you're up for it Mom," Matt suggested. Linda was not surprised that Matt suggested an outdoor activity. The next day though Linda was surprised that she felt a stiffness in her right knee at the end of the third mile. She took a couple ibuprofen, which completely took care of the pain, and she thought no more about it.

They picked up Casey and ate dinner that night at the burger joint of eating contest fame. The hostess smiled at the group as they entered, "Here's the duo who almost put us out of business."

"Do you have an all-you-can-eat special tonight," Matt asked with a grin.

"No, the owner banned those after you and your buddy did us in," the hostess quipped as she led them to a table.

After dinner, Matt requested that Linda drop him off with Casey without the slightest hint of sheepishness, "Casey will get me back to the base before it gets too late. Do you mind dropping Rico off though?" Rico gave the couple a sly smile as they got out of the car. He chatted politely with Linda about his hometown on the way to base.

Casey must have dropped Matt off as promised because he was at his base housing when Linda picked him up for breakfast. Linda ate a bowl of oatmeal with fruit while Matt polished off three eggs, half a pig's worth of bacon and a stack of pancakes. "Did I underfeed you as a child or something," Linda teased him.

Matt didn't answer, only forked in another mouthful of pancakes. "Everything seems to be going really well for you here, though, and you're not putting on extra weight no matter how much you eat so you must be keeping busy," Linda continued.

"I love it here. Iraq and Afghanistan were tough, but we've got such a good team, and we haven't seen any of the really bad stuff that other guys have. And with Sergeant Wilson headed out, that's one more sergeant position open. I've got enough time in for a promotion, but there's still two guys who've got more time in grade than me who haven't made sergeant yet. One of them may not be re-upping his contract though."

"Well, you deserve to make sergeant. I'm sure you'll get it as soon as there's an opening," Linda responded.

Linda dropped him off after breakfast and headed home. She contentedly sang along to oldies the whole way home.

* * * * *

Now in 2009, Linda chewed over Matt's changed condition for the six-plus-hour car ride, and still had reached no satisfactory conclusions when she reached home. She shared her worries about Matt with her twin sister Laurie, "He's way too quiet except for when Casey pisses him off, and that's not like Matt. And Casey isn't going to put up with him for long if he stays like this. You can tell she's a social girl, wants to hang out with everyone in the bar. When I was down there back in 2007, she soaked up every bit of the attention Matt and his teammate Rico got."

"What do you think's going on?" Laurie asked.

Linda mused, "It could certainly be depression. I knew something had changed after his concussion. Before that, when I talked to him he couldn't get enough of Army life. But I only heard from him a handful of times after he got out of the hospital and before he was sent back to the States and discharged. And when I did he would say he didn't think he'd be re-upping his contract, that he didn't want to be deployed again, didn't think he could take seeing how miserable 'these people over here' are. When he told me that back then, I was just happy to think he might not be deployed again, that I wouldn't have to worry about him anymore, but now when I think about it, maybe I should have seen it as the beginning signs of depression."

"You can't Monday morning quarterback this. Just because he said he was done with being in the Army doesn't mean that he was clinically depressed. People get tired of their jobs all the time without it meaning there's something wrong with them."

"You're right, of course, and even if I had guessed, there was nothing I could have done for him while he was in Iraq. I'll just have to keep an eye on him as best I can from Maryland."

Linda was not surprised when Matt moved home with all of his stuff a few months later, courtesy of a buddy whom he had cajoled into giving him a ride. Matt hadn't even called to inform her he was coming home. He just showed up in the kitchen with a large Army duffel bag and two dingy backpacks. Linda had been making a sandwich in the kitchen when he clambered through the door.

"Hey Mom," Matt greeted her from where he stood with his back pressed into the only corner of the kitchen not covered in cabinets, not even coming over to give her a hug.

"Hey yourself. I didn't know you were visiting," Linda noted. Matt was already turning to go up the stairs, and only then could Linda see how much stuff he was carrying.

"Not visiting," Matt mumbled as he went upstairs. Linda heard something that sounded like "not working out with Casey" as he continued to ascend.

Linda decided not to push for an explanation. She suspected that Casey had gotten tired of the lifeless Matt she had seen on her most recent trip to North Carolina, and she knew from having lived with Matt's father that if you poked a MacDermott male's pride asking questions, you weren't going to get anywhere.

"Want a sandwich?" she yelled up the stairs instead.

"Nah," she heard come floating down the stairs.

Linda had expected that Matt would eventually emerge from his room, but by the time she was heading up to bed he was still upstairs behind his closed bedroom door. She knew he was avoiding the third degree, and she decided it wasn't worth pushing him. If he had moved back in, she'd have plenty of time to find out what was going on.

She turned on the TV in her bedroom and nodded off during some banal show or other. She awoke to Matt's screaming. Linda had become so accustomed to living on her own that the sound of someone screaming in her house sent her heart rate soaring. She popped out of bed wondering in the fog of almost sleep who was in the house, then remembered it was Matt. She ran down the hall and threw open his bedroom door and turned on the light.

"Hey, knock it off," Matt complained.

"I heard you screaming. I was worried," Linda defended herself, then wondered why she was defending her actions in her own house.

"I had a nightmare. Have'em all the time since I got back," Matt admitted sullenly.

Linda switched gears into nurse voice, "I'm sorry to hear that. I didn't realize."

Matt stood up. He was wearing only a T-shirt and boxer shorts, and he quickly wrapped the worn twin comforter that had been on his bed since adolescence around himself and moved toward Linda.

"I'm gonna go watch TV. I won't be able to get back to sleep for a while."

Linda moved out of the doorway to let him pass.

"We got any beer here?" he asked as he moved toward the top of the stairs.

"I'm not sure. If we do, it's in the fridge."

Linda went back to bed and turned back on her own TV, which had shut itself off earlier via its sleep timer. When she had visited Matt in North Carolina a few months earlier she had seen the signs of clinical depression. The nightmares were something additional. Linda wondered if Matt was suffering from post-traumatic stress disorder as well, but in her half-doze she couldn't remember the diagnostic criteria. She knew she would have to very gently probe into whether he was getting any treatment. She guessed not.

Linda was grumpy when the alarm went off the morning after Matt's return, unaccustomed to having her sleep interrupted. Matt was asleep on the sofa bed in the sunporch. She made her coffee and unwrapped a pastry for her breakfast. She left a note on the kitchen table indicating when she'd be back from her shift.

When she returned home from a day at work made miserable by the electronic health record system going down, forcing her to write out paper charts and then having to rush to enter all the data when the system came up a half-hour before her shift was over, Matt was still on the sofa bed on the sunporch. Linda would have guessed that he hadn't moved at all that first day except for the case of Miller Lite in the can hogging the bottom half of the fridge. As a teenager Matt would never sit still inside the house for longer than it took to consume all the leftovers in the fridge and couldn't even be bothered to sit through an entire football game on Sunday. He had always been wandering the neighborhood, or out in the field with the dog, or cleaning his hunting gear out by the shed.

"Hey Mom, where's Caesar?" Matt called out from the sunporch.

Linda walked to the door of the sunroom and leaned on the door frame, "Oh honey, I'm sorry I hadn't told you. I had to put him down last week just before you came home. He had several strokes, couldn't even stand up straight. I couldn't let him suffer anymore. I wasn't sure whether to tell you over the phone or not. I thought it might be better to tell you in person. I'm sorry sweetie."

The German Shepherd Caesar had been brought home as a puppy when Matt was in middle school and was the only pet the family had had. When she found Caesar one morning obviously having had a serious stroke overnight, she was afraid she was going to have to enlist one of the neighbors to help lift him into the car in order to take him to the vet. To her relief, when she called the vet to tell them she needed to bring him in to be put down, they offered to send a vet and a tech out to take care of him in his own home without the trauma of a final trip to the vet, for an extra fee of course. She had considered calling Matt, but she had been worried about calling someone who was clinically depressed and telling him that she had put his childhood best friend to sleep. She had figured she would find a gentle way to break it to him, but then he moved back home with no warning.

"That sucks," Matt pouted. He increased the volume of the TV.

Once she had showered and changed out of her scrubs, Linda called her sister, "Hey, you off work?"

"Yeah, I just got home from my shift," Laurie worked as a nurse at the local hospital. "What's up?"

"I need to get out and have a drink. Can you meet up somewhere?"

"Sure. Where?" The sisters agreed to meet at a waterfront bar near the South River Bridge in a half-hour.

Linda had ordered cosmos for herself and Laurie before Laurie arrived. The bartender placed them on the bar as Laurie walked in.

"Perfect timing," Laurie grinned. The sisters clinked their glasses and took sips.

"Amen," Linda sighed.

"What's with you?" Laurie asked.

"Matt's moved back. Looks like his girlfriend threw him out."

"Yikes. What'd he say?"

"Absolutely nothing. He showed up with his duffel bag and marched right upstairs. Mumbled something about Casey."

Laurie took a big sip of her cosmo in sympathy, "Well, you said they didn't appear to be doing too well when you visited."

"Right. And then last night he woke up in the middle of the night screaming. According to him he does that all the time. He does other weird stuff too, like always having his back to a wall, never standing in the middle of a room, like he's afraid someone will sneak up on him. My best guess is a solid case of post-traumatic stress disorder."

"Ouch," Laurie said wincing. "Surprised you didn't take a cab here, so you could have a few of those." Laurie pointed at the martini glass in Linda's hands.

"I hadn't thought that far ahead. I was too focused on getting a drink and getting out of there."

"You said that he had a concussion and was hospitalized after the explosion. Does he have TBI or is it just PTSD or is it both?" Laurie asked.

Linda took a sip and thought about her sister's very pertinent question. As she recalled from some continuing education program she took in the past, traumatic brain injury or TBI is the result of a physical insult to the brain whereas post-traumatic stress disorder or PTSD arises from a non-physical exposure to trauma. PTSD is the more refined understanding of what used to be called "shell shock." Shell shock was first observed with enough frequency to be named as a medical condition in World War I. Linda didn't remember what treatments were available for either PTSD or TBI.

"Great question. When his squad mate Rico called me the day after the explosion, he said that Matt had been thrown backwards by the explosion and hit his head on a wall. So he definitely had a physical injury at one point. But whether he had the sort of injury that constitutes TBI, I don't know. And I don't know whether TBI is associated with nightmares years later. I kinda remember from some continuing education session at work that people can actually have both TBI and PTSD," Linda knew she was giving her sister a vague answer but she hadn't thought Matt's problems through yet.

"So, what are you going to do?" Laurie queried.

"What do you mean?"

"With Matt?"

"What can I do? He only got home yesterday after his girlfriend kicked him out. I can't throw him out of his home, and part of me is a little relieved that he's back in Maryland so I don't have to worry about how he's doing down in North Carolina. I'm going to try to get him to see a psychiatrist and maybe a neuro person if it's TBI. I'm sure he hasn't thought far enough ahead about what he wants to do with himself. And quite frankly, unless he gets some antidepressants or whatever the current treatments for PTSD or TBI are, he's not likely to be successful at getting a decent job. If he came home from Iraq missing a leg, I'd take him in and do what I could to help him. Why should it be any different because his brain is hurt, not his leg?"

"Easy, easy," Laurie soothed. "No need to defend yourself. You seemed a little frazzled. I just wanted to know what you had in mind."

"Oh, ignore me. I had gotten used to not having any smelly males in my house, be they human or canine. I'm allowed to be a little grumpy about having my space invaded. Guess I'll need to drink more," Linda held up her martini glass.

"Excellent decision. And it'll be warm enough soon to get out on the boat. You can leave Matt at home and we'll party on the boat."

"Cheers to that," Linda replied

CHAPTER TWO

Linda and her twin sister Laurie glory in being on their 33'
Grady-White cruiser whenever possible. On this particularly
gorgeous day, their boat is rafted-up in Harness Creek off the
South River, an estuary of the Chesapeake Bay. Harness Creek, as
always on a sunny July weekend, is filled with boats tied up to a
central heavily anchored boat, or rafted-up as the locals call it. The
rafted-up boaters don't even need to be acquainted to party
together, although the regulars at Harness Creek all recognize each
other. The only requirement is a desire to drink, swim and chill on
a boat deck for an afternoon.

Linda decided to switch to beer, already having had two
margaritas, grabbing a can from the small fridge in the galley. Linda
despises the tinny taste of beer in a can, but respects that glass is
taboo to avoid any chance of having a broken glass land in the
water where everyone is swimming. Linda had already turned away
from the fridge when she belatedly decided hydration was also in
order. She made a quick turn back to the fridge to grab a bottle of
water right as the boat rocked, causing her to lose her balance and
slam her right knee into the unyielding fixed bench next to the

galley table. The beer hit the ground and rolled to the far side of the cabin. Linda screamed in pain, "Oww, oww, oww." She grabbed the galley table and lowered herself onto the offending bench.

Laurie's voice traveled down the stairs into the cabin, "You OK down there? What happened?"

Linda replied, "I banged my knee on the blasted bench. I'm going to sit here for a minute or two until it stops smarting."

A few minutes later, the knee still stings and Linda can see the swelling beginning. "Shit," she cursed out loud. "I would have to hit my bad knee."

Laurie came down the stairs, "You must have done a number on that knee if you're still sitting there." She knelt down next to Linda's knee and gently examined the contusion.

Linda answered, "I was already worried about that knee. I mean I've had a low grade ache in both knees for years, but over the last couple months I've noticed this right knee's definitely getting worse. I'm putting all the strain on the left knee when I get out of a chair. You know all these news reports about the poor pro football players wanting compensation for their brain injuries. What about all us former high school field hockey phenoms who need knee replacements? Who's going to pay for them?"

Linda and Laurie had both been active field hockey players all through high school. Neither of them could count the times they had banged or strained their knees, showing up to practices and matches with ace bandages on one or both knees.

Laurie agreed, "You said it. Knee replacement is undoubtedly the most common surgery at our age. I've had three co-workers in the last year go out for surgery, and I'm sure my left one's going to have to be replaced eventually. Here, let's get some ice, and I'll help you up on deck. You can prop your leg up on one of the benches."

"Alright, thanks. I think I am going to need help. Thank God I don't have a shift at work until Monday night. Hopefully the swelling will go down before then." Even in the brief minutes that the two women had chatted, the knee had swollen further.

With Laurie's help Linda climbed out of the cabin and settled herself on one of the benches on the back of the boat with her right leg swung up. She placed a towel full of ice on the knee and turned to Laurie, "Any chance you feel sorry enough for me to grab me a beer and a water? I dropped my beer when I fell." She paused then added, "Fortunately, I hadn't opened the beer yet, so no alcohol was wasted."

"Well, thank God for that," Laurie joked. She emerged a minute later with two beers and two waters. The women sat on the back of the boat silently sipping their beers for a while. The couple rafted-up on the port side of the boat started undoing their lines. They called over to the two women, "Time for us to head home."

"See you next time," Laurie called back. The couple motored off, leaving a swath of open water.

Laurie queried Linda, "You think you can get in and out of the water with your knee? A swim would feel good right about now."

Linda responded, "Well, I'm sure I can get into the water. Whether I'll be able to get myself back in is another story, but I'm game to try. I suppose you can always tow me home on the raft."

On standing, Linda found that she couldn't put much weight at all on the knee. Contrary to her statement, getting down the stern ladder into the water was not easy. The water was worth the exertion though, with its temperature right around a perfect 80 degrees. She floated on her back with her leg suspended, and with no weight on it, she could almost pretend it didn't hurt.

Laurie brought their beers down, and they relaxed in the water until the cans were empty. Laurie sighed, "I suppose we should be getting back. You may not have a shift tomorrow, but I do. Can you get back up?"

"I hope so," Linda answered, but her first attempt failed miserably. She grasped the boat ladder with both hands, put her left foot up and lifted most of her weight out of the water. But when she put the right foot on the next rung, pain shot all the way up her thigh and down to her foot. The pain was so intense that she lost her grip on the ladder and fell back in the water.

Laurie looked around and yelled over to the boat rafted-up on the starboard side, "Hey Rob, you still over there?"

The Clint Black music drifting from the next boat was abruptly turned off, and a big dark-bearded man came out of the cabin of the adjacent boat with a beer in his hand, "Yup, what's up?"

"My sister hurt her knee, and she can't lift herself back in. Can you help?" Laurie asked hopefully.

"Sure thing." The man named Rob climbed down the stern ladder of his boat and flopped into the water. He paddled over to the sisters. "I'll push, you pull," he said to Laurie.

With Rob's assistance from below, and Laurie tugging from up top, Linda gracelessly rolled into the boat. Laurie lowered down a six-pack of beer to Rob as thanks. She pulled up the anchor, undid the lines tying her to Rob's boat and slowly maneuvered out of Harness Creek.

"Thank goodness for Rob," Linda commented.

"Yeah, he's a good guy," Laurie agreed. "He's the first one out here every weekend of the summer, and he always sets his anchor with dozens of feet of chain." Securely anchoring even one boat requires substantially more line than most people appreciate, approximately seven times the depth of the water, although having a large amount of chain rather than rope line can reduce the length a bit. To serve as a central anchoring point for a pile of boats requires more line than many people carry on their boats.

Linda settled herself back on the stern bench with another towel full of ice on her knee. Laurie observed, "You're not going to be able to drive home with that knee, you know."

"Oh God, you're right," Linda replied. "Can I borrow a couch? If it's not better in the morning, it's a good thing you're a nurse at the local hospital. You can drop me off at the ER on your way in. Man, I've been trying to baby this knee hoping I can avoid a replacement."

Laurie steered out into the South River, then into her creek off the South River, putting the twin engines in neutral once she had lined up with her lift, allowing the momentum and the tail wind to push her the rest of the way. When they had set out earlier in the day, Laurie had anticipated the approximate time of their return and lowered the lift to match the afternoon low tide. Now, she expertly pulled onto the boat lift in between the padded beams that would cradle the boat once out of the water. She hopped on the dock, lifted the plastic cover protecting the boat lift controls, and raised the lift to make the smallest step possible for Linda to get out. Then she raised the boat the rest of the way putting the keel up above the high tide line. "You OK if I hose the boat down?" she asked her sister.

"Sure, you mind if I head up to the house? I'm going to call Matt. I'll make him take Goldy out for a walk."

After having had the ice on the knee for the last half-hour, Linda was able to limp herself up the short walk from the dock to her sister's sleek contemporary house, her glassy reminder of a disastrous marriage that Laurie never brought up.

Opening one of the glass sliders, Linda gratefully entered the air-conditioned white-tiled great room and flopped on the upholstered couch. She stuck her arm up to her elbow in her Vera Bradley carryall, rummaged around and emerged with her phone.

Matt answered his cell phone sleepily on the fifth ring, "Huh?"

"Oh great," thought Linda. "4:00 and he's passed out. Guess he bailed early from work today." Matt had been working part time at one of the marinas in walking distance from the house, but lately he seemed to be home at hours inconsistent with his shifts.

Into the receiver she said, "Hey Matt, I need you to take Goldy out for a walk."

"Huh?"

"Matty, wake up." She paused for a few seconds. "You there, Matty." Matt had declared at the age of twelve that he despised being called by the baby name Matty, and he wanted to be called Matt from then on. Now whenever Linda felt Matt was ignoring her she pulled Matty out of her hat.

"Yeah, yeah, cut the Matty stuff. What?"

"I banged my knee out with Aunt Laurie on the boat. It's swollen up big time. I'm going to snooze on her couch until the swelling goes down. I need you take Goldy out for a walk."

"Oh man, the game's about to start," Matt complained.

"Oh stop, Matt. All Goldy needs is ten minutes down at the field. And then let her out in the morning if I'm not home by the time you get up for work." Linda hung up, hoping Matt wouldn't fall back to sleep without letting the dog out.

Thrusting her arm back in her bag again, Linda this time brought out a bottle of ibuprofen and a half-empty plastic water bottle. She popped two tablets in her mouth, swallowed and leaned her head back against the couch, closed her eyes and sighed. She wasn't pleased that an injury necessitated the night at Laurie's, but she wasn't sorry to have a night off from her 28-year-old son.

Over the last two years that Matt had been back with her, his mental health issues had become worse, and Linda wasn't sure how much more she could take. When he first moved home, he quickly got part-time jobs, one at a local skeet club where his expert shooting skills were in great demand, and the other at the local marina in walking distance of the house. The job at the skeet club disappeared after about a year with no explanation to Linda, and Matt started spending even more time on the sofa bed. Linda imagined she had made a mistake by not pushing Matt for more answers. However, her one attempt to broach the subject by noting that a skeet club couldn't possibly not need a skilled shooter like Matt as an instructor had been met with such an inexplicable outburst of rage that she never brought the issue up again, even though she was pained to see him doing nothing more with his life than washing boats at a marina. She cursed herself yet again for being the proverbial enabler.

Laurie came in the house, interrupting Linda's reflections, "You reach Matt?"

"Yup, Mr. Enthusiasm. It was all I could do to get him to agree to take Goldy out. I'm worried that he's getting even worse. I mean he's been screwed up since he came back home, but at least when I first got Goldy, he showed a spark of life at least when it came to the dog."

"I remember. I thought you were nuts getting another puppy, and we both knew it wouldn't fix Matt, but it was good to see him kinda like his old self."

Linda vividly remembered Laurie's reaction to her bringing Goldy home. "Why on earth did you get a puppy, Linda?" Laurie had asked with exasperation. The twins, although expectedly similar in many ways, differed significantly in their love for animals, particularly canines. Laurie tolerated them and acknowledged that they brought value to some people's lives; she just didn't happen to be one of those people. Linda on the other hand loved dogs.

Linda had resisted getting another dog for a while after she put Caesar down, conceding that life was easier without a dog. But easier doesn't mean better, and she missed the companionship.

"Well, I wanted at least one living creature in my house that was happy to see me," Linda answered her sister sarcastically. "I loved living on my own, but if Matt's going to be back, and I have to clean up after him, I might as well have a dog."

"OK, but why a puppy? I mean you have to potty-train them or housebreak them or whatever it is you do with a puppy."

"I've got the housebreaking licked. I bought a case of Chux at the medical supply shop in Annapolis, and I covered the laundry room floor. And God knows I've changed enough Chux." Both sisters had. Chux is the informal name for the plastic-backed absorbent underpads used in hospital beds with bedridden or otherwise incontinent patients. Learning how to safely roll a patient off an old soiled one and onto a new fresh one is a skill learned early in a nursing career. "Besides, by getting Goldy as a puppy I don't have to deal with someone else's baggage. I train her, and I'm responsible for her bad behavior."

"Sort of like your son?" Laurie quipped.

"No," Linda replied with a snap in her voice. "His time in Iraq screwed up the training I did."

"Fair point. I hope you didn't get the puppy expecting it would fix Matt."

"Oh hell no. I know better than that. What's wrong with Matt can't be fixed by a puppy. I got the puppy to help me, to give me something to look forward to when I come home, not just seeing gloomy Gus rotting on my sofa bed."

"Is he still refusing to consider help of any sort?" Laurie asked carefully.

"He insists that since he's a veteran he's entitled to his medical care at the VA, and he doesn't want me or anyone else to pay for care he should already be getting. Allegedly he's put in his paperwork to get his medical benefits. I can't force him to see some private doctor."

"Right. Well, let's hope his paperwork comes through soon. All I know about what happened to Matt is what you've told me, but my favorite nephew sounds like as classic a set of PTSD symptoms as you can get. He's got the flashbacks and nightmares, he can't sleep, and he's on edge all the time or hyperaroused if we're using our good nurse technical speak."

Linda did realize that depression and PTSD could not be fixed by a puppy, but she was happy to see that Matt initially took a fair amount of interest in Goldy. He did not grumble at first about taking Goldy out for bathroom breaks. And when Linda was upstairs, she could often hear Matt talking to the puppy, "Here girl, want the ball? Go get it."

Matt was even slightly more social with Linda once she had the puppy. For instance, on one occasion Matt brought a tennis ball down to the field with them trying to entice Goldy to play ball, even though Goldy kept barking at the flock of mallards she scared away. "No bird is going to sit still for a mile around with you, little pup," Matt crooned with a tenderness in his voice that Linda hadn't heard for a long time.

"Oh, not true, that blue jay is still sitting on the piling over there," Linda pointed toward the remains of the old community dock, a sorry mess of pilings with no decking.

"That's a kingfisher, Mom. Blue jays don't sit at the water."

"It's blue and it's got the pointy back of the head," Linda protested.

"Mom, it's a kingfisher."

Linda gave up as she was sure the Boy Scout and hunter in her son was correct.

Drifting back to the present from her reminiscences about the puppy, Linda suggested to Laurie, "How about we order Chinese? My treat, since I'm crashing on your couch."

"Sounds good to me," Laurie responded. She went over to the fridge and came back to the couch with a kitchen towel, a gallon-sized plastic freezer bag of ice cubes, and the menu for the local Chinese restaurant which delivered.

"God bless you, you are an angel," Linda said with genuine appreciation.

"Nope, just force of habit from thirty plus years of nursing. I'm going to shower up, and then we'll get the Chinese going."

The sisters ate Chinese food in front of the TV locked onto the latest reality TV contests. Linda slept on her sister's couch.

The swelling had greatly diminished by the time Laurie's pre-work routine awakened Linda, who popped another two ibuprofen down for good measure. She made sure that her sister didn't need her to help with any cleaning up and then drove home.

Matt was sound asleep on the sofa bed on the sunporch flat on his back with his mouth open when Linda got home. She observed to herself how much Matt with his lanky muscled frame looked like his father Jimmy at that age.

Before the divorce Jimmy did contracting work for convenience stores. When the work required that the electric or the plumbing be shut off, the convenience stores insisted that the work be done at night to minimize the impact on business. When Jimmy had been doing night shifts, Linda had always tried to get a day shift at work so that one of them could be home with Matt instead of paying a babysitter. Linda remembered many times getting up for a morning shift to find Jimmy sleeping on the couch after finishing his night shift, looking exactly like Matt did now.

For a long time, Linda had missed having Jimmy around the house. When she had complained to Laurie that she missed the sex, Laurie had told her she merely needed to go to more singles bars and she'd have no problem picking up somebody for at least decent sex. But when Linda had grumbled that she also missed having Jimmy to take care of all the little things around the house, like changing the furnace filters, replacing the leaky faucets, and shoveling snow, Laurie had conceded, "Damn, it is much harder to replace a good handyman. I mean there's plenty of men who are decent in the sack, but most of them aren't nearly as good around the house. Last winter, during that blizzard, when my generator froze up and I couldn't get it to fire up when the power went off, I would have killed for a good handyman."

Linda joked back, "But you can get a service contract to take care of the generator. Last I heard it's illegal in Maryland to have a service contract to take care of the good sex part."

CHAPTER THREE

SUMMER 2012

Linda wasn't surprised that her house's automatic generator was faithfully chugging along when she woke up because the previous night's thunderstorm had been unusually intense. Overnight Linda had been vaguely aware that the power had gone off amidst the lightning flashes that lit up her bedroom, but when she heard the generator fire off, she had let herself drift right back to sleep. When thunderstorms caused widespread power outages, the power company usually got to the houses closest to the water like hers last, focusing on the major housing developments and commercial centers first. That's why Linda and most of her neighbors had generators in the first place. The generator wasn't quite the same as running on full power, as she couldn't start the dishwasher or wash clothes, but the air conditioning worked and the fridge was cold. Linda decided, however, that the generator could handle running the coffee pot. She had just finished the first cup when her cell phone rang at around nine. It was Laurie.

"Hey, how 'bout that storm last night," Linda started off.

"Well, sis, that's exactly why I was calling," Laurie responded.

"You have power? You OK?" Linda asked.

"I'm on generator. And yes, I'm OK. But I was a dumbass. I left my chairs and umbrella out on the dock during the storm, and they're all in the drink."

"You never forget to bring your stuff in," Linda was surprised. Her twin's OCD need for organization was a family legend.

"My relief didn't show up at work. It took them four hours to get a replacement in. I was so flippin' tired by the time I got home, I completely forgot. Anyway, I can see most of the stuff on the bottom of the creek but I don't want to be wandering around in the water lifting stuff without a spotter."

"Sure, no problem. I'll be there in about a half-hour, is that OK?"

"Yup, thanks Lin."

Linda finished her coffee and put the newspaper away for later. She used the kitchen table to help herself up, using her right knee as little as possible. Then she changed into a swimsuit, put a T-shirt and shorts over top, and threw a pair of water shoes and a change of clothes into a small bag. She stuck her head in the sunporch, "Hey, Matt, I'm heading over to your aunt's. She had some minor problems in the storm." As her eyes adjusted to the dark she realized she was talking to herself. "Where the hell has he gone this time," she wondered to herself.

On the drive over, at least half the traffic lights were out. Even the main roads were covered with debris ranging from clumps of leaves to large branches that drivers were having to swerve to avoid. Linda flipped from her satellite oldies station to a local news channel. The reporters were talking about widespread power outages, flooding, and even a dozen or more deaths from the storm. Linda counted herself lucky that all she had to deal with was a power outage and Laurie's dock furniture.

Laurie had Danishes plus a fresh pot of coffee on the kitchen counter when Linda got there. They snacked and chatted, and then they put on water shoes and walked down to the dock. Laurie pointed to where a momma duck and her babies were feasting on seagrass on the surface near the end of her dock, "At least a couple of the chairs are there."

As the sisters walked toward the ladder at the end of the dock, the mother duck paddled off quickly leaving a widening V-shaped wake behind her, which the baby ducks used to follow her like a bike racer uses the forerunner's vacuum to suck him forward.

Laurie chuckled, "I had four chairs out. I couldn't tell if they were all there or not."

Laurie lowered her dock ladder and the two women went down one after the other. Three of the chairs were only a few feet past where the women had entered the water, and they lifted the chairs up onto the dock. Seagrass had already wrapped itself around the arms and legs, and the parts of the chairs that had been on the bottom were muddy.

"Alright. We're missing the fourth chair, the umbrella and the umbrella stand," Laurie observed.

"The umbrella stand went in? It's cast iron," Linda was surprised.

"The umbrella was still in it. I had put the canopy down but left it in the stand. The wind must have tilted it over."

"Then it probably didn't go far. What part of the dock was it on?" Linda queried. On her first attempt to climb up the dock ladder, she started with her right leg. The knee didn't hold and she fell backward in the water. Thankfully, Laurie hadn't noticed. Linda started the ladder again with her left leg and climbed back up onto the dock.

"That corner over there on the other side, the one closer to the shore, back behind the boat," Laurie pointed as she spoke.

Laurie's dock was a standard four feet wide for the first fifty feet from the yard and then broadened out to a large square at the end. The boat lift was on one side of the square. Linda walked over to the indicated corner and looked down in the water.

"I see the umbrella. It's half under the boat. Good thing you like yellow." Laurie's favorite color was yellow, the brighter and more neon-like the better. Linda could see the bright yellow peeking out from under the boat.

"How the heck'd it do that?" Laurie asked without expecting an answer as she went under the dock to reach the umbrella.

"Guess the tide could have moved it around once it went in. Doesn't matter how it got there, does it?"

"Here, I'll lift it toward the dock, and you pull it up." Laurie tried to use her foot to lift the umbrella enough to grab it. The silt on the bottom acted like a suction cup, and Laurie was forced to stick her head under the water to get a good grip on the umbrella. She emerged from the water and lifted the umbrella up to Linda who pulled it up on the dock.

"Uggh," Linda exclaimed as orangey-brown silt covered her hands. The umbrella needed a good hosing off before it would be useable. "Alright, one chair and one umbrella stand to go. Good thing the table didn't go too."

"Nope, I picked that fake wrought iron on purpose. All the holes mean the wind goes right through. Can you see…" Laurie broke off swearing, "Owww. Dammit. I found the umbrella stand." Laurie had kicked the umbrella stand as she walked around in the water looking for it.

"Oh, it's heavy!" Laurie swore as she tried to lift it. "I'm gonna scooch it closer to the shore so I don't have to lift it as high."

"Want me to get in and we both lift?"

"No, I think I got it. Keep looking for the chair."

Linda walked back to the side of the square of the dock that faced the opposite side of the creek. She scanned the water looking for the fourth chair. She heard a grunt and a clunk. When she twisted her head back, she saw that Laurie had succeeded in the lifting the muck-covered umbrella stand onto the part of the dock closest to the shore.

The two sisters were about to give up on the final chair concluding that it must have been sucked by the wind and the tide into the channel dredged in the creek, where if it sank the water would be too deep for them to see it.

"Wait, wait, wait. There it is!" Linda pointed at the water near Laurie's next door neighbor's dock.

"Yup, woohoo!" Linda got back in the water to help her sister carry the last chair across the distance between her and her neighbor's piers.

"Looks like the boat survived OK," Linda remarked.

"Oh yeah, I checked her out first thing. I was actually checking her out when I realized the chairs and umbrella were gone. At first, I walked right past the table and then when I was done with the boat, I looked around and realized. I saw a couple of the chairs right away. Thanks for coming over. I could get most of it myself, but you never know what a storm like that throws around on the bottom, and I didn't want to go mucking around by myself."

"No problem. When I was driving over here, the radio was calling the storm a derecho or something like that."

"What the heck's a derecho?" Laurie asked.

"Beats me. Some new term they came up with. Most of the traffic lights on the way over here were out though," Linda replied.

"Damn, that means people will call out for their shifts. Maybe I'll pretend my cell phone ran out of power. I'm sick of being the only one who's always available when people don't feel like doing their shifts. Makes me wish I stuck with the case management work." Case managers are generally nurses employed by insurance companies who are supposed to help seriously ill patients coordinate their care. The hours are predictable and the pay is decent, and both sisters had done brief stints. Both had promptly returned to bedside nursing after becoming a bit jaded about the insurance companies' underlying motive to keep costs down rather than help patients get better care.

"Ha, you were bored stiff, just like I was. I, however, was smart enough not to go back to acute care, although I still get more than my share of shifts. But I'm off 'til Monday." Following her stint at an insurance company, Laurie had gone straight back to the hospital, working first in the ER, then in ICU or telemetry units, liking the adrenaline rush of dealing with fairly ill patients. Linda, on the other hand, had chosen the calmer atmosphere of the orthopedic center, which was thrilled to have a bachelor's level registered nurse willing to hang around for more than six months. Such centers often had trouble competing with hospitals for higher level nurses meaning Linda had a leg up in the interview process on other nurses such as LPNs without four-year college degrees.

"I'm supposed to be off 'til then too," Laurie said.

The women hosed the mud and the seagrass off the deck furniture. Laurie suddenly piped up, "Well, we're both off work, and we're here, and we're wet. Why don't we take the boat out?"

Linda considered for a second and replied, "Great idea. Why not? You got any sandwich makings in the house?"

"I'm sure I have some tuna and bread. Lunch on the water sounds great."

The women finished cleaning up the deck furniture and then hosed off their legs.

"Hey Laurie, you've got blood on the back of your leg."

"Huh?"

Linda took the hose and sprayed the back of Laurie's calf. There was a small scrape, oozing some blood. Linda touched gently around the area, "Is this where the umbrella stand found you?"

"Must be," Laurie said as she twisted her neck and calf to take a look. "I'll get Neosporin and a bandage on it when we make the sandwiches. My tetanus shot is fresh enough, so I should be good to go."

The two women walked up to the house leaving their water shoes outside and wiping their feet off with a towel Laurie had left at the back door. They grabbed a soft cooler, put in ice packs, diet sodas, and two beers. Laurie tore open blue foil packets of StarKist and spread them on pita bread. She added mayo and garlic salt, then packed the sandwiches in foil and added them to the cooler.

During the warmer weather, the sisters' social life centered around their excursions on the boat. Laurie had never entered into another serious relationship after she divorced her surgeon husband. When Jimmy and Linda were still together, Jimmy joked that he had every man's dream of twins because Laurie was around so often. The three of them took Matt out in the boat whenever their work schedules allowed. By the time Matt was ten he was an expert at tying the boat up at the dock and wanted to drive the boat desperately. Laurie was too much of a stickler about the boating safety regulations to let a ten-year-old handle a cruiser, but Jimmy had taught Matt how to handle his little duck hunting boat.

* * * * *

Linda vividly remembered a bygone late June day in the early 1990s when Matt brought Jimmy's boat alongside Laurie's dock while she and Laurie had been getting the boat ready to go out. Jimmy and Matt had gone on their first men-only camping trip the night before, which consisted of pitching a pup tent on one of the few farms with a smidge of waterfront left on the Mayo Peninsula, but they could have been in the backwoods of upper Canada as excited as Matt had been. Jimmy had befriended the farm owner when he built him a new workshop, and now Jimmy was allowed to go duck hunting on the farm in the late fall. The owner had asked Jimmy to check on the property while he was on summer vacation, and Jimmy had received permission to camp there one night with Matt. Jimmy had motored off from the community dock the night before, an overnight set of gear stowed in his hunting boat.

Linda had not been expecting to see them until after she and Laurie got done with the day's boat trip, but she looked up to see Jimmy's boat pulling up to Laurie's dock with Matt at the rudder.

"What are you all doing here?" Linda called out.

"We thought we'd surprise you lazy boneses. Matt and I have been up since sunup, and we figured we had enough time to get over here before you two got your act together," Jimmy answered as he and Matt tied lines to the dock.

"Yeah, you're even in time to help get the boat ready."

Matt climbed up the ladder on Laurie's dock like a monkey and ran up to hug Linda around the waist.

"I did it all by myself, Mom," he exclaimed.

"You did what all by yourself?"

"I did the whole boat trip. I started the engine and let the lines loose, and I drove us all the way here. I knew exactly where to go too," Matt's face was pink with excitement. Jimmy, standing behind Matt, nodded his head in confirmation.

"Wow," Linda exclaimed. "That's amazing." Linda was genuinely impressed. She and her sister had been taught to handle a small sailboat fairly early on, but for a ten-year-old boy to be that good with a boat was rare. For the moment, her pride in Matt's abilities outweighed her worry about how the Coast Guard or State Department of Natural Resources would have reacted to Matt's age and lack of a boating safety education certificate had they stopped the boat.

Without allowing the disapproval Linda knew her sister felt to show, Laurie chimed in, "Well, there's a box of Hostess donuts on the kitchen counter. I'm sure your parents wouldn't mind you having a donut as a reward for your captaincy skills."

Matt glanced briefly at Linda to make sure she wasn't going to deny permission, and took off down the dock at full speed. He came back a few minutes later with powdered sugar all over his face and a half-eaten donut in one hand.

"Well, since you two have finished the camping, are you all coming on the boat?" Laurie asked.

"Any chance we can go swimming somewhere?" Jimmy answered with a question.

"Oh, heck yeah, only way I'm going to have two stinky male campers on my boat is if I can dump your butts in the water and clean you off at some point," Laurie joked.

They rafted-up at Harness Creek and swam in the water for over an hour. When Matt had been too small to notice, they enjoyed their swimming excursions at smaller less popular sites where they could go skinny-dipping. With Matt being ten, however, they were more circumspect about keeping clothes on, and Harness Creek was as good a spot as any.

After Linda and Jimmy split, Laurie hauled Linda out on the boat as often as possible. Linda had grumbled at first, "It's not the same. Being out here just reminds me he's gone."

"Exactly, we need to make as many new memories as possible. Matt's always off with his friends now, which means we can even start going skinny-dipping again." Matt was in tenth grade, and Laurie was correct that he was seldom home. Once the first of his friends had a driver's license and a car at his disposal on the weekends, Matt was always out and about.

After a few trips out on the boat with just Linda and Laurie, the two sisters agreed that in some ways they enjoyed having all-female time after years of Jimmy's not quite overbearing masculine presence. Linda also began to realize that she could have a life of her own outside of raising Matt. By the time Matt returned at the end of 2009, Linda had become so accustomed to her single life that she had to remind herself not to resent her own son's presence in her life.

* * * * *

Matt was still not home by the time she got back from her present day post-derecho boating excursion with Laurie. Linda ate leftovers for dinner, not too concerned. When she got up for her shift the next morning, Matt had not yet returned to his makeshift den on the sunporch. Still she didn't worry too much. However, by the time she got home from her shift to find no evidence that Matt had been back to the house at all, Linda became genuinely apprehensive. What if he'd been caught out in the derecho and had some sort of problem? She called Laurie who was far more sanguine, "He probably got lucky at a bar. He'll be back."

Another two days passed before he came back. Linda practically leaped on him when he came in the front door, "Oh my God, Matt. Where have you been? Your cell phone goes straight to voice mail."

Matt looked like hell, bags under his eyes, unshaven, filthy clothes, slightly glassy eyes. He scanned the entire room as he always did, a habit that Linda assumed was related to his military training, then stared at her without answering, walked past her and collapsed on the sofa bed.

Linda followed him in, "You could at least answer me."

"Oh piss off Mom. I'm a grown man. Can't a guy go out partying?"

"Don't you ever tell me to piss off in my house again!" Linda roared back at him. "You got that, mister?"

Linda got a reluctant low volume "Sorry."

"And leave a note next time you decide to go partying for three days. You may be a grown man, but you're still my son and this is still my house you're living in."

Matt didn't answer, just turned up the TV volume louder.

Matt spent the next thirty-six hours on the sofa bed, getting up only to use the bathroom or grab a beer from the fridge. He didn't shower or shave, and Linda didn't think he ate anything. He probably would have continued for longer if he hadn't drank all the beer. Linda had seen the beer supply diminishing and placed herself at the kitchen table with a book and a cup of coffee after the last Natty Bo was gone.

Matt lumbered into the kitchen, opened the fridge and realized the supply was gone. "Didn't you get any beer on your way home, Mom?" Matt complained.

"No, Matt, I didn't. Do you realize you're self-medicating, hon?"

"What are you talking about?" Matt growled at her.

"Matt, I try not to play nurse with you, but you are clinically depressed. I also think you have PT….."

"Oh, Mom, leave off," Matt cut her off and headed back to the sunporch.

Linda followed him, "Matt, I know you don't want to hear this, but you cannot spend your whole life on this sofa bed drinking beer."

"What do you mean? Are you throwing me out?" Matt sounded slightly panicky.

"No, Matt, that's not what I'm saying at all. I'm saying we need to get you some help. There are medicines that can do a lot better job than beer at making you feel better."

"I've already told you I've tried to sign up for my VA medical benefits. I've heard nothing. The Army fucked up my life, they should fix it." Linda was almost relieved to hear anger creeping into Matt's voice. Anger was better than the lifeless dispassionate Matt melting into the sofa bed.

"Matt, I don't know anything about getting VA benefits, but you've been waiting for the VA for months. You can't wait forever. I'll pay for you to see someone."

"I don't want you paying for anything, Mom. It's bad enough that I'm twenty-nine years old and living with my Mom with no job. I was a squad designated marksman, and I was next in line for any sniper position that opened up. I'd finished all the training for it. I was great at my job, and then that damned bomb went off. My girlfriend dumped me because I didn't want to start popping out kids. I can't get a job. Those assholes at the marina fired me so they could pay some Mexican half my hourly wage under the table. You want to make it worse by having my Mommy pay for my whack job medicines," Matt's voice kept rising in volume.

"No, Matt, the last thing I want is to make things worse," Linda used the calm voice she reserved for unreasonable patients. She would have loved to point out to him that Casey dumped him because he sat on the couch all day doing nothing, not because he didn't want kids. And that the marina fired him because he was pouring shots of Jack Daniel's into his Cokes at work making him a liability to have around, not because they wanted to underpay some immigrant. However, she knew if she tried to counter his self-pity with facts or chastise him for his inappropriate and newfound racism, she would lose any chance of getting him to listen to her about seeking treatment.

"Then just give me twenty bucks so I can go get more beer."

"Matt, you're asking me to help you get worse. I want to help you, but in the right way."

"Oh, for Christ's sake, stop lecturing. You sound like one of those AA crazies. If you don't give me the money, I'll take it out of your purse once you go to bed."

Linda gave up. She grabbed her Vera Bradley dump bag off the back of the kitchen chair and pulled a twenty out of her wallet.

"I love you, Matt."

Matt took the twenty silently and walked past her and out the front door, not even giving Goldy a pat on the head when she leaped out of her dog bed hoping he would take her out with him.

Linda sat down in a kitchen chair feeling defeated. If there were any beer in the fridge she would have had one. Truthfully, she would have enjoyed a cosmo or an appletini, something with a little more punch than a beer.

She had been a nurse for close to thirty years, but she felt completely unable to help her own son. Linda tried to console herself with the notion that as a nurse she saw people who had already entered a medical setting, voluntarily or not. She had no experience with trying to get people to make that first step. She hadn't therefore contemplated exactly how hard it would be to see her own child mentally ill and have him refuse to get the help he needed.

As she reflected back over her attempts at conversation, she tried to think if she could have said anything different or if she failed to say whatever it was that would have finally gotten through to Matt. She also remembered the panic when Matt had interpreted her as suggesting he might have to move out. Would telling him that he couldn't stay here if he didn't get help force his hand? Or would he take off and she'd find out he was living in a tent under a bridge? The problem with tough love was it was a gamble. When it worked and you induced the desired positive result, everyone cheered for what a great thing tough love was. But no one wanted to talk about when tough love failed. In a depressed person, could forcing that person to seek help end up pushing them to suicide? Could she live with herself if Matt got hurt or killed because she had insisted that he seek help?

She told herself she didn't have the answer to that question and grabbed her purse off the back of the kitchen chair to prevent Matt from helping himself to her wallet while she was asleep. She climbed up to her bedroom with her left knee bearing the weight and only swinging the right leg up to the same stair without bending the knee rather than using both legs to climb the stairs. As she was lying in bed waiting for the dull ache in her knee to subside allowing her to fall asleep, she realized she had lied to herself. She did have the answer to her question, but she didn't like how weak the answer revealed her to be. She couldn't live with her guilt if something bad happened to Matt because she demanded that he seek help. That's precisely why she still allowed him to live with her doing nothing but watching TV and drinking beer on her sunporch. Over the next year, these scenes with Matt repeated over and over again, and Linda lied to herself that this status quo would just continue. But she ignored the signs coming from her knee that would rob her of her ability to cope with the status quo.

PART TWO

GIVING UP GROUND

CHAPTER FOUR

Despite having sufficient seniority to avoid night shift, Linda always volunteered to work nights on Labor Day weekend, and this year was no different. Labor Day boating was unenjoyable with the water crowded with everyone trying to get in the last cruise of the summer, and her colleagues with younger children were always grateful to have the weekend off for the last hoorah of summer. Further, Linda did not seem to suffer from either the insomnia or overwhelming drowsiness that plagued some staff if they switched between day and night shifts. She also found it a painless way to earn brownie points with the management as they otherwise had difficulty staffing the holiday weekend.

Night shift ends at 8 a.m. A few minutes before the end of her shift, Linda headed into Mrs. Nelson's room to assist her out of bed and into her wheelchair. Mrs. Nelson, who wakes up no later than 6 a.m. every day and resents every minute she stays in bed after that, had already arranged herself in a sitting position with her legs hanging off the side of the bed, fidgeting with her impatience to wheel herself down to the lounge. Linda pushed the wheelchair against the bed next to where Mrs. Nelson's legs were, lowered the arm of the chair on the side closest to the bed and locked the wheels. Then she used the motorized controls to lower the bed to the same height as the seat of the wheelchair.

"Alright, Mrs. Nelson. I'm going to help slide you over onto the chair." Bracing her legs the same way she had hundreds of times, she put her arms under Mrs. Nelson's and helped slide her posterior ninety degrees onto the chair. Mrs. Nelson was safely seated in the chair, and Linda tried to move her right leg a bit further away from the wheelchair and straighten herself up. She felt a muscle spasm in her right leg though, and then her knee suddenly felt frozen. Linda lost her balance, banged her right arm painfully on the arm of the wheelchair and went down on the floor next to the chair. She yelled out in pain.

Mrs. Nelson was clearly alarmed and screamed as well.

Their joint cries brought the teenaged volunteer from the room across the hall. She stared with her mouth open at the sight of Mrs. Nelson in her chair and Linda sprawled out on the floor beneath her. "Go get whoever's sitting at the central desk," Linda ordered the girl who seemed prepared to continue gawking.

While waiting, Linda apologized to Mrs. Nelson, "I'm so sorry, Mrs. Nelson. That must have scared you. Are you OK?" Mrs. Nelson nodded.

The girl came back with Renee from the desk and Mark, one of the orderlies. "What happened?" Renee asked.

"My knee locked up," Linda replied.

Renee took charge like the pro she was, "Mark, you help Linda up and get her over to the break room. Then get an ice pack for her knee. I'll finish up with getting Mrs. Nelson ready to go to the lounge. Heather, you can go back to what you were doing."

Linda got herself in a sitting position. Mark bent at the knees and picked Linda up from behind, supporting all her weight as Linda tested to see if her knee would hold. With any weight on it, pain radiated up and down her leg. Mark put her right arm up on his shoulders and helped her hop down the hall to the break room, where she lowered herself with relief into a chair. Mark moved another chair across from her and lifted her leg onto it.

"Thanks so much, Mark," Linda said on an exhale of relief. Mark grunted and went to get the ice.

Linda waited for about ten minutes before Renee showed up, surprisingly with their supervisor Nancy in tow as Nancy was seldom seen before 9 a.m. Nancy had a clipboard with the "Incident report" paperwork; she was the sort who had a stack of such clipboards with the paperwork already in place on top of her file cabinets, available the instant a patient or staff injury occurred.

While Renee checked to see if Linda's knee was still frozen, which blessedly it wasn't, Linda answered the questions on Nancy's incident checklist and described how she'd felt a muscle spasm or cramp and then her knee had frozen up. On querying Linda about whether she knew her knee had problems, Nancy pounced on Linda's admission that she had previously seen an orthopedist, "After you saw him, did he clear you to keep working?"

Linda answered honestly that the orthopedist at that time had given her a cortisone shot, but told her that the cortisone was only relieving the pain and she would ultimately need the knee replaced.

Nancy scowled, "Well, this counts as a near miss with the patient. If you had dropped Mrs. Nelson or fallen on her, corporate would be all over me for letting someone seeing an orthopedist keep working without a specific signoff. As it is, I can't let you back to work until you've had that knee examined and a doctor signs off on it. Do you want me to call an ambulance to take you to the ER? I don't see how you can drive with that knee."

Renee piped up, "We're both off shift at eight. As soon as I make sure day shift's here, I'll drive her to the ER." Linda frowned and started to demur. On Labor Day weekend, the ER would be packed full of people dealing with the consequences of backyard misadventures.

Renee countered, "The ER's the only way you're going to get somebody to look at that knee on a holiday weekend, and it's blowing up like a balloon."

Linda looked at the knee and admitted to herself that Renee was correct, "Thanks, Renee. I can have my sister or my son grab my car later. My orthopod's practice is the consult for the ER anyway."

Nancy left, still ticking boxes on her clipboard. Renee and Linda shook their heads at each other. "I realize she's just doing her job, but her delivery is so abrasive," Linda remarked.

Renee went out to check on the arrival of the next shift and grab both her and Linda's things from the staff lockers. She came back with Mark, who helped Linda walk out to Renee's car.

At the ER, Linda was in luck. First, she arrived early enough in the day that the waiting room was not yet overfilled with the mishaps of the holiday weekend. Second, she and Renee both knew the triage nurse behind the desk, who knew that Linda would not show up with her knee injury unless she was worried that she had done significant damage. Third, when she finally did get taken back, the attending ER physician looked up the orthopedist on call, who happened to be Linda's orthopedist; even better Dr. Rosen was on site doing rounds and came down to check her out. Linda had known Dr. Rosen since he was a fellow in training and she was a brand new floor nurse at her first full-time position. When he pushed aside the curtain to enter her ER cubby, he gave her a deprecating look and said, "I can tell you what needs to happen with that knee without even looking at it. I told you cortisone was only a temporary fix. It's time for you to get over being a chicken and get that knee replaced."

When the ER released her, Linda took a cab to her work to pick up her car, which would have horrified the ER staff had they seen her leaving without assistance. She drove home and was able to put a bit of weight on the knee now that it was tightly wrapped in a temporary brace.

She made sure that no cars were coming and that none of the neighborhood fussbudgets were in the park, and then she opened the front door for Goldy to go flying out to the park. Linda was not going to try to manage a 70-pound dog on a leash in her current condition. Linda hobbled across the street to the park. As she was making her way slowly, Siobhan appeared at the far end of the park with her two chocolate labs. Siobhan released her two to play with Goldy and then walked over to Linda.

"That's a pretty good limp you've got there," Siobhan commented.

Linda shook her head in disgust, "I used to play field hockey in high school and both my knees are about shot. This one, and she slapped the braced-up knee, is going to need surgery real soon. I fell at work today, and good old Nancy, she doesn't want me back until an orthopedist clears me."

Siobhan smiled knowingly. Siobhan had worked with Nancy on a number of occasions while auditing at Linda's facility. "I can imagine."

"Bad news is my orthopedist is not going to clear me to go back to work without surgery. He says I've put off the surgery as long as I can get away with, the cortisone shots aren't doing it, and it's time."

"Ugh, sorry to hear that."

"I have an appointment at his office tomorrow to get surgery and all the pre-op junk scheduled."

"How long will you be down for the count?" Siobhan asked.

"Probably six to eight weeks."

"If you need any help with Goldy, let me know. You've done plenty of dog sitting for me. I couldn't take her for the whole time you're down, but I can certainly help out."

"Thanks, Siobhan. I really appreciate that. I've got to talk to my sister tonight. I'll be bunking with her during the initial recovery, and I doubt she'll put up with a dog for as long as I'll be down. I fantasize that my grown son may finally behave like a responsible adult and take care of the house and Goldy. Even with all that though, I may need to take you up on your offer for help."

When the three dogs had had their fun and taken care of business, Siobhan got enough plastic bags to clean up and then helped Linda get Goldy back on the deck.

"Thank you so much, Siobhan. I'm not sure I could have made it across the field to be a responsible dog owner."

"No worries. Like I said, you've certainly watched my babies often enough, and I'm sure you've cleaned up after them. Good luck with the surgery, and call if you need any help with Goldy."

Linda went in the house to call Laurie and update her.

* * * * *

Linda was out of work for eight weeks with the surgery. She was discharged into Laurie's care with a prescription for Percocet, which she was determined not to fill. The street derelict overdoses she had seen in her training years in the ER had instilled plenty of respect for opiates' power, but the quiet addicts, the middle class soccer moms and former high school football quarterbacks, were the ones who had given Linda a healthy fear of the addictive potential of the synthetic prescription opioids. Those ordinary patients had not set out to become hooked. Almost universally they started out with an injury requiring painkillers. And Linda could always tell when she had an unadmitted prescription addict on her hands; the physician would prescribe a reasonable dose for an opioid-naïve person, but an hour later the quiet addict would still be in pain. Linda would then have a conversation with the patient about how tolerance for both street opiates and prescription opioids builds up and how the patient needed to be honest with the physician about any past or current usage; otherwise the patient would never get a dose strong enough to help them.

Linda therefore loaded herself with as much ibuprofen as was safe, but she wasn't going to touch one of those damned Percocets. Laurie tried to convince her to take the advice Linda dished out to her own patients about not being able to heal with too much pain and filled the prescription for her anyway. Laurie put the bottle on the end table next to the couch where Linda camped during the day. "I told you I'm not taking those damned things," Linda said.

"Well, it doesn't hurt to fill it. If you don't need them, you don't need them," Laurie responded.

"How did you get the pharmacy to give you a narc anyway? You don't have the same last name as me," Linda asked.

Laurie smiled a cat-licking-the-cream smile. She fished in the handbag still on her shoulder and pulled out Linda's driver's license. "Did you forget that we're twins? I lifted your license from your wallet and picked it up."

Linda laughed, "Nursing's finest breaking federal law to illegally get opioids. They didn't even ask you about your long hair."

"Nope," Laurie replied. Linda and Laurie both had their mother's thick black curly hair which showed not the slightest bit of gray even as they approached the tail end of their fifties. Linda, however, had long since lost patience with taming the curly mess and had chosen a short no-maintenance cut ending just below her ears. Laurie still held onto shoulder length locks on which she applied a straightener on a regular basis.

Linda's insurance paid for one week of in-home physical therapy visits. Laurie then took Linda to her first outpatient physical therapy session. Even after a week of rest with therapy, bending the knee was only OK, and straightening the leg out to full extension was impossible. Discouraged, Linda realized how slow the progress was and that she was weeks away from being fully functional again. On the drive back, Linda looked at the clock on the dashboard noting that she was at least an hour away from being able to take another ibuprofen.

Laurie helped her to the bathroom, then the couch and brought her a sandwich, "Are you sure you're OK if I go to this electronic health records training session at work? I already told them they'd have to let me make up the training if you weren't able to be alone yet."

"It's only a few hours. I just used the bathroom, I've got food, and I'm sore enough from that therapy session that I don't want to move for a while. Go ahead. You might as well get it over with," Linda replied. Laurie headed out.

Linda mindlessly surfed through channels anxiously waiting for an hour to go by in order to take the next dose of ibuprofen. Her knee throbbed and throbbed and throbbed.

The appointed hour finally came and she scooched her rear to the edge of the couch closest to the end table with her medicine. She pulled the bottle of ibuprofen out of her purse and only then remembered that she'd finished the little container with her previous dose. She looked down the hallway toward the bathroom where the large bottle of ibuprofen was in the medicine cabinet. She thought to herself, "How am I going to make it that far?"

Laurie had left the walker in the hallway near the front door. The cane with the four prongs at the end was on the floor in front of the couch, but Linda hadn't worked much with it yet. Linda picked it up and positioned herself to push with her good left leg and her left arm. She got herself most of the way upright, her butt resting lightly on the arm of the couch. She positioned the cane and tried to start shuffling forward toward the bathroom, but her knee would not hold the weight after the physical therapy session. She tried to sit back down on the couch, almost made it, but her butt caught the edge, held for a second and then slid down to the floor. Her right foot kicked into the leg of the coffee table. The contact sent tidal waves of pain up her leg. Tears poured involuntarily out of her eyes. She twisted part way around to rest her head on her arms on the seat of the couch and gave into self-pity. Wiping the tears from her eyes, she looked toward the hallway again. The idea of slithering on her belly like a snake the whole length of the hallway for the ibuprofen brought a fresh wave of tears to her eyes. She looked up to the coffee table for the tissue box. In front of the tissue box was the bottle of Percocets that Laurie had picked up.

She had sworn she would never ever take one. But damn she hurt. She had never hurt so much in her life, giving birth to Matt included. She tried to get her breathing under control and stop the tears. She couldn't count how many times she'd spit out advice to her patients: "Pain is the fifth vital sign. Your body can't heal if you ignore the pain signals it sends you."

She reached for the bottle and read the dosing instructions. Two tablets by mouth every four hours, thinking, "I can't possibly need two of these pills at once even if they are the lowest dose out there." The Deer Park bottle was on the far side of the tissue box. She hooked the tissue box with two fingers and swung it toward the bottle. The bottle moved. She repeated the maneuver. The bottle of water was now in reach. She grabbed it gratefully. Pushing down on the top of the Percocet bottle, she twisted until it opened. Before she could have any further second thoughts, she grabbed one little white pill, popped it in her mouth and gulped down several swallows of water.

The knee continued to throb. She leaned back against the couch, closed her eyes and prayed for relief. The pain rolled up her legs to her hips in waves and then rolled back down like water sloshing in a bathtub, hitting one end of the tub and then having no further to go, reversing and rolling back the other way. If she could have opened her eyes she would have looked at the clock to see how long she waited for the waves of pain to diminish in amplitude. Finally, finally, the Percocet forced the pain waves to subside. Her breathing slowed, the natural consequence of an opioid. She watched an episode of *Forensics Files* while still sitting on the floor.

After another forty-five minutes, she was able to pull herself up onto the couch. She could have kissed the bottle of Percocets. She was blessedly able to take a nap for a bit over an hour, and she didn't care in the least that the orthopedist's staff had cautioned her about how daytime naps increased the difficulty of getting a full night's sleep during recovery.

"Feeling great still, huh?" her twin teased lightly when she returned.

"Actually, I gave in and took one of the damned Percs," Linda replied.

"Good, you took your own advice!" Laurie approved.

"Well, I only took one. And I'm waiting a full six hours before I take any more, if I need it. But, yes, it is helping," Linda insisted as much to herself as to Laurie.

"Great, then you're feeling well enough for us to do your at-home exercises," Laurie said with a falsely cheerful smile. "I'll get you the cryo machine so you can be suitably iced up before exercise time." Linda groaned in response.

Linda and Goldy stayed at Laurie's for the best part of two more weeks. Linda still hadn't been released to drive when she convinced Laurie to take her home, but she was worried about the state of the house with only Matt in it. "I got that evil compression sock on all by myself this morning which I won't need for much longer anyway, and I can always use ice packs if I have trouble with the cryo machine, so I should be able to manage at home. And I swear I'll do my exercises like I'm supposed to," Linda argued with her sister.

"How are you going to get food?" Laurie demanded.

"The way God intended, delivery. I can even have Peapod bring groceries."

"What the heck is Peapod?" her sister asked.

"It's a grocery delivery service. One of my ortho rehab patients who loves to cook swore by it."

"And how are you going to get upstairs to your bedroom? You may have been practicing stairs during physical therapy, but you still look pretty shaky to me climbing."

"I'll go up on my butt if I have to. Or if I can't manage it, I'll throw Matt off the sofa bed in the sunporch and make him go up and down the stairs."

"And how are you going to let Goldy out?"

"I'll make Matt do that. And my neighbor Siobhan with the two labs I dog sit offered to help if I needed it too."

"In that case you're right, get your stuff packed up and get the hell out."

Laurie drove her home. Linda lived in the house in which she and Laurie had grown up. The house is on Lord's Creek on the Mayo peninsula in Maryland, at the back of a neighborhood of what used to be vacation cottages. Before the Chesapeake Bay Bridge was built in the 1950s, Ocean City and the other Delmarva Eastern Shore beaches were quite a trek from the Washington, D.C. area. The Western Shore of the Chesapeake, however, could be reached in an hour, making it a perfect weekend getaway for Washingtonians. Places like North Beach and Chesapeake Beach that boasted accessibility by train service and a sandy beach had developed a resort hotel business. Then, after the Second World War, small communities of basic vacation cottages had started to spring up in areas accessible by car rather than train, like Lord's Creek. Linda's family home was in one of those developments; the development's land had originally been a large farm deeded by Lord Cecil Calvert to Quakers whose descendants got tired of paying the property taxes and sold off the waterfront land to the developers, leaving only the name of the creek remaining to remind folks off the original provenance.

Linda's house was directly across the street from the community field and beach area. She had a full open view of the water which would never be blocked by new houses, but because her house was non-riparian she didn't have to pay the taxes on a waterfront house. She considered that she had the best of both worlds.

Matt was not home when the sisters arrived, which was probably good because Linda was so angry at the state of the house she might not have held back from chewing him out. He hadn't taken the garbage out the entire time she had been gone. The bag in the trash can was the same one she had left. Rather than taking it out, he had started a new trash bag on the floor next to the can when he filled the first one up. Laurie dragged Goldy away from the miasma of smells in the festering garbage and took the bags out to the cans on the deck.

The kitchen sink was full of dishes. He hadn't even bothered to put any soap or water on them, leaving grimy crusts of food which would take steel wool to remove. The stench was vile, and a colony of fruit flies was in nirvana.

"I'm gonna kill him," Linda swore to her sister. "I am not his goddamned maid." She leaned against the kitchen counter for support to avoid putting too much weight on her knee, opened the dishwasher and started throwing the dishes forcefully in.

"Hey, you don't need stitches to add to your misery if you break one of those dishes in your hand," Laurie quipped as she came returned from taking the garbage out. "And Mom would be appalled. One must fully wash dishes before putting them in the dishwasher."

Linda smiled. They had always unsuccessfully argued with their mother that the point of a dishwasher was to wash the dishes and that washing them before putting them in was robbing the dishwasher of its role. "Well, I've secretly been recruited for one of those dishwasher soap commercials to see if their product really can get baked-on caked-on grease off with no scrubbing. I instructed Matt to make as big a mess as he possibly could in order to thoroughly test the soap. I'm proud of what a good job he did."

Laurie laughed, "Oh you should be. Seriously though, we need to get him into treatment. I'm sorry to be critical, but you're letting him get away with murder."

"I know. He says he still hasn't gotten a response from the VA, and he doesn't want to let the government off the hook and pay for treatment himself since he says everything that's wrong with him is all their fault. He's more obsessed with placing blame than fixing what's wrong, and he's existing like an animal. And it's not like he'd be paying if he went to a private doctor. I would. I'm just afraid that he'll pull one of his extended disappearing acts if I push too hard, and then something bad will happen to him."

"Linda, something bad is already happening to him," Laurie sighed and then resorted to humor as she always did when she sensed she stepped over the line in criticizing how Linda was handling Matt. "Well, I'm glad I convinced you to come back home. Another week at my place and we'd have had to bring in a pest control service to clean the joint up."

Linda scowled at her twin for taking credit for the idea of her coming home.

Laurie looked into the sunporch, "It looks like a mangy fox made its den on your porch. His clothes reek. Well, he's gonna have to sleep upstairs for a while. I don't want you going up and down the stairs all the time. And that's your nurse talking." Laurie proceeded to throw all of Matt's filthy clothes into a pile in the laundry room. "And don't you dare wash even one sock for him. He can damned well do a load of laundry for himself." Laurie stripped the sofa bed and threw the sheets on the pile. She brought down a fresh set of sheets from upstairs for the sofa bed and opened all the blinds. When she was done, she looked over at Linda and mocked, "Well, you boasted about your ability to order delivery food. Let's see it."

"Alright. Italian?"

"Sure."

The sisters were eating their calzones and salads when Matt came in. The clothes he was wearing looked no better than the ones Laurie had picked off the floor. He started to head straight to the sunporch. Laurie stood up and blocked his way, "Oh, no you don't, mister. Your mom doesn't need to be going up and down stairs unless someone is spotting her. You can sleep in your old bedroom until she's in better shape."

"What," Matt started to protest, looking over at Linda, trying to ignore Laurie.

"Don't you what me," Laurie retorted, putting her face right up to Matt's. "Your mom just had surgery, and the way you've treated this house is a disgrace. Since you're not even working, you could have at least taken the trash out so the mice and roaches wouldn't move in. It won't kill you to sleep upstairs for a couple weeks. And don't you dare let me come back over here and see a pile of filthy laundry upstairs."

"Fine," he sulked and went upstairs.

"And take a shower. You stink!" Laurie yelled after him.

"Thanks," Linda said. "I wasn't up to yelling yet." Linda knew she was kidding herself. She didn't have the guts to yell at Matt the way Laurie just did. When she saw how depressed he was, she worried herself sick that if she made things worse for him he might do something to harm himself.

"No prob. You sure you're OK here?"

"Yup. It's good to be home. Thanks for the help cleaning up."

"I'll be by tomorrow to take you to physical therapy."

"Thanks, sounds good."

Linda hobbled onto the sunporch and propped herself up on the sofa bed with piles of pillows around her back and under her knee. She dozed off at some point.

Linda woke in the middle of the night, she wasn't sure when. Matt was screaming. Alarmed, Linda yelled up the stairs, "Matt, Matt, are you OK? What's wrong?"

Linda couldn't see Matt come barreling down the stairs, but she could hear him. "Matt, what's wrong?" Linda repeated.

He looked over at her, "See I told you I can't sleep up there. I can't sleep without a TV. I wake up with bombs going off and kids' body parts in front of me. Oh God, do we have any beer here?"

Linda hadn't realized Matt's sudden infatuation with TV when he'd always been too much of the restless outdoorsy type to sit down long enough to watch TV was allowing him to escape from his nightmares. She struggled over the best way to approach him about letting her pay for some psychiatric visits. Meanwhile, Matt was opening every cabinet door in the kitchen.

"I can't believe there's no beer here. We must have some sort of alcohol somewhere."

While part of Linda was wrenched by seeing her son in such distress, a devil in the corner of her brain pointed out that since he was the only one who'd been in the house to drink it in the last two weeks he should know if there was beer in the house.

"Oh, thank God!" She heard Matt exclaim from the kitchen. "Where the hell's the corkscrew?" She heard him banging drawers open.

To save the kitchen from destruction, she yelled out, "The drawer to the left of the sink."

One more bang. About thirty seconds later, she heard the sound of a cork popping out of a wine bottle.

Matt came into the sunporch and sank onto the sofa bed next to Linda. His weight on the mattress shifted her knee painfully, but Matt didn't notice. He leaned against the arm of the sofa bed and took several deep gulps directly from the bottle.

Linda could barely see the label by the light of the kitchen filtering in. It was a bottle of Chianti that she'd received in the anonymous holiday gift exchange at work last year. As Linda was not much of a red wine drinker, she had stuffed it in the pantry cabinet for a future spaghetti sauce which had never materialized.

Matt reached across her and grabbed the remote off the bed. He turned the TV on.

"Matt, I didn't realize the TV was so important to helping you sleep."

Matt was silent.

"You know there's a TV in my room, don't you?"

Matt looked at her, "I forgot."

"Well, I can't risk going up and down the stairs yet, and you're way too big to be crawling into bed with me like you did when you were three," Linda gave him a playful nudge in the side. "So, until I can do the stairs, how about you use my bed?"

"I can do that," Matt took a smaller sip of the wine out of the bottle. He leaned over and in a display uncommon since his discharge from the service hugged Linda. She heard him mumble, "I'm sorry Mom" into her shoulder. He sat back up and commented, "These nightmares are no joke. It's like I'm back there again. I keep seeing a kid getting blown up in front of me. Sometimes it's a street urchin dressed in rags like we saw over there, but other times the kid looks like my old buddies Jonesy or Alan or even Casey or my high school girlfriends. Sometimes the kid picks up a grenade, other times the kid's chest gets torn apart by a rooftop blast. I've had so many different versions of the nightmare, I'm not even sure which version is what I actually saw back then."

"I'm so sorry you're dealing with this." Linda had a flash she considered brilliance, "Hey Matt, Dr. Samuelsson is still practicing. Maybe while you're waiting for your VA benefits, you could see if he can give you some sleeping pills. It's no big deal for me to pay for one primary care visit." Linda knew perfectly well that sleeping pills were not a proper treatment for PTSD, but all her prior attempts to get Matt medical help had failed. Maybe if she could get him to see the doctor he had seen all his life he'd be one step closer to getting the right kind of help.

Matt didn't answer for a few seconds, during which Linda held her breath. "It would be nice to sleep through the night."

Linda exhaled, "I'll look up his number in the morning and see if they can get you in."

"OK," Matt acquiesced as he stood up.

"And Matt," Linda continued.

"Yeah?"

"Please take a shower before you sleep in my sheets. Your aunt was right. You do smell."

Matt smiled at her and headed upstairs. She heard the water running a few minutes later. She rearranged herself back on her pillows and turned off the TV. As she drifted off to sleep she thought about Matt admitting he'd had so many different variations of the nightmare, he didn't even know which one was real any more. No wonder these poor kids with PTSD had such a hard time getting the military to take them seriously if their story changed constantly. Hopefully once she got him some proper help, the psychiatric personnel who were expert in PTSD would recognize the inconsistencies as a symptom of the disease.

* * * * *

About two weeks after Linda had returned to her own house, she poured out into her hand the Percocets remaining in her bottle in the medicine cabinet of the upstairs hall bathroom. Only fifteen remained, and she knew she should have more left. She took one.

When she went to bed that night, she left her bedroom door cracked. The digital red numbers on the alarm clock face read 3:27 when she heard footsteps down the hall. She could tell from the weight of his slightly shuffling footsteps and his breathing that it was Matt. He went into the bathroom and shut the door. She knew he opened the medicine cabinet because its door gave its customary squeak. After a minute or two, he shuffled back down the hallway and went downstairs. Linda laid in bed for a few minutes and then figured, "What the hell, I've got to pee anyway." She went into the bathroom and with the noise of the toilet flushing as cover, she opened the squeaky medicine cabinet. She counted out eleven pills. "Damn, he just stole three of my Percs."

Linda had to snap herself back into perspective. She was recovering from knee surgery. She wouldn't need the pills after she had healed. The bigger problem wasn't her supply; it was the fact that her son who had no medical condition requiring an opioid had just scarfed down three times her normal dose. A string of expletives marched through her head as she climbed back into bed. After two hours of lying on her back with a bolster pillow under her right knee, Linda was unable to return to sleep, her brain whirling with the ramifications of this latest manifestation of her son's mental health issues. Even more worrisome, she knew he was at least drinking beer and possibly sipping at whiskey earlier in the evening; if he kept popping too many Percs with his alcohol consumption, the Tylenol in the Percs would blow his liver out. She tried to remember exactly when she went to bed and whether she was due for her next dose. Then she decided, "Oh screw it." She got back up, went to the bathroom and took the first Percocet dose of the day. She laid back down. After the usual half-hour or so, the paradoxically calm euphoria set in and she fell back to sleep.

Waking much later than her norm, she headed back into the bathroom. Her knee was sore, and the muscles in her right leg were still tight from the physical therapy session. It was a little early for her next Perc, but she wouldn't want to work her way back upstairs when it was time to retrieve the bottle from its hiding place. Rather than just take the pill downstairs with her to take later, she decided to go ahead and take the next dose and returned to her bedroom to find a good hiding spot for the bottle. The nightstand was too obvious. Of course, if she hid the bottle too well, Matt would realize she was on to his theft, and she wasn't sure she wanted to confront him about it yet. She wanted to mull over how to handle this for a little while. Her well-worn house sweater was hanging on the hook on the back of the bedroom door. She slipped the bottle into its oversized pocket. If Matt did go rummaging through her room when he didn't find the bottle in the medicine cabinet and he found it in her sweater, he would think nothing of it. Linda had been known to wander aimlessly out of a room with the TV remote or kitchen utensils in the pockets of that sweater.

Linda stewed. Three Percocets wasn't a huge dose for a full grown man like Matt, but she assumed he must have tried them somewhere before he grabbed them out of her medicine cabinet. She remembered the end table at Casey's father's house with its array of amber prescription bottles and wondered if Matt might have started helping himself to his girlfriend's father's supply. If he had been caught, that could have been a final nail in the coffin of his relationship with Casey.

Linda hadn't needed to worry about anyone taking things out of the house in which she grew up since Jimmy moved out and she changed the locks, a move which her mother would have applauded had she been living at the time.

* * * * *

Her Mom had never liked Jimmy, not from day one. The best Linda ever got was Mom's acknowledging that Jimmy was a good father and a good handyman; even by the time her mother had encouraged Linda and Jimmy to move in to the house with her she was still no more than lukewarm in her feelings to Jimmy.

The dislike understandably started with the fact that Linda was pregnant before they got married. As she had endlessly tried to tell her mother right up to the day of the wedding, Jimmy had proposed before they found out she was pregnant; therefore it didn't qualify as a shotgun wedding.

She had told her Mom about the pregnancy sitting on the front lawn of the house in cheap white plastic lawn chairs with her Mom and Laurie, back before the deck had been added. Laurie was recently engaged, and in her mother's eyes Laurie's budding transplant surgeon fiancé was several notches up the ladder from Linda's self-employed general contractor.

"Mom, you don't understand, he's…." Linda tried to explain.

"You're absolutely right, I don't understand," the twins' mother interrupted. "I don't understand what you see in him at all, or why you let yourself get knocked up and now you're stuck with him. Look at Laurie, she's marrying someone with a future."

"Mom, not everyone wants a surgeon for a husband. Jimmy is practical and hard-working, and he treats me very well. I don't have to want the….."

Laurie stepped in between the two of them and stared them each down in turn, "You two are not going to agree on this one, and neither one of you is going to change your mind. Arguing about it is only going to be unpleasant without serving any purpose whatsoever. So can it, both of you, please."

Linda refused to believe her mother's concerns that Jimmy was cooking the books for his business, despite the fact that her mother was an accountant. After her Mom got over her initial complaints about the marriage, she ordered Linda in no uncertain terms, "You make sure that man sets up an actual business for that general contracting of his. Don't you dare get married if he's still running it as a sole proprietorship. He can ruin your lives if something happens to his company. And all his nonsense about how these guys he hires are contractors, not employees. He's going to run into IRS problems one day."

Mom had been the tiniest bit more tactful when she talked to Jimmy on the eve of the wedding about the need to set up a business entity. Jimmy bought into it, not because he wanted to do the right thing, but because he thought he could hide some of his profits better if he had the company. He swore up and down for the first years of their marriage that he was doing his books exactly the way Mom had taught him to do them.

Linda was pleased to prove her mother wrong by starting off idyllically happy in their decent but unremarkable apartment in Annapolis. Jimmy was a terrific father without a chauvinist bone in his body when it came to taking care of Matty. He changed diapers and carried Matty around while pushing the vacuum to make the humming noise that would put Matty to sleep. If Matty woke in the middle of the night, Jimmy would retrieve him from the crib to bring him to Linda to nurse. Once Matty started to try to walk, if he fell and needed comforting, Jimmy was his first choice, even over Linda.

Mom's inability to maintain her house in the handful of years since Dad had died propelled the first minor rapprochement between her and Jimmy. During a heroic snow storm, an ice dam had formed in her gutters and shoved up under the eaves of the house. Mom had called Laurie first when she saw a river of water pouring down the living room wall. Laurie had said, "Mom, call Linda, she's the one married to the contractor."

Mom swallowed her pride to find out why her living room suddenly had a water feature, "Linda, it's Mom. I've got a little water problem in the living room."

"What do you mean by a little water problem, Mom?"

"Well, there's water coming down the inside of the wall."

"You mean the wall is sweating?" Linda knew no more about construction her mother did.

"No, there's a waterfall coming down from the ceiling to the floor from the picture window over to the front door."

"Do you think a pipe burst?" Linda had asked.

"I don't know. I called Laurie but she told me to call you." Then Linda caught on. Her Mom wanted to ask Jimmy, but wasn't comfortable asking directly for him.

Jimmy had been in the process of putting on his long underwear and boots. He had insisted on being one of the first contractors to buy one of those four-wheel drive pickup trucks with its own snowplow. Linda had initially viewed it as a ridiculous expense, until she realized how much Jimmy was charging his convenience store owner-customers per hour to come clean out their parking lots. He had come home for about four hours of sleep and then was getting ready to go do more plowing when Linda's mother's call came in.

Linda put her hand over the receiver and informed Jimmy, "Mom says she has water coming down her wall from the ceiling to the floor between the picture window and the front door. Could a pipe have burst?"

Jimmy snorted, "Well, I hope to hell no one put the plumbing in an exterior wall. More likely she's got an ice dam."

"What's an ice dam?"

"It's what happens when your gutters fill with water, usually because they haven't been cleaned, and then freeze. Ice takes up more room than water. The ice has to go somewhere, and it usually goes up under the roof."

"Oh. Should I ask Mom to look at her gutters?"

"No, I'm heading to that quickie mart store at the end of the Mayo peninsula later today. I'll go by her place on my way."

Linda returned to her mother, "Mom, Jimmy says it may be water backing up from your gutters. He's plowing snow out on Mayo later today and he'll take a look at it."

Jimmy had been correct. Mom, who declaimed in an innocent voice that she had no idea that gutters needed to be cleaned, took Polaroids of Jimmy standing in the front yard yanking the old gutters off the house. When the weather let up, he fixed the damage to the roof, the interior wall and put new gutters on.

Mom would probably rather have eaten nails, but she did thank him for doing a nice job. Two weeks later Mom's twenty-five year old water heater died and flooded half of the first floor. Mom called Sears at first but they told her that the laundry room didn't have sufficient air flow by current code to put in a new gas heater and to boot estimated it would be two weeks for a code-compliant electric water heater to come in. Jimmy got a gas water heater the next day at half the price that Sears had quoted her. He used the wet-vac throughout the whole lower floor, installed a vent, and put down a new linoleum floor in the kitchen because the flood had pulled the old one up. Again, Mom thanked him, but Linda knew it killed her to do so.

Then at Easter dinner a few weeks later, Mom nonchalantly asked Linda, "Your lease on your apartment is coming up soon, isn't it?"

With a mouthful of ham, Linda had garbled out, "At the end of June."

"Well, you know Matty needs a yard to play in and your apartment doesn't have enough room."

Linda had kept chewing on her ham, not quite sure how to respond.

"I was thinking that maybe you all, you move in here with me. I'll take Laurie's old bedroom. You all can take the big bedroom, and then Matty can be in the room next to you all. That way Matty can play in the yard, and he's right across the street from the park, and he'll be in a better elementary school when he gets to be old enough."

Laurie played her usual smartass role, asking, "How much rent you gonna make 'em pay, Mom?"

"None," Mom had snapped back a little testily. Linda was astonished and was still trying to figure out where this came from. Then she got it as her Mom continued, "Well, you know, the grass will start to grow soon, and the faucet in the upstairs shower keeps leaking, and my water bill was through the roof last quarter. Maybe Jimmy takes care of those things for us instead of paying rent."

Linda had the aha moment. This was as close to an admission as Mom would ever make that she couldn't or didn't want to handle the house. So, Jimmy's work must have impressed her, and she had thought up a way to make a good deal for everyone.

"Wow, Mom, that's very generous of you." Linda hadn't met Jimmy's eyes yet, "I think Jimmy and I should talk about it when we go home. It's not fair for me to put Jimmy on the spot in front of everyone. But we'll definitely talk about it."

That night as she and Jimmy discussed her mother's offer, Linda had far more reservations than Jimmy did. "Jimmy, I grew up living with her, you didn't. Mom wants everything to happen like clockwork. She'll never be able to cope with our schedules, with dinner not being at six o'clock on the dot every night, and she'll hate it whenever one of us has a night shift."

"We'll just have to do the best we can to let her know when we'll be around," Jimmy shrugged. "Think how much money we can sock away for Caribbean vacations if we aren't throwing away half your take-home on rent every month."

Trust Jimmy to count the money. He would move in with just about anyone if it meant he didn't have to pay rent. The extra money would be nice though, as well as the better school district for Matty. "And for Matty's college."

"Huh?" Jimmy questioned.

"We should be socking some of that money away for Matty's college, not just our beach trips."

"Yeah, yeah, of course." Jimmy had not gone to college and since he was making what he considered a good living, he didn't seem too concerned with Matty's going to college. Linda didn't push though as there was no need to argue about college with Matty not even out of diapers yet.

"So, we're in," Jimmy stated in confirmation.

"We're in. I'll call Mom when I get off work tomorrow, and then we can tell the landlord we're not renewing."

"Great news. Hope the walls of those bedrooms aren't too thin," he leered, snaking one of his long arms around Linda's waist and pulling her to him.

When they moved in with Mom, Mom had put the house in a trust with Mom as the original trustee and beneficiary, and Linda as the subsequent beneficiary but with Laurie as a trustee as long as Linda was married to Jimmy. Mom had seen all the future money problems coming and had used a lawyer to set up a trust to keep Jimmy from being able to touch the house in a divorce. She had also ensured that the trust prevented Jimmy from sucking all the equity out of the house to sink into his business.

Not that Jimmy was a bad contractor. He was actually quite competent at the work. He had completed the carpenter's union's apprenticeship program while working for his uncle. Jimmy, however, had seen that residential construction was a lot less profitable than commercial construction, and he left his uncle's business to hook up with one of the big contractors to learn commercial work. Then he struck out on his own, doing remodels and building cooler boxes and walk-in freezers for convenience stores.

The problem was that Jimmy was greedy and didn't want to play by the rules. Although he had sworn to Linda and her mother that he was doing his books exactly the way that Mom had taught him to do them, he would not let Mom or Linda see any of his paperwork. He kept it all at the little office he rented off the back of one of the marina buildings. But as it turned out, he wasn't playing by the rules. He wanted to call all of his employees "independent contractors" to avoid covering them under his insurance and withholding taxes, even though not a one of them carried their own liability insurance or met any of the other IRS tests for independent contractor versus employee. Somehow Jimmy deluded himself that he was smart enough to outfox the IRS on this, as if the IRS doesn't see this thousands of times every year.

And he insisted that even after Mom had explained it all to him, he hadn't believed that what he was doing was actually illegal; he claimed he believed he was merely picking a cheaper route to go.

Linda's Mom had already passed away by the time Jimmy's business got its audit notice. Mom would have loved it. And the IRS nailed him in the audit. They found he owed six figures worth of back taxes from more than a decade's worth of playing it fast and loose.

And that was when Jimmy tried to get his hands on the equity of the house. He tried to convince Linda to take out a home equity loan to pay the back taxes, promising that he would make all the payments on the house. Linda could see her mother's ghost predicting Jimmy's skipping town, scot free of damages owed to the IRS and Linda's holding the bill in the form of the mortgage.

"Look, Linda, if my business goes under it's bad for both us," Jimmy cajoled. "You can see that, can't you? When haven't I paid my share of the bills around here anyway? But there's no way I can come up with that kind of money in one lump without the house. And look at all the work I've done on this house over the years. I've made this house worth lots more than it ever was the way your mom had it."

On that point, Jimmy was correct. He had built the large deck on the front, giving them a spectacular waterfront vista and barbecue space. He had also winterized the prior screened in porch on the back adding hundreds of square feet of living space.

Linda had felt guilty enough at that point that she started to waffle, "I'd have to check with Mom's lawyer. You know Mom put the house in a trust so we wouldn't have to do probate when she died. I don't have a clue how you get a loan for something owned by a trust."

Jimmy pleaded, cajoled, encouraged for a further twenty minutes until Linda agreed to call the lawyer. Fortunately, by the time she agreed, it was after business hours, but she had to swear on a virtual Bible that she would call the next day. True to her promise, she did call the lawyer the following day after Jimmy was already out working. Linda was stunned to find out from the lawyer that Laurie was the one who had to approve any mortgaging of the property. Linda tried to reach Laurie right away hoping she could stall Jimmy about her conversation with the lawyer until she could talk to Laurie. Fortunately, Linda was on night shift, and she was already headed to work by the time Jimmy got home; during her break at work that night Linda tried Laurie again.

Laurie had been aware of her mother's intentions, "You know Mom didn't trust the way Jimmy handled his business. She learned to put up with him well enough once she saw what a good father he was to Matt. But she still swore one day he'd get you all into trouble with the way he ran his business."

Linda acknowledged, "Yup, and she sure nailed that one. IRS has stuck him for over $100,000 in back payroll taxes. He nagged me half the damned weekend about how the only way out was to take a loan out on the house."

Jimmy was furious when Linda relayed the news that she couldn't take out a loan on the house without Laurie signing off. "That goddamned stuck-up bitch of a sister of yours gets to decide how we manage our lives," he fumed. When Jimmy and Laurie were getting along, Jimmy teased Laurie about her fancy house in Annapolis and her tendency toward more stylish clothes than Linda bothered to don. While he always did so in a joking manner, Linda could see now that Jimmy did have a bit of a grudge against Laurie.

Linda had tried to reason with him, "Jimmy, Mom didn't have to leave us this whole house. Laurie would have been entitled to half of it, but Laurie agreed she didn't need it. And besides Laurie is just doing what Mom wanted her to do, making sure that the house eventually gets to Matty free and clear."

"Well, what is Matty supposed to eat all this time if his Dad's business goes under? He can't eat a house. And it's not like you're in the clear, we filed joint tax returns." With that, Jimmy stormed off, leaving Linda with a sick feeling in the pit of her stomach. Could the IRS get the house because she and Jimmy were married? She knew Jimmy would be furious if she went behind his back and asked the lawyer, but he hadn't exactly been above board with her, all this time pretending he was doing his books the way Mom taught him. She therefore felt justified calling the lawyer who had drawn up the trust again, expressing her concern that she was tied into Jimmy's problems.

The lawyer told her, "I'm not a tax expert, but I'm going to give you the name of a colleague of mine. If you haven't been involved in your husband's business, you should be able to qualify for innocent spouse relief if the individual tax returns are implicated. And, your mother specifically set up the trust to protect the house if your husband's business ran into trouble, so your house should be OK. But definitely call my colleague."

Linda did, and she ended up retaining the tax lawyer to make sure she didn't get caught up in Jimmy's bad bookkeeping. Jimmy exploded when she finally got up the nerve to tell him, "Oh, that's great. My own wife won't try to help us out by getting a loan on the house to pay off this debt. No, she goes and hires her own lawyer to save her own ass. Well, if that's how you think a husband and wife are supposed to act, we're through. Go hang out with your uppity sister. You've both turned out exactly like your miserly selfish mother who hated me anyway." Jimmy stormed out of the house, roared off in his truck and didn't return for almost a week.

CHAPTER FIVE

Matt had been gone for five days this time with no note. Since Linda had yelled at him last year for disappearing he had at least been scrawling partially illegible, uninformative notes on her kitchen board when he wasn't there, such as "Gone for the weekend." And lately Matt had been so touchy that part of Linda was relieved when notes indicated he wouldn't be around for a few days. She figured if he's not here, he can't be mooching more cash off me or flying into a drunken rage or befouling the back sunporch. On the other hand, with this multi-day unannounced disappearance, she couldn't turn off her maternal worry instinct. What if he overdoses? What if he tries to get drugs from the wrong person? Linda wasn't sure how there could be a right person from whom to get drugs illegally, but some must be wronger than others.

Linda stood on the deck shivering in her sweater and made sure no cars were coming. Then she opened the gate leading from the deck to the yard and let Goldy run ahead of her to the park.

Joe, who lives two blocks back from the park, showed up about ten minutes later with his Rottweilers. "Are you having duck for dinner?" Joe asked.

"Huh?" Linda responded, confused.

"I saw Matt out with the decoys yesterday while I was fishing," Joe offered.

"Really," Linda said, trying not to sound too surprised or worried. "He didn't mention anything to me, and he didn't take his crack assistant Goldy with him. Where'd you see him?" Linda inquired, trying to sound casual and unconcerned.

"Oh, I was trolling the boat over around the county park lands, you know, the ones we pay taxes on, but they keep the gates locked to," Joe answered.

Linda knew exactly where he meant. The county owned a fair amount of waterfront acreage in between her community and the next one down river. Walking by it on the road, a brown sign announced that it was a county park, but the chain link gates on the driveway were always locked. She hadn't taken a boat around there lately, but on the water side, numerous signs prohibited trespassing on fragile wetlands. Cynically, she had always thought the county was holding out for a high enough offer from a developer to buy up the chunk of land, but until then, they were calling the park protected wetlands.

"I'll have to give him a hard time about missing my duck a'l'orange dinner," Linda joked, but inwardly her engines were racing.

Siobhan entered the park from the far side and unclipped her two chocolate labs, who made a beeline toward Goldy. Linda and Joe waved at Siobhan, and the three chatted amicably while the five dogs roughhoused.

Once the dog party broke up, Linda brought Goldy onto the deck and locked the gate. Then she grabbed a towel out of the small plastic storage box on the deck and rubbed Goldy's wet paws.

Back inside, Linda went up to her Dad's old gun safe in the closet of the spare bedroom. She reached up onto the top of the closet door frame and grabbed the key. Her knees protesting the whole time, she sat on the floor, then laid back and inserted the key into the lock on the underside of the inch-thick door. The lock clicked, she pulled the handle downward, and the door popped open.

"Dammit," she cursed out loud when she saw that one of the shotguns was in fact missing. Jimmy had been, and for all she knew still was, an avid duck and deer hunter, and had instilled those skills in Matt at the earliest possible age. When Jimmy moved out, he had tried to take all the guns and the safe as well.

Using Linda's mother's inventory of her Dad's guns on the homeowner's insurance, Linda had insisted that Jimmy leave those guns that had originated from her Dad for Matt. Linda herself would have been happy to be done with the guns, but since Jimmy had instilled his love of hunting in Matt, Linda wasn't about to let Jimmy take all the gear away from his own son.

Linda closed up the gun safe and returned the key to its usual spot. Darkness was already fully set in, and Linda was not going to venture to the park to see if she could locate Matt's hiding spot. Coming up on a man with a gun in the dark was suicidal. And she had another eight-to-four shift tomorrow. If he wasn't back by the day after tomorrow though, she was going to have to sneak into the county park and find him. Although she suspected she knew roughly where he was because there were only so many places at which Joe could have spotted him from his boat, Linda did not relish the trek through the overgrown paths with her knees.

Linda was surprised she hadn't considered the possibility of Matt hiding out in the woods before. Jimmy and Matt had camped out on their hunting expeditions dozens of times when Matt was a teenager. Now that she thought about it, Linda was sure that if she ventured out to the shed, the pup tent, orange hunting vest and duck decoys would be missing as well. Jimmy and his uncle had made most of the duck decoys themselves. When Jimmy and Linda separated, she could not claim any right to the duck decoys as she had with the guns, but she did suggest that Matt would be hurt if his father didn't leave him any of them. And whatever quarrels Linda and Jimmy had had, Jimmy would never intentionally hurt Matt. Hence, a half dozen of the duck decoys had remained.

When Linda returned from work the next day, Matt was back in the cave he had made of the sunporch. Later that night when she could hear him snoring, she went into the spare bedroom and checked the gun safe. The shotgun was back. She wondered whether to take the key. If she did, he would probably fly into a rage. On the other hand, if she didn't, she was allowing someone she knew to be mentally unstable access to guns. In the wake of the plethora of school shooting events, Linda concluded that she was going to have to live through his temper tantrum when he found out. Linda was not going to have an overeager news reporter thrusting a microphone into her face asking her if she had done anything to prevent her son from going on a shooting spree.

* * * * *

Linda didn't mean to steal the pill the first time. Actually, she didn't steal it technically speaking. Her actions in her mind fell in the limbo land of a happy accident.

Her patient Mr. Jacobson had been having an episode. The 74-year-old man had compression fractures in three vertebrae in his lower spine, T10, T11 and T12. With that kind of pain, even the sweetest person is a difficult patient. However, Linda was still annoyed when she heard Mr. Jacobson screaming at the medical assistant from three rooms down.

"You're just trying to dope me up and keep me in here."

Linda apologized to the patient whom she had been attending and hurried down the hall to calm things down. To her utter surprise, Mr. Johnson was standing on his bed. With the condition of his spine, he had no business being in such a precarious position, but moreover, Linda had no clue how someone in his condition had managed to stand up unaided on a spongy mattress.

Linda put on her best placating voice, "Mr. Johnson, I'm sure we can take care of whatever the problem is. We don't want you to hurt yourself any worse than you already are though. So, if I could please help you to sit down on the bed. Then I'll be happy to listen to whatever you have to say."

The medical assistant had backed off to the side wall of the room, eyes wide and confused.

Linda approached the bed and with her eyes and a motion of her chin she signaled the medical assistant to move to the far side. She reached her hands up toward Mr. Johnson hoping he wouldn't tip forward and was pleased that the MA had caught on that she was supposed to prevent him from falling backward if at all possible. Linda kept using her calmest, quietest voice.

"If you can grab my hands, Mr. Johnson, and then let's slowly lower you to your knees."

Whatever burst of internal chemicals had allowed Mr. Johnson to attain a standing position seemed to be wearing off because he did take her hands. Amazingly, he made it to his knees without incident. Before Linda could explain how she wanted to get him safely back in a supine position, he flopped himself over and miraculously landed in the bed.

"OK, Mr. Johnson. Good to have you back lying down. Your spine is very fragile right now. You'll get out of here a lot faster if you move around more carefully. Now, what was the problem?"

"Her trying to force feed me pills," Mr. Johnson stabbed a finger at the MA, who was clearly taken aback.

"All I did was ask him to take his OxyContin. I noticed it was still in the cup when I came in." The MA started to defend herself, holding up the translucent plastic cup containing a green pill. Mr. Johnson swung his hand in a circular motion, hitting the MA in mid-forearm, and knocking the cup out of her hands. The cup hit Linda in her sternum.

"Now, Mr. Johnson. Let's try to be a little more careful," Linda motioned the MA away from the bed. The MA got down on her hands and knees, retrieved the plastic cup and looked all over for the pill, but was not able to locate it.

"Well, the pill is gone Mr. Johnson, so it looks like you get your wish. I am going to have to let the doctor know that you haven't gotten your dose so he can order a replacement." Linda was going to have to do more than that. She was going to have to fill out an incident report. The patient had hit a staff member. She didn't believe that Mr. Johnson had intended to do anything more than push the pill away. But he did, inadvertently or not, hit the MA's arm and struck Linda with an object, albeit only a tiny pill cup. And, a Schedule II drug was missing.

"Oh, piss off. I'm not taking any pills no matter how many you get the doctor to order," Mr. Johnson grumbled back at her.

Linda and the MA left the room. The MA commented, "At my first hospital, they just hooked patients up to on-demand morphine IVs. Then we didn't have to fight with people to take their pills. If they were in pain and didn't use the IV, that was their business."

Linda replied, "Well, there are certain advantages to the on-demand drips, but they're really better for breakthrough pain, and even then most patients aren't patient enough, no pun intended. They're in pain, and they hit the button expecting that their pain will be gone five seconds later. When it's not, they hit it again, and again. Then when the meds finally kick in, they've taken too much. You can partially stop that by only allowing the button to work once in a particular period of time but patients with the severe spinal damage Mr. Johnson has need constant pain control. With an extended release pill like an OxyContin, once you get the patient on a regular schedule, they should have some relief for a twelve-hour period, unless they have a breakthrough pain episode."

The MA shrugged.

Linda and the MA arrived at the office where Nancy, their supervisor, was doing paperwork. She told Nancy, "I need an incident report form."

"What happened?" Nancy demanded, the pitch of her voice rising. Nancy lived for reporting misdeeds.

Linda and the MA both went through their stories. They both swore up and down that they had looked for the missing OxyContin pill to no avail. They both filled out paperwork for management, and Nancy filled out her paperwork. Linda then went down to the pharmacy and filled out their paperwork for a missing controlled substance. She pulled up Mr. Johnson's chart at a computer at the nursing station and recorded a brief description of the incident, noted that the morning OxyContin pill was not taken and that the patient wanted to refuse a replacement. She called the on-call physician to ask him to order a replacement anyway.

Linda wasn't surprised that within an hour or two Mr. Johnson was howling in pain. He wasn't prescribed OxyContin for nothing. Compression fractures hurt as badly as just about anything other than burns. Although his blood level of the OxyContin shouldn't have dropped enough in a couple hours for him to be in severe pain, he more than likely caused himself some damage with this antics on top of his bed and was experiencing breakthrough pain.

When the physician did his rounds and got to Mr. Johnson, he listened to the patient rave about the care he was getting. Then the physician questioned Linda about what she had typed in the chart. He finally decided that Mr. Johnson was going to have to go to the ER to have scans done to make sure he hadn't hurt himself flopping on the bed.

Linda spent the rest of her shift trying to catch up on all the other work she hadn't been able to do while dealing with the Mr. Johnson incident. She grabbed her sweater and purse from her locker and headed home.

Not until she was in the bathroom at the house and took her scrubs top off did she find the OxyContin pill. It had lodged into the V at the center of her bra. She ignored the little voice in her head that said that failing to turn the pill in the next day would be defined as drug diversion by any professional standard. But if she turned it in, the pill would go in the incinerator, so she convinced herself that keeping just this one pill which would end up in the trash anyway wasn't doing anyone any harm.

Because she wanted that pill. She wanted to try taking it although at the same time she was afraid to take it. OxyContin had sustained release as opposed to the Percocets whose effects wore off in four to six hours. She knew that OxyContin was meant to be taken as a long-term chronic pain strategy but part of her hoped that just one such pill meant that she could have one day where with one pill she didn't have to think about discomfort in her right knee or the increasing pain in her left knee for an entire shift. But she had no idea what the dose of the pill was in relation to her Percocet dose. Mr. Johnson had been on pain medication for spinal problems for years. By this point, he could be taking a dose way higher than what Linda could tolerate, and even with the slow release she could get a dose that would kill her.

She resolved to sneak a look at Mr. Johnson's chart the next time she was at work and see what his prescribed dose was even though she knew she wasn't supposed to look at a patient's chart unless she was doing so in service of the patient. She looked around her bedroom for a place to hide the pill until she'd figured out if she could handle taking it. She decided to hide it in the bottom of her jewelry box.

The wooden box on top of her dresser opened up like an accordion with three layers, each layer with a different configuration of felt to accommodate rings, necklaces, earrings, etc. The first things she noticed when she looked at the open box was that her engagement/wedding ring set was gone. Obviously she hadn't worn the set since she and Jimmy got divorced, but a half-carat diamond set in 14K gold was worth money. Linda seldom wore jewelry because at work, jewelry was a nuisance. Rings tore the nitrile gloves. Necklaces dangled in the way when leaning over patients, not to mention the fact that a patient might grab onto the necklace. She therefore stared at the open box wondering when the last time she'd had it open and when the last time she'd seen the wedding ring was.

"Matt couldn't have taken it, could he?" Linda wondered to herself. He lived here for free, and she brought groceries and beer. After he got fired from the marina, he had been getting spending cash washing and waxing some of the neighbors' boats. She was also reasonably sure that he'd occasionally helped himself to a twenty from her wallet when she left her purse in the kitchen at night. What else could he need money for? Then she looked down at the pill in her hand. But he was stealing her Percocets that she conned out of Dr. Rosen by complaining about the left knee with the right knee so recently replaced. Could he have enough of a problem that he was stealing her jewelry to pay for more drugs than what he was already stealing from her? She had never dreamed that his experiences overseas could mess her son up so badly leaving her and Matt in such a weak shadow of the happiness that used to pervade their house.

* * * * *

Thinking back to the early 2000s, Matt hadn't given either her or Jimmy a clue that he was enlisting. He gave Jimmy the news first and before Matt could even tell Linda, Jimmy had called Linda, ballistic. "What the hell did you let him go and join the Army for?"

Linda was clueless, "What are you talking about Jimmy MacDermott?"

"He hasn't told you?"

"Who hasn't told me what?"

"Our son. Our son has signed up for the Army!"

"What? When did this happen? When did he tell you?"

"About an hour ago. He took off when I told him what I thought. What'd he expect me to do, hug him and cheer 'way to go' like all those parents in those phony recruitment ads?"

"I'm not sure it's such a bad idea," Linda noted.

"Are you nuts?"

"Well, he hasn't figured out what to do with himself. At least he'll be collecting a paycheck and getting some experience."

"He was gonna get plenty of experience with me. Jesus, I can't believe you're supporting this."

"What choice do I have? He hasn't even bothered to tell me yet," Linda replied calmly.

Jimmy hung up in a fury.

Linda knew that Jimmy had big dreams of taking Matt under his wing and teaching Matt the contracting business. As much as Matt idolized Jimmy the outdoor man, Linda was sure that Matt was smart enough to have figured out that Jimmy was not running his business on the up and up. Since the disastrous IRS audit and their subsequent breakup, Jimmy took small cash-only jobs. Linda was wise enough not to criticize Jimmy's business practices in front of Matt or discourage Matt from joining his father's business, but Linda suspected that Matt had his own reservations about tying his career to Jimmy. When Jimmy talked about working with him, Matt merely nodded his head as if hoping Jimmy would drop the subject.

Matt had not mentioned any other career thoughts though. He had done OK in high school, but more because he was intelligent enough to get by, not because he put any work into it. What Matt loved was the outdoors. He loved hunting and fishing, and he loved them most when it was with Jimmy. Even his girlfriends had to be outdoorsy, and not in a pompon cheerleader way. For instance, in his junior year of high school he had brought home an attractive 19-year-old blond girl who raced motocross with all her spare time, of which she seemed to have a lot.

Linda decided to have pizza waiting for whenever Matt got home to see if she could get him to engage in conversation about his Army plans. When Matt did arrive around eight o'clock and sat down immediately to gorge on pizza, Linda prodded, "I hear you have some news for me."

"Oh man, not you too," Matt moaned.

"What do you mean, not me too? I think the Army's a great move for you," Linda pushed as much enthusiasm as she could into her voice. Great might be overstating it, but she certainly wasn't opposed to it.

Matt looked up from the cold pizza he was eating and asked, "Really?"

"Yes, hon, if the Army's what you want, I'm with you."

Matt still had a shadow of disbelief in his eyes, "You're not just saying that so I won't be mad at you too, are you?"

"Why would I just say that? In fact, when do I ever just say something so you won't be mad at me?" Linda chuckled.

Matt laughed too, "Never. You really think it's a good idea?"

"Yes, you love being outdoors. You're in great shape. You're a great shot. The Army'll barely have to teach you anything about shooting."

"I know. I would love to be a sniper or some sort of marksman. That would be awesome."

"I didn't realize you were so interested. Are you sure you'll be OK if you have to point your rifle at something other than a deer?"

"I used to think I wouldn't be able to do something like that, but man, those bastards who attacked New York aren't human. They're worse than the animals I shoot. I'd have no problem evening the score on what they did to us."

Linda cringed inwardly a little bit, "Well, that's one way to look at it. So, what's the timeline for all this?"

"I put in my application a little while ago, but man, that thing is huge. It's pages and pages long. They want info on every job you've ever had, all your relatives' names, character references. I snagged your address book one day while you were at work to fill out part of it. I guess it's for the security clearance, or at least that's what the recruiter told me. Of course, since I've only had two part-time jobs before, I could leave a lot of the stuff blank. But anyway, I was waiting to make sure everything was all set before I let either you or Dad know," Matt was stuffing bites of pizza in his mouth as he was talking, somehow managing to speak reasonably clearly around the balls of dough.

"I figured you would be the one who was pissed off. I was sure Dad would be thrilled. That's why I told him first, I thought he could help me tell you. But he went apeshit."

"Hey, watch the language."

"Yeah, sorry. He went ape. Said I was gonna get myself killed or maimed."

"He'll calm down after a while. He had all these fantasies that you were going into the business with him. He was picturing adding '& Son' to the company name. Once he realizes how happy you are about this, he'll be happy for you."

"Ya think?"

"Definitely. And you still haven't told me when all this gets started?"

Matt answered, "Oh yeah, I leave for basic training in two weeks. Isn't that great?"

Linda and Matt probably had the best two weeks of their relationship since Jimmy moved out. Matt seemed to walk taller, with his chest puffed out with a little bit of pride that he was going to be serving his country. Once he realized that Linda's support was genuine, he talked endlessly at the kitchen table in the evenings about what his friends who had gone in the service were doing and what job he might end up with in the service.

When Matt left, Linda had expected to feel lonely. Instead, she found that she loved living by herself. She had lived with her parents until she had gone to nursing school. Then she and Laurie had lived together during nursing school, first in a cramped generic dorm room at their small college out in Western Maryland and eventually in a beat-up apartment off campus which had seen way too many students. Linda and Laurie both moved back in with their parents when they first got out of school. Laurie had then moved in with her transplant surgeon fiancé, and Linda moved from her childhood home to an apartment with Jimmy. Jimmy and Linda had then moved in with her Mom. Even after her Mom died and she kicked Jimmy out, she had still lived with Matt. All of which meant that this was the first time in her life that she had lived by herself.

On the phone with Laurie one night, she asked, "Does it make me a bad mother that I'm deliriously happy to have the house to myself?"

Laurie answered, "Oh no. And now that you have it to yourself, you will even resent it when Matt comes home on leave. I'm sure. I couldn't live with anyone at this point in my life, not even you, not for any length of time."

"You mean we're not gonna grow old together with 50 or 60 cats?" Linda joked.

"No," Laurie replied firmly. "Besides, you're not really alone. You've still got Caesar."

"Caesar doesn't count. All he cares about is his trips to the park and my table scraps."

Matt called episodically from South Carolina during basic training. His enthusiasm vibrated through the phone. They had been taught to shoot this or that large gun. He was running miles and miles each day. The spaghetti wasn't as good as Mom's, but there was tons and tons of food. Could Linda believe that you could bounce a quarter off his bunk? And he always got perfect marks for cleanliness, which considering how he had left his bedroom in Linda's house was nothing short of a miracle.

"Mom, you won't believe it. I scored expert on rifle and pistol."

"Well, that's hardly a surprise, honey, you've been shooting with your dad since you could hold a gun."

"Yeah, but expert! I mean, I knew I'd at least score marksman or maybe sharpshooter, but I thought I might need more practice on their rifles before I could score expert. But you were right when you said I'm a really good shot. I mean some of these kids in training with me, they've never even picked up a rifle before. And they were lucky if they could hit the target at all. The sarge was trying to keep it cool when he pulled my first target back in on the first day of the basic course. Only one shot missed center. 'Not bad, son, but you need to try to get that last shot in.' I knew he was just hiding how impressed he was. And then, when the sarge saw that I already knew how to break down a rifle and how to clean one up and keep it absolutely spotless, I could tell he wasn't expecting that.

"And then we did our tests. I was pretty sure I was going to score at least marksman. But when they brought the targets in, I knew I'd done better than marksman. I'm hoping that means I'll get put in for sniper, but I keep telling myself not to get too fixed on being a sniper, because the Army can give you whatever job they want, and sniper jobs don't come up that often. But the sarge says he'll definitely recommend me for the squad designated marksman course down at Fort Benning. And if I can't get a sniper job, it'd still be pretty cool to be the squad designated marksman."

"I'm thrilled you're doing so well Matt. I'm sure you'll get whatever job you want if you keep shooting so well. And I'm sure your dad will burst with pride no matter his first reaction to your joining the Army."

When he called her from his posting in North Carolina a few months later to tell her that he was being prepared for deployment to Iraq, she suffered in the same way that mothers have been suffering for centuries when their sons get called to battle. She worried about his getting killed. She worried about his getting hurt. But she never realized she needed to worry that her son would be hopelessly traumatized by what he saw and did over there, and that PTSD could send him back to her a crushed fragment of the sunny young man who'd almost choked on his pizza in his excitement about heading off to serve his country.

Matt was given leave before his first deployment in order to make a visit home. Linda was looking forward to seeing him again, but was somewhat surprised when not only Matt showed up but also his new girlfriend Casey. In what was probably an unconscious gesture, Matt had his arm around Casey's waist and was rubbing the outside of her hip in the exact same way Jimmy had used to do to her. "Hey Mom," he greeted her, giving her a quick hug. "This is Casey. She's a fitness instructor at a gym near the base."

"Nice to meet you," Linda said politely, extending her hand to Casey. "I was going to order pizza tonight since I didn't know exactly what time you'd get here, but then tomorrow night I thought we could go to a crab house."

"Oh, we're going out with Jonesy and his girlfriend, and Alan and his girlfriend tonight. Crabs tomorrow sound good though."

Matt and Casey threw their backpacks on the sofa bed in the sunporch. Within ten minutes, Alan, Jonesy and their respective girlfriends had arrived.

"Hey, Mrs. MacD," came from a chorus of voices that headed straight to the sunporch and for a half-hour Linda's house was filled with the exuberant voices of her son and his friends. She then watched them all pile into Alan's old sedan to head out for their evening.

Linda heard Matt and Casey return late in the night. She heard them giggling, and then she heard other noises. Although Matt had had girlfriends in high school, Linda had never allowed them to sleep over. She guessed if the U.S. Army felt that Matt could go to Iraq to defend our country, he could probably sleep over with his girlfriend. And Linda had no specific complaint with Casey who was voluble, perky and athletic, the same sort of girl to whom Matt had always been attracted. Linda did remember Laurie's warning that she would resent the invasion of her privacy when Matt did return home, realizing her sister had been absolutely correct.

Matt and Casey slept until early afternoon and then according to them spent the afternoon prior to dinner roaming the neighborhood with Matt showing Casey all of his favorite spots in the woods

To the detriment of Linda's wallet, Alan, Jonesy and their girlfriends all came to the crab house with her, Matt and Casey. "So, what did you all do last night?" Linda inquired.

"Went skinny-dipping off the community beach," Matt answered.

Casey blushed, "Matt, I can't believe you told your mother that!"

"Oh, please. Dad and Mom and Aunt Laurie all used to go skinny-dipping off the boat when I was a kid," Matt looked up from the crab he was cleaning for Casey. "And don't even deny it, Mom, 'cuz Dad told me you did."

Linda raised her eyebrows at him and replied, "It beats ruining perfectly good bathing suits with all the silt that's in the Bay."

After dinner at the crab house that night Matt and Casey took the pup tent from the shed to the county park to complete the experience. Although overnight camping was not permitted at the county park, Linda knew Matt knew the place better than any of the rangers or police and would be camped out where none of them could find him.

Despite her worries about his upcoming deployment, Linda was smiling as she watched Matt and Casey back out of the driveway to head back to North Carolina.

CHAPTER SIX

A few weeks later, Matt pulled another disappearing act. After he had been gone for 48 hours, Linda went out to the shed to look for the pup tent, which as she suspected was gone. Blank spots on the coat hooks and shelves across the back suggested that a hunting vest and several decoys were probably gone as well. Then she noticed the letter-sized piece of paper on one of the blank spots on the shelf. The paper looked like it had been tented to stand up, but that its weight had pulled it almost flat. She pulled the paper off the shelf and read, "Mom, I still have my guns I bought in the service."

Linda swore to herself after reading the note. Clearly, he had gone up to the gun safe and found the key missing. Linda had not been aware that Matt had guns he brought home with him from the service. Had she known, she would have insisted that they go into the safe with all the hunting guns. She wondered where he kept them. Hopefully locked securely in the trunk of his car, not anywhere in the house.

Linda had just finished up a night shift and had been hoping to get some sleep. However, at this time of year, by the time she woke up darkness would have long since fallen. And she wanted to see if Matt was camping out in the county park while she had plenty of light for it.

Back in the house, she changed out of scrubs into heavy duty jeans, a warm hooded jacket and good walking shoes. She popped two Percocets to stop her left knee from protesting, only absentmindedly noticing that the right knee didn't feel as unnatural as it had for the first months after the surgery. She made two ham and cheese sandwiches and threw them plus two Diet Cokes in a plastic grocery bag. She drove the car over to the local tennis courts, the closest spot to the entrance of the county park. On her phone, she pulled up a Google map of the area and got her bearings.

Her neighbor Joe had seen Matt out by the point in his fishing boat. Linda figured from the Google site that she should be able to walk in a fairly straight line from the park's driveway to the water and reach the point. The trails weren't too badly overgrown, in part because the vegetation had died off for the winter. Linda turned her head around every hundred yards or so to see if she could still see the park entrance. After about ten minutes though, the trees closed off the view. She started listening for waves slapping against shorelines. If nothing else, as long as she found the cove, she could walk along the shoreline until she found the point. Besides, there was no guarantee Matt would be in exactly the same place as Joe had seen him.

She spotted the decoys floating in the water first. He had brought the wood ducks even though the season for that species was past, and Linda again admired anew the artistry Jimmy had put into the amazingly realistic decoys. Once she knew she was close, Linda called out, "Matt, hey, it's me, Mom." She did not want to startle someone with a gun.

No response. But she did hear rustling off to her left and headed there. Matt was wearing full camouflage. Linda wasn't sure whether it was old Army fatigues or ones he bought for hunting. The shoreline was eroding badly where he was standing, slightly stooped underneath an overhang created by the water cutting into the orange clay-like soil. A small tree with a sizeable portion of its root system dangling in the air was about three feet over Matt's head.

He didn't say anything as she came into view. She tried a joke, "I was hoping for duck a'l'orange, but in case it wasn't ready, I brought ham sandwiches." He at least smiled.

Without waiting for an invitation, she sat down in the dirt next to him and offered him a sandwich and a Diet Coke. He took it, and they both started eating without speaking. Having forgotten to put napkins in the bag she wiped her hands on her jeans when she was done.

Matt finished his sandwich quickly. "How'd you find me?" he asked.

"One of the neighbors saw you out here from his boat while he was fishing. He teased me about whether I'd had duck for dinner."

"Figures. Can't sneeze in this damned community without six people saying Gazootite and three more handing you tissues."

"Where's the pup tent?" Linda queried.

"Back up on the higher ground where it's still stable," Matt responded, jerking a thumb back up over his shoulder. "This section's eroded so badly the tree with our old rope swing even came down." Matt pointed next to a large gum tree lying on its side about thirty feet away. Linda wouldn't have noticed if Matt hadn't mentioned the rope swing, but the tatters of a dirty thick rope remained tied to one of the larger branches, almost completely blending into the clay-rich orange soil. Linda could still vividly remember the 1990s day when nine-year-old Matt and Alan had burst through the front door of the house supporting Jonesy between them.

* * * * *

Jonesy's face was that awful combination that came from being flushed from crying and having smeared dirt around with tears. "What's wrong?" Linda had asked.

"Jonesy's sprained his ankle. You need to fix it Mom," Matt had answered.

"How do you know it's not broken?" Linda questioned, at the same time moving her gaze down to the subject ankle.

"Cuz it's just swollen. There's no bones sticking out," Matt had replied. "You have to fix it before he goes home so his mom won't get mad."

"Matt," Linda said firmly. "I'll look at it, and I may be able to wrap it up to keep it from hurting as much, but the only way to be sure it's not broken is an x-ray." Linda wasn't sure if having Matt believe she was a superhero who could fix anything was a blessing at this point.

Linda moved her stern nurse glance to all of them as she probed, "How did this happen?"

All three boys met her with silence. Linda tried again, with a little bit of dissembling, "If I don't know how it happened, I may not fix it right." She stared pointedly at her son, betting he would crack.

"He let go of the rope swing too soon and didn't land in deep enough water," Matt finally ventured.

"A rope swing, huh," Linda started. "That means you came straight down on it, rather than twisting it?" This time Linda turned her nurse stare on Jonesy.

Jonesy gave a pained shrug, "I guess."

Linda had the boys to help Jonesy to the couch, where Linda probed gently at the ankle, comparing it to its companion. The ankle was at least twice as big as the other one, quite red, and unfortunately warm to the touch. There was no hiding this accident from Mrs. Jones. The boy was going to have to go to the ER to have it checked out.

Knowing Matt would never tell where the rope swing was in front of his friends, Linda tried another tactic, "The ankle is very swollen. How long did you boys have to walk to get him home?"

"I dunno, almost forever." Linda gave up. Boys their age didn't have a particularly good sense of time.

Linda decided that the ankle was in bad enough shape that she didn't want to keep moving Jonesy. The boys were aghast when she told them she was going to have to call Jonesy's mother to come get him and take him to the ER.

"No, Mom, you've got to just fix it. Jonesy's dad will kill him for getting hurt," Matt protested.

"I'm sorry, honey, but I can't keep moving him. He's already walked too much on it. Jonesy, you need to go to the emergency room. They'll put your leg in an x-ray machine. It will be kind of cool, you'll get to see your bones."

"Really?" Jonesy asked, temporarily distracted from his fear of his parents.

Mrs. Jones was a nervous Nellie sort of mother. Linda knew that her own job as a nurse made her somewhat dispassionate in the face of injury, but good Lord, Mrs. Jones overdid it. She was half-hysterical on the phone, and Linda had to cut through with her sharpest voice to make her understand that she needed to get off the phone and drive over here. By the time Mrs. Jones pulled up in her station wagon, she had been crying more than Jonesy.

"Rose, you need to pull it together. Your son will be fine if you do what I tell you. Take him to the emergency room and have them x-ray the ankle. If it's only sprained, they'll wrap it up. If it's broken, they'll get you in touch with a doctor who can set it." Linda had absolutely no intention of wasting her free afternoon escorting a hysterical mother to the ER. She spent enough time at the hospital as it was.

She helped Mrs. Jones put Jonesy in the back seat, with his leg up on the seat. After she finally got them moving, she sent Alan home.

"OK, Matt, spill the beans, where's this rope swing?" Linda questioned.

"No, I can't tell you. I'm no tattle-tale."

"Matt, one of your friends has already been hurt. If the rope swing isn't hung up right, one of you could get hurt worse. Look, your aunt and I used to play on one when we were kids. But only after my Dad had made sure it was safe."

Matt wouldn't budge though.

When Jimmy got home that night, Linda informed him about the rope swing and the ankle, "I'm betting the swing is somewhere they aren't supposed to be."

Jimmy answered, "When I check the crab pots this weekend, I'll motor around and see if I can find it. There's only so many places that they could have walked from with Jonesy between them that have the right kind of shoreline for one."

Jimmy swore to her he couldn't find the rope swing, although Linda was never sure that she believed him. The rope swing was just the sort of boyish fun that Jimmy would not want to deny his son, and having Mom know the location of the swing would take the fun out of it. However, Linda consoled herself with the realization that if Jimmy had found it he would either have secured it well enough to make it safe or if he couldn't secure it, he would have taken it down and told Matt not to tell his mother.

* * * * *

Now, nature had saved the twenty-tens generation of boys from the rope swing. Linda could see that the tree on which the swing had been secured had been a good solid tree, big enough that two men probably couldn't have touched hands if they reached around it. Linda felt sad to see it lying on its side, done in by the erosion that plagued the Chesapeake.

"So that's where the damned swing was. You would never squeal."

Matt grinned.

"Planning on staying here much longer?" Linda ventured.

"I feel better out here. The constant nightmares in my head sorta stop. I can just stare out at the eagles and listen to the water and not have any bad memories for a while."

An actual response. Linda was encouraged, "What brings you back when you do come back then?"

"Run out of beer. Or can't stand the stink of myself."

Linda chuckled.

"See the eagle headed to his nest right there," Matt pointed to a tall dead tree on the far side of the cove. A brown eagle was circling preparatory to landing.

"What type of eagle is that?" Linda asked.

"It's a bald eagle," Matt answered with a slight sigh for Linda's ignorance.

"But his head's brown," Linda protested.

"Their heads turn white as they grow up. Their heads don't turn fully white until they're five years old," Matt explained.

Linda hmmphed.

"That one snatched up a baby starling the other day," Matt said.

"Huh?"

"Mostly eagles eat fish but the baby fell out of the nest. I heard something chirping on the ground but I hadn't figured out what it was yet. And then the eagle swooped down and grabbed it, and I could see the baby in its talons. The adult starlings were going nuts. They wanted to chase the eagle, but they were afraid of it, so they would start to follow it, but then back off."

"Oooh. Poor baby bird."

"Well it fell out of the nest, it didn't have much chance anyway."

Linda decided she should head home. She had come to the park with grand plans for being able to truly connect with Matt and get him moving in the right direction again. But she found herself sitting on the ground with him not having a clue what to say.

"Guess I should head back now. Just wanted to make sure you were OK."

No response.

Linda tried to push herself up with one hand on the ground and another on a nearby rock. During the time on the ground though, her left knee had stiffened up. "Actually, Matt, you're going to have to help. Guess my knee won't let me sit on the ground anymore."

Matt moved around behind her and easily lifted her to a standing position. "Thanks, hon. You know, Matt, I do need my pills for my knees. I've gone back to physical therapy because my left knee is bothering me so much. I'm scared I'm going to need surgery on the left, and I don't want to have to get it so soon after having the right knee replaced." Matt remained silent behind her while she steadied herself. "If you need medicine to feel at peace, I'll get you an appointment with someone. I can pay for the medicine."

Linda hadn't planned to bring up the stolen Percocets, but her knee had given her the best opportunity she'd had yet. She hoped that she had sounded helpful and that seeing Linda struggle with her knees had shown Matt what his mother was going through.

Still silence.

She hugged him and started to set off, limping a fair amount. Matt caught up to her with two of his strides, "I'll make sure you get out of the woods. You're not walking too good."

As they walked along the path back to the entrance to the park, Linda's left knee loosened up and she could walk almost normally. She pointed to the car at the tennis courts, and Matt helped her the rest of the way. He hugged her briefly and loped back to the woods without even a good-bye.

Linda drove home, not sure what she'd accomplished. Faithful companion as always, Goldy was delighted to see her, and Linda realized she needed a park visit. As it was the middle of the day, no one was around. She let Goldy loose from the deck, and then made her own way slowly to the park. She hoped she didn't need to clip Goldy back on the leash as she was a little worried that a good tug on the leash would unbalance her.

When Goldy had had her fun and Linda returned to the house, she tried to remember what time she had taken the last Percocets before heading out to find Matt. She couldn't, but decided it had to have been long enough. She popped two with a glass of water and then parked in front of the TV.

Matt came home two days later while she was at work. She was not sure how he managed to time his arrivals to her work schedule, since she had long since stopped writing her shifts on the eraser board in the kitchen. He never made his returns from his little adventures while she was home though. For that matter, she wondered what he did with his car when he went off. Of course, he had enough buddies in this neighborhood that the car could be anywhere.

CHAPTER SEVEN

To keep Matt from poaching her pills, Linda had gotten in the habit of taking her Percocet bottle to work with her, and she kept it in the bedroom with her while she slept. But all she did this time was go to the bathroom in the middle of the night and five or six pills disappeared from the bottle on her nightstand. What was he going to do when she couldn't come up with any more justifications for getting Percocets from the orthopedist anymore?

Linda was still stewing over Matt's most recent theft of her Percocets the next day when Laurie hosted a nurses-only party on the boat. Although she would have preferred to bow out, Linda played first mate, and found places to stow the drinks and food which people brought in the small cabin of their boat. Up on deck, Laurie called for attention with her best charge nurse voice, "Alright, folks, we're having an in-service." Groans from on deck filtered down to the cabin. All nurses got their fill of in-services, the euphemism for the training that nurses receive any time a hospital has a new piece of equipment or a new patient procedure.

"Before we go out on the water, everyone's going to know where the emergency equipment is and how to call for help on the radio." Laurie then proceeded to go into excruciating detail about where every life jacket, air horn, and flare on the boat was stored.

As she was going through the instructions for calling Mayday on channel 16 on the VHF, Linda was heading up the stairs to the deck after packing the lunch in the fridge. "Jesus, Laur, the crabs swimming under the boat can use the radio by now. We'll never make it out to the Bay if you keep going on," Linda gave her sister's right hip a bump with her left as she reached her to lighten her words a little.

"OK, OK, but if anyone drowns on this trip, it's not going to be for lack of an in-service," Laurie conceded.

"When you said you were having a nurses-only boat trip, Laurie, you didn't tell us it was because only nurses would put up with an in-service," joked one of the nurses whose name Linda had missed during the introductions.

Laurie lowered the boat lift until the boat was floating and then some to accommodate the expected low tide for the return. She started the engines and backed the boat out into her little creek. Generating no wake, she motored at a crawl until her creek let out into the South River. Laurie scanned for boat traffic and in particular for swimmers and kayakers. Then she pushed the throttles forward and headed down the South River toward the Chesapeake.

Despite her funk, Linda had to admit the day was glorious for boating. The sailboats were getting enough wind that most of the ones out on the Bay were actually under sail, not just using their back-up engines to get around. Small power boats were plentiful as well. As they entered the Bay, Linda could see several container ships parked on the south side of the Chesapeake Bay Bridge, waiting for their time slot in the Port of Baltimore. The channel is dredged all the way to the Port of Baltimore but on the north side of the bridge, the channel becomes narrower as the Bay reaches its upper end. When the big container ships arrive early for their berth at the port, their designated Maryland pilots keep them waiting a little south of the Bay Bridge so as not to impede traffic through the narrower parts of the channel, turning their bows into the tide to keep securely anchored. As the spot these enormous vessels anchors is parallel to the Naval Academy and its security systems, Linda had always assumed that having the large foreign vessels stuck there also served a security purpose.

Laurie took the boat under one of the small passages between piers of the two spans of the Bay Bridge. As she approached the Bridge, she pointed out the logjam of cars on the eastbound span. Both sisters found the four-mile-long spans impressive from the underside as well as the top side, and most guests in the boat did as well. Laurie stayed far enough away from the beach at Sandy Point State Park to avoid the day Jet Skiers and non-motorized craft. She did point out to her guests the park's long stretch of imported yellow sand dotted with beachgoers. "They do a charity polar bear plunge from that beach every January," Laurie added. "But I've treated enough hypothermia in the winter that I have no interest whatsoever."

The waters of the Bay had enough chop that Laurie decided to tuck back into the edge of the South River where it was a little calmer to stop for lunch.

Rosa, Laurie's colleague from south of the border, had brought homemade tamales as her contribution. As if the tamales weren't enough, she brought out sour cream, pico de gallo, a fiery looking thin red sauce, and a thicker smoky burnt-sienna-colored sauce.

Linda inquired, "Are those hot?" pointing at the two unfamiliar sauces.

Rosa answered, "I call my grandmother's secret sauce the oxycodone, and the adobo OxyContin." Rosa pointed at each of the sauces in turn as she spoke, "You get heat with both. With the first one it's all up front. With the second one it's a long slow burn. Pick your poison."

The women laughed. Janet, another colleague of Laurie's, said, "I can't believe you went to so much trouble for lunch for us."

Rosa demurred, "Oh no, tamales were the original pack up your lunch in a corn husk and go to the field food. My grandmother would keep making them like an assembly line until she ran out of ingredients."

Janet responded, "But still, all I did was bring margaritas from a bottle of mix."

"I have no complaints about that," Linda piped in. "A perfect bebida for tamales." Linda, however, found herself thinking more about the concept of OxyContin than margaritas, dreaming over the notion of a long-acting painkiller that would keep her left knee in check for a whole shift at work.

"Oh, icky seagulls," one of the nurses exclaimed. She pointed up over her head where a handful of the birds were circling. They had obviously seen the lunch set out on the boat deck.

"Don't worry," Laurie pronounced in an affected haughty tone, "birds don't shit on my boat."

Even as she made this remark, Linda could see a trail emanating from the rear of one of the seagulls which landed with a splat right next to the foot of the nurse who had originally screamed.

"They don't, huh? If my foot had been two inches to the left, I'd have been hit."

Laurie sipped a small amount of margarita from a plastic cup while most of the other women filled up the infamous red plastic Solo cups with theirs. After the lunch was put away, Laurie offered the swim-and-sun option, "Now that all our blood is flowing to our guts, I can drop anchor over at Harness Creek, maybe raft-up with another boat or two depending on who's there. Then we can all sunbathe or swim. All in favor."

Seeing all hands go up, Linda motored back up the South River and turned into Harness Creek. As usual for one of the first glorious boating weekends of the year, a dozen or more boats were already anchored there. Laurie rafted-up to the empty side of Rob's boat, promising him that no one would need to be lifted back on board today.

Several teenagers in the next clump of boats were standing up on their paddleboards. Linda admired the ease with which they popped themselves from a kneeling position right up to a standing position, holding a paddle, without even a bobble.

Linda remarked to the group, "Well, my knees are thirty years too old to try that."

One of the other nurses commented, "But it looks like so much fun."

"Not me," rebutted Laurie. "Give me a good old-fashioned motor anytime. Besides if I fall in, the water's not as warm as I'd like it yet."

"Me too," echoed Linda. "Last time I tried to go out in a non-motorized craft I made a jackass out of myself in front of my teenaged son."

"Anything a mother does makes her look like a jackass to a teenaged boy, Linda. What did you do that was so special?"

"It was right after my ex had moved out, and I was trying to show my son that we would still do fun things even with his father gone. With Matt being the quintessential outdoorsy boy, I borrowed a canoe from one of the neighbors and packed a picnic lunch. We got the canoe off the community rack and loaded ourselves up, and we were doing fine paddling around in our little creek," Linda pointed downriver to her creek on the opposite side. "But a big tropical storm was passing off the East Coast, and the winds were gusting over 30 miles per hour. My creek was a little choppy, and the South River had the beginnings of whitecaps. But we made great time getting out of the creek and heading up toward Glebe Bay.

"My son had friends over in London Towne which is on Glebe Bay, and Matt decided it would be a hoot to paddle up on the community beach and go knock on his friend's door, but the friend wasn't home. Instead we ate our picnic lunch on the London Towne beach. Everything was great until we started paddling for home. We got to the mouth of Glebe Bay and tried to head back down the river to go home. But now, the wind had picked up even more and we were going against it. We kept looking at the shoreline as we were paddling, and we were moving backwards toward Glebe. I felt like one of those people in the commercials for those exercise pools with a continuous current. We paddled and paddled and paddled. It did us no good whatsoever, and this cormorant floating nearby with no difficulty whatsoever probably wondering what we was wrong with us."

"How'd you get home?" Rosa asked.

"Good thing Matt had more sense than his mother. I was starting to panic. First, Matt says to me, 'Mom, we're only fifty feet off shore. It's not like we'll die; we can swim to the closest shore.'

"Little did he know that when I was home for the summer from nursing school, a teenaged boy from our community did die in a canoe accident, probably no more than fifty feet offshore. So, I said to Matt, 'You're wrong my boy, you know Mrs. Barrett, who runs all the pancake dinners with the Boy Scouts and her church?'

"'Yeah, what's that got to do with it?' Matt questioned back, as we both still paddled furiously but vainly.

"'Her son died in a canoe accident on the Fourth of July, no further off shore than we are right now, so don't tell me don't worry we can't die.'

"I couldn't see Matt's face, but as if I were the biggest idiot on the planet he said, 'But Mom, all we have to do is turn around and go back. We'll find someone in Londontown to make a phone call for us or drive us home.'

"Of course he was right. I calmed down, and we paddled back to the beach where we'd had lunch. By this point, Matt's friend was back home, and we borrowed their phone. I called the neighbor from whom I borrowed the boat and told him what had happened. He came to get us with his pickup truck. He strapped the canoe on the top, and drove me and Matt home. It could have been a perfect bonding moment, but instead while we were waiting for the neighbor, Matt's friend started teasing him about not being able to paddle against a little bit of wind. Matt was so embarrassed that his friend in Londontown was going to tell all his other friends that we hadn't been able to paddle home that he didn't speak to me for days. I cooked my neighbor a gigantic pan of lasagna as a thank you, and I vowed that I would never go out on a boat without a motor ever again."

The group of women laughed. When the teenagers got bored of the paddleboarding and were lying on their rafts sunbathing, one of the women got brave enough to ask if she could borrow one of the paddleboards. A couple of the nurses tried it out. Only one of them was completely unsuccessful in getting to a standing position, but none of them had much staying power once up. The slightest boat wake and over they would go into the water, although the afternoon was hot enough that no one minded that the water hadn't quite warmed up to its balmy summer temperature yet.

At the end of the afternoon, Laurie got unhitched from Rob's boat and headed back to her dock at Harness Creek. After the other nurses had left, Linda helped Laurie wash the boat down and clean up the cabin. Then she drove home, thankful she didn't have a shift until the day after. Her left knee hurt even after a Percocet, and she lay in bed with a mental picture of the high-dose OxyContin nestled in the bottom of her jewelry box, hidden under the costume jewelry that even Matt would know wasn't worth pawning, but still worrying about where she would get enough Percocets to keep her knees from aching.

* * * * *

The second time Linda had deliberately acted to take pills, she had acted out of her growing lust for the relief from the stress of her world, but she still succeeded in convincing herself that she hadn't stolen pills.

Her patient Lisa Marie Daniels was an auto accident planning to happen. Ms. Daniels' chart noted this was her second car accident in less than six months. The chart continued by indicating that by patient's report her first accident had left her with "severe whiplash" from which the patient claimed she was still recovering. In this second accident, while still driving the rental car the other driver's insurance had to provide while her car was fixed from the first accident, she had been rear-ended by a tractor trailer that had pushed her into the car in front of her. Unfortunately the subcompact rental car when smashed between a tractor trailer and a large limousine had collapsed from the front, breaking both of her legs and putting her in Linda's orthopedic rehab unit.

Linda walked in Ms. Daniel's room right as Ms. Daniels was pulling an amber plastic prescription bottle out of the small purse she'd been keeping in her bed table.

"Ms. Daniels," Linda spoke sharply. "What's in the bottle?"

"Oh, nothing," Ms. Daniels demurred, trying to shove the bottle into her blankets.

"Ms. Daniels, I'm going to need to see that bottle. You're on several medications here, and we can't have you taking another pill that might interact with the medicines we give you," Linda placed her hand gently on the blanket next to the spot where Ms. Daniels was still attempting to conceal the bottle.

Ms. Daniels just stared at Linda. Linda calmly repeated, "Ms. Daniels, it's dangerous to have medicines we don't know about."

When Ms. Daniels reluctantly released her grip on the bottle, Linda read the label, "Percocet. Ms. Daniels, you're already taking Vicodin here. Do you realize that both Percocet and Vicodin contain Tylenol?"

Ms. Daniels did not answer. Linda continued, "Ms. Daniels, if you add your Percocets to Vicodin, you could be taking enough Tylenol to bake your liver. I'm going to have to turn these pills into the pharmacy, advise your physician of what I've seen, and make a note in your chart."

Now Ms. Daniels was angry, "Hey, I paid for those pills. You can't take them from me."

Linda responded, "Ms. Daniels, the pills will sit in the pharmacy until you and your doctor work out an appropriate pain management strategy for your issues. I cannot let you have these in your room when I'm bringing you Vicodins. It's not safe. This is not about money."

Linda walked out before Ms. Daniels could say anything. On her way to the pharmacy, Linda ducked into the staff bathroom and poured half the pills into her key pouch. Then she took the bottle to the pharmacy and brought the pharmacist up to speed. The pharmacist filled out some paperwork and took the bottle from Linda. Then Linda sat down at the round desk in the middle of the facility and documented the issue in Ms. Daniel's electronic chart. With perfect timing as she was finishing her notations in the chart, the orthopedist doing rounds on the orthopedic rehab unit came out of a nearby patient room.

"Dr. Mahmoud," Linda stopped him with a hand up. "Have you already been in to see Ms. Daniels?"

"Yes, she was my first patient," Dr. Mahmoud replied. "Why?"

"Well, when I went into her room she was helping herself to some Percocets that she had in her purse. Since we're giving her Vicodin, I told her she could be baking her liver with all the Tylenol. I took the bottle to the pharmacy. I have no idea how many Percs were in the bottle before she was admitted here, and I don't know how many she's had since she got here. I looked in her chart to see what meds she said she was on and what the hospital discharge papers listed. The hospital discharge note indicated they were giving her Vicodin. She denied any outpatient medications except birth control pills."

"Not another one," Dr. Mahmoud shook his head. "I guess I should get pain management in to see her. Do you think you scared her enough?"

"Oh, no way, she was pissed. Told me she'd paid for those Percocets, and I had no right to take them from her. I assured her the pharmacy would keep them for her."

Linda finished up her shift and went home. Linda had made sure to note the dose of the Percocets before she turned the bottle into the pharmacy. The pills she stole from Ms. Daniels were the same strength she'd been taking. She put the stolen pills in a plastic baggie and hid them in her underwear drawer. She didn't believe Matt was desperate enough yet to rummage through her underwear for pills.

Snapping the leash on Goldy because a gaggle of neighborhood kids were walking on her block, she walked Goldy to the far side of the park close to the beach hoping she could get Goldy's exercise in before the storm clouds massing on the far side of the river made it across. Only at the far side of the park did she unsnap the leash. As Goldy chased the tennis ball Linda threw for her with one hand while trying with the other hand to protect her eyes from the sand on the beach that was being blown about by the incoming storm, Linda internally debated whether she should feel guilty about the Percocets. The first time, Mr. Jacobson had thrown the OxyContin at her, and she hadn't even discovered until she got home that the pill was in her bra. So, she hadn't actually stolen that pill. She may not have run back to work and deposited the pill with the pharmacy and documented her find, but she hadn't intentionally stolen the pill.

With the Ms. Daniel's incident, Linda had indisputably intentionally taken the pills. However, she tried to convince herself that she didn't feel guilty. Ms. Daniels was either incredibly unlucky as a driver, or was a dangerously bad driver, or she was one of those drivers who deliberately got into minor fender benders to get the insurance money, only with this particular accident she'd gotten more than she'd bargained for. On top of her failings as a driver, Ms. Daniels's behavior suggested she had an opioid problem. And the dumb bunny hadn't even realized she could toast her liver, not to mention OD on the opioid itself. Therefore, she shouldn't have the pills, and Linda tried to rationalize to herself that by taking them away Linda was preventing harm to a patient. All true. And since the pills shouldn't go back to Ms. Daniels, the pills would have to go into the incinerator, since her facility could not do anything with pills once a patient had handled and potentially contaminated them. Hence, ignoring everything she'd learned in every work training session on opioid diversion, all Linda was doing was taking trash. And once something was in the trash in the garbage cans out on the street, it didn't belong to anyone. By the time Goldy was tired of chasing the tennis ball and they were making their way back across the field as quickly as her knee would carry her away from the first rain drops being blown in by the storm, Linda had deluded herself into believing that she hadn't stolen anything, merely taken something out of the trash, fair game.

And besides the Percocets she had taken from Ms. Daniels came just in time. Her orthopedist had not refilled her Percocet prescription at her last visit, where he declared the right knee on which she had had surgery to be sound. When she had tried to casually ask, he told her to take an ibuprofen if she had any incidental pain, and he scolded her that if her left knee was causing her that much pain she needed to consider her second surgery. Linda counted out the stash she had acquired from Ms. Daniels and convinced herself that she would cut back to two a day and by the time she ran out, she should be fine. She'd also almost convinced herself that she would never need to resort to such a method for obtaining pills again.

Now all she had to do was make sure that Matt didn't get hold of any of them. She again wondered somewhat maliciously whether Matt had picked up the habit from his ex-girlfriend's family, the one with whom he had been living in North Carolina when he first got discharged from the Army.

CHAPTER EIGHT

Linda and Laurie went out on the boat almost every weekend of every summer unless one of them was stuck working both weekend days. The boat was titled in Laurie's name but Linda gave her a check for the boat insurance once a year and paid for half the gas, the inevitable repairs, and the winterizations, hence they considered it a joint asset. Many days they did nothing more than raft-up directly at Harness Creek or take a short foray out into the Chesapeake and then end the day at Harness Creek. On the way back from one of these forays they stopped to watch three kids tacking their Sunfish on the South River.

"Oh look," Laurie commented. "They're practicing tacking."

Linda countered, "Tacking nothing. They're trying to flip her. Look, every time they jibe, they all throw themselves to the side of the boat with the sail and let the sheets run all the way out."

Linda and Laurie had learned as kids to sail on a Sunfish. A single mast sailboat with a lateen or triangular sail and a single sheet or rope, the Sunfish was about the easiest sailboat on which to learn. The summer camps dotted around the Chesapeake all had small fleets of them, as did many of the community beach marinas.

Learning how to bring a capsized sailboat upright again is part of basic safety training with a Sunfish, but for kids the capsizing is as much fun as the sailing itself and once most kids get the hang of it, they intentionally flip the boats at any chance.

"Yup, yup, yup." Laurie agreed. "There they go." The kids had executed a jibe turn into the wind, let the sheet run out and thrown themselves to that side of the boat. Over the Sunfish went, kids as well. The kids, all of whom were wearing neon-colored life jackets, all emerged safely on the stern side of the capsized vessel. The biggest of the kids swam quickly to grab the bottom side of the centerboard.

Another feature ensuring the enduring popularity of the Sunfish was the lack of a fixed keel. Fixed keel sailboats typically need at least six feet of water. Once off the rivers of the Chesapeake, most of the creeks and coves had channels cut out to depths sufficient for large pleasure boats but then quickly shallowed near the shorelines leaving many waterfront homeowners without enough depth at their docks to moor a fixed keel sailboat. The Sunfish, however, had a removable wooden centerboard instead of a fixed keel; the centerboard was thrust through the hull of the boat from the footwell. A larger block of wood at the top of the centerboard prevented the centerboard from slipping all the way through. The trick to righting a capsized Sunfish was to throw the weight of one's body on the centerboard from the hull side and let Newtonian physics do the work of lifting the sail out of the water and into an upright position again.

What looked to be the oldest boy of the trio was attempting to pull off this trick in front of the twins' eyes. But even the oldest one was a scrawny little thing and with the bulky lifejacket he wasn't able to propel himself with enough momentum to execute the uprighting. The other kids started to scream at the boy, although Linda and Laurie couldn't make out what they were saying.

Of course, capsizing a Sunfish wasn't completely safe. For one, when jumping on the centerboard to bring it back up, the jumper has to get out of the way of the hull of the boat as it comes back upright. And for another, if enough water starts to wash onto the sail, the weight of the water could push the sailboat toward 180 degrees from upright rather than 90 degrees. A completely upside-down sailboat, called a turtle, is a whole different level of problem because the entire surface area of the sail is fighting against you. A good-sized man can still put enough force on the centerboard to pull it up, but a few scrawny kids, no way. And, if a Sunfish turtles in a shallow part of the river, the top of the mast could get stuck in the alluvial silt forming the bottom of most of these waters.

After watching the kids struggle for several minutes, Laurie asked her sister, "Should we go help 'em out?"

"If you're up for it. My knee is definitely not, but I'll handle our boat."

Laurie gently brought the boat up behind the stern of the capsized sailboat at a safe distance from the swimming children and called over the side toward the kids, "You need a hand getting her back upright?"

"Yes, please," came the immediate answer.

"They're polite, what the hell," Laurie noted to her sister. She pulled on a life jacket and left Linda in charge of their boat. Laurie jumped over the side and swam over to the kids. She grabbed the centerboard that the oldest boy was still holding and made the kids swim out of the way. Then she lifted herself onto the centerboard slowly. Showing off, she didn't simply bring it back upright. She put enough of her body on the centerboard that she could reach over the edge of the hull. She slowly increased the pressure on the centerboard and brought the Sunfish up while managing to land her body on the top of the hull as it came back to top rather than flopping into the water. She grabbed the tiller and the sheet and got the boat under control. Then she waited until all three kids had scrambled back aboard the Sunfish before slipping back into the water herself.

The three kids were all thanking her profusely as she started to backstroke toward the motor boat. Linda heard her telling them to stick to come-abouts, turns into the wind that were inherently much safer than and much less prone to capsizing than jibes, and get themselves home.

Linda cut the engines and lowered the ladder of the stern of the boat to let Laurie back on board. "Oh, what a show off you are. Not just uprighting the boat but landing yourself on the boat."

"Oh, come on. We did that a thousand times a summer when we were kids."

"Yeah, well sailing is for young folks. I'm all for engines these days."

"No argument there. Sailing is work. I want a boat for recreation, and I could use a soda."

Linda went down to the galley to grab the sodas for them. She also grabbed a Percocet out of her bag. Laurie had come down to the galley without Linda's hearing, "Still poppin' those Percs, ay?"

Linda almost jumped out of her skin, "What are you talking about?" she croaked a little too defensively.

Laurie backpedaled, "Just teasing you. Thought I saw you popping a pill there."

Linda lied about the pill, "It's a Claritin. My eyes are itching like hell." Linda wasn't lying about the itching. Her face was itching, but she knew that was a side effect of the opioids. In her ER days, she had seen heroin addicts come in complaining that they had bugs crawling out of their nose, when what they were really experiencing was a common side effect of the opiates. Linda had been surprised when she started noticing the effect with her Percocets a few weeks ago; she had thought that itching as a side effect was limited to the street opiates and was related to the garbage used to cut the heroin, but when she had done a little internet searching, she found the side effect was caused by the opioid itself.

Laurie grabbed a bag of chips and dropped the subject, but Linda knew her twin well enough to realize that Laurie wasn't completely convinced.

The twins went back up on deck and watched the kids head their Sunfish toward one of the coves off the river.

Laurie looked at Linda as she walked over to the edge of the boat, "You're still limping, you sure you're not still in pain?"

Linda answered, "Unfortunately, I'm limping because of the left knee. I doubt I have too much longer until I'm going to have to do the next surgery."

Laurie groaned, "That sucks. That means I'm going to have to take care of you again."

"And here I dreamed I might be getting sympathy out of you, but no, you're worried about my being a burden to you. You know I don't have anyone else to take care of me. What am I gonna do, ask Matt?"

They both shook their heads at that thought. "I'm just giving you a hard time. You'd do it for me if I needed it, and I may, as another former field hockey star. Besides, you've done plenty for me."

And that was as close as Laurie ever got to bringing up her failed marriage. Laurie had been married to a transplant surgeon just long enough to be impregnated and then miscarry at the end of her first trimester when he knocked her down a flight of stairs after she caught him in their bedroom with an ICU nurse.

* * * * *

After her surgeon husband had knocked her down the stairs, Laurie had called Linda even while her husband was calling 911. Linda moved Matty's basinet next to Jimmy's side of the bed, left a note because Jimmy hadn't woken up enough to remember where she told him she was going, and hurried to Laurie's. She got there at the same time as the ambulance. The asshole was already trying to tell the EMTs that Laurie had gotten up in the dark to get something to drink and had lost her balance and fallen down the stairs. He hadn't seen Linda come up behind him as he started his cover story.

Linda jumped right in, "Don't you listen to his horseshit. This cretin got caught in bed with his latest bimbo, and he knocked my sister down the stairs. Don't fall for any of his smooth story about her needing water and tripping. She called me right away and told me what happened."

Jordan looked like he would have happily knocked the other twin down another set of stairs, but he wasn't stupid enough to stand around arguing. He disappeared into the house, and a few minutes later his convertible sports car backed out of the garage and took off. Linda wasn't one hundred percent sure, but she believed she saw a head in the passenger seat, the bimbo she guessed.

Linda would not allow Laurie to downplay her husband's actions. As the initial 911 call had not indicated any emergency requiring police presence, Laurie was already at the hospital before the police were summoned to get a report from her. Linda stayed in the room and squeezed Laurie's hand whenever Laurie faltered. Linda called her Mom, waking her up, and asking her to get in touch with one of the attorneys for whom she did taxes to get a referral for a good divorce attorney.

The hospital kept Laurie for a day and a half as the bleeding from the miscarriage was considered excessive. Their mother did track down a divorce attorney, who barged her way past the nurses into Laurie's hospital room.

The lawyer advised Laurie, "First, you have to go back to the house as soon as they release you from the hospital and make him leave. He's going to want to argue that because the house came from his family's money, he should keep it. If you don't insist on residing there, your argument for keeping it or making him sell it to give you your half is weaker."

Laurie protested, "I can't go back there. What if he shows up? What if he tries something else?"

Linda jumped right in, "I'll stay with you. Or I'm sure Mom will. Heck, I'll even make Jimmy stay there if I've got to work."

When they released Laurie, Linda drove her back to the beautiful waterfront home. Linda's Mom was there with Matty in his bouncy seat. Mom had already scrubbed up any blood on the floor and cleaned up whatever mess there had been. Linda arranged for her Mom to stay with Laurie and Matt while Linda ran home to talk to Jimmy and get a change of clothes, even though she and Laurie could still wear each other's.

"What a bastard!" he cursed as Linda filled him in on what happened.

"No kidding. The divorce lawyer says she needs to stay in the house because she thinks she can get the house for Laurie. The lawyer's going to lean on Jordan's parents to settle quickly to save his professional license. But Laurie's afraid to stay by herself. She's afraid he'll come back. I promised her I'd stay with her. I'll keep Matty with me too, so you don't have to take care of him. I hope you're OK with that."

Jimmy replied, "I'm OK with you helping her out, but I think Laurie's right to be worried that he'll come back. I want you to take one of the shotguns with you."

"Jimmy," Linda exclaimed. "What are…."

Jimmy cut her off, "Linda, don't be stupid. Mr. Silver Spoon in his mouth, God's gift to surgery isn't going to roll over and let Laurie and her divorce attorney ruin his life. He'll come back and try to scare Laurie into going away quietly. He'll try to convince her that his family's $500 per hour attorneys will squash her divorce lawyer like a bug. And, if he was angry enough to knock her down the stairs once, he might hit her again. The only way you're going over there is if you take the .410."

He didn't even wait for her to reply. He got out one of the shotguns from the safe, the one he mocked as the ladies' weapon of choice. He handed her a box of shells and demanded, "Now, show me you remember how to load it."

Linda decided to humor him even though he knew quite well that her Dad had taught her to handle a shotgun as a teenager. She easily loaded in a shell, pointing the muzzle at the floor. She packed a bag with diapers and clothes for Matty and a change for herself. Jimmy put the shotgun in the trunk of the car, and as he kissed her goodbye, he ordered, "And, don't you dare leave that shotgun in the trunk when you get there." After promising him she wouldn't, she drove back over to Laurie's. Linda waited until their Mom was gone to bring the shotgun into the living room, where Laurie was reclined on the couch.

"If you had any doubt that my husband was a redneck, rest assured," Linda joked. "He wouldn't let me leave the house without a loaded shotgun. I waited until Mom left to bring it in."

Laurie laughed weakly, "You're right. Mom still hasn't fully warmed up to Jimmy and telling her his solution to my abusive husband was a shotgun wouldn't help."

"At least, I can hope for a reprieve from Mom telling me I should have found a husband more like yours," Linda hoped it wasn't too soon to joke with her sister.

Laurie may have lost the baby and her husband, but not her dark sense of humor. "Right," she snorted. "You've got a great comeback if she does. And anytime in the future when she's royally pissing you off about Jimmy, you need to stick it in her face that she told you you should find a hubby exactly like Jordan."

"Whaddya say to ordering in a pizza," Linda suggested, figuring it was time to change the subject.

"I'm not real hungry, but order whatever you want. I can nibble on a piece. Take some cash out of my wallet, I owe you for all this anyway."

"Don't worry, I already had every intention of letting you pay."

They ordered a pizza. Linda nursed Matty and then put him down in the upstairs guest room. The twins watched a movie on TV. Laurie decided to sleep in the downstairs master, claiming she was too sore to climb the stairs, but Linda knew that Laurie didn't want to return to the marital bedroom.

With the downstairs master and the guest room spoken for, Linda was left with the upstairs master, Laurie and Jordan's bedroom. Linda's Mom had thankfully already changed the sheets where Jordan had taken his lover. Linda carried the shotgun, which had been lying next to her overnight bag, upstairs with her. She propped it up between the bed and the nightstand. Linda slept poorly. The upstairs master had large skylights and a large wall of windows to take in the views of the creek, while Linda was used to a much darker bedroom. Also, not knowing how Matty would do in a strange room, she had left both her and his door cracked with the hall light on in case he woke up.

She wondered if she was just spooking herself when she first heard the creaking on the modern metal staircase with all tread and no riser. She heard it again though, and cursed to herself, "Shit, Jimmy was right. The bastard's come back. Oh God, what do I do?" Linda propped herself up in the bed and careful not to make any noise, she laid the shotgun across her lap, releasing the safety.

And then more quickly than she imagined possible, Jordan had opened the bedroom door and stepped in, a shadow in the light from the hallway, "Alright, you money-grubbing whore, we're going to have a long talk about you trying to ruin my life and steal my house."

Linda should have been terrified, but the arrogance with which Jordan delivered those words infuriated her, "Wrong sister, you bastard. There's a shotgun pointed at your chest, and if you take one more step forward, your life will be far more ruined than it is right now."

"Like I believe you've got a gun, even if you are the fucking redneck twin. I'm sure this idea to steal my house was yours."

Linda turned on the nightstand light, making sure that Jordan could see that she was serious about holding a shotgun.

"No, not my idea, but I assure you this shotgun is very real. And it's going to be here every night until you get it through your arrogant spoiled rotten head that you can't beat up women because you're rich and you believe you're God's gift to surgery. Now get out of this house and don't come back unless you've got a court order and a police escort. Otherwise I will not only put a pile of buckshot in your chest, I will take out an ad in the *Capital Gazette* telling all of Annapolis society that you beat your wife and killed your unborn baby after she found you in her bed with your lover," Linda never lowered her gaze for one second.

Jordan backed out of the bedroom. Linda got up quickly and turned on lights as she went. She was worried that he would figure out that Laurie was in the downstairs room and would go after her. Linda called out after him as he descended the stairs, "You do know where the front door is. Use it quickly."

He slammed the front door as Laurie came out of the bedroom. She saw Linda halfway down the stairs holding the shotgun, "Oh God, he came back, didn't he? Oh God oh God oh God, I told you he would. Oh my God. Oh God, I'm so sorry he came after you thinking it was me."

"Laurie, relax. Turns out my redneck husband was right on the money. Jordan's gone. Let's hope he doesn't come back, but we'll tell the lawyer what happened in the morning and get Jimmy to send over a locksmith buddy of his."

Matty woke up with the commotion. Linda grabbed him and gave him a tit to suck on. Linda poured her and her sister a shot of

Johnnie Walker Red, Linda figuring that the alcohol wouldn't have a chance to get to her milk before Matty finished suckling. After the drink, Linda and Laurie both went to bed in the downstairs king bed with Matty in between them.

When Linda went home, she hugged Jimmy and falsely cooed, "You are the smartest husband ever."

"Huh?"

"The bastard did come back. He mistook me for Laurie because I was in her bedroom. I pointed the shotgun right at his chest and ordered him to get lost. And he did," Linda could feel a memory of the adrenaline rush she had felt holding the shotgun.

"Good girl," Jimmy smiled, beaming with pride and squeezing her ass. "See, I'm always right."

Linda shook her head but let him have his moment and asked him to find a locksmith.

The divorce attorney had a field day with Jordan's visit in the middle of the night. Just like she ultimately did for the property settlement, she called Jordan's parents and advised them that they needed to rein in their son if they didn't want to be all over the pages of every newspaper. Laurie's divorce attorney eschewed seeking permanent alimony from a Maryland court; instead she went to the surgeon's wealthy Annapolitan parents and offered to let them buy Laurie's permanent silence about their son's sociopathy for the price of the couple's lovely waterfront home and a generous cash settlement. Concerned not only for their social standing but also for the reaction of the Maryland Board of Physicians to their son's criminal acts, they paid up. Whenever Linda experienced an occasional twinge of jealousy for her twin's financial felicity, she reminded herself that Laurie had paid heavily for it with a lost child and a fall that could easily have killed her as well.

Laurie had come a long way since then. Of course twenty-five years of nursing, particularly in ERs, ICUs, and telemetry units will toughen up anyone. Now Linda was the sister who needed the help even if she didn't accept her need yet.

* * * * *

The third time Linda took pills, she again convinced herself that she wasn't taking anything more than trash. All of the nurses knew that the new medical assistant Veronica was trouble from the first day she came on board. During orientation, Veronica had barely focused on the training. She showed up ten to fifteen minutes late for every shift, and she was changing out of her scrubs in the staff room ten to fifteen minutes before the shift ended and walking out the door the second the clock struck the hour.

The patients hated her too. They complained to the nurses that Veronica didn't fill their water pitchers for them, didn't stick around to help them in the bathroom if they needed it, frequently checked her long brown hair and excessive makeup in the patients' bathrooms, and was routinely checking text messages on her cell phone in patients' rooms despite the facility rule that personal cell phones were required to be left in staff lockers.

Even as bad a medical assistant as Veronica was, Linda never expected what happened in the dispensary. The dispensary is an offshoot of the pharmacy created when the management saw the need to tighten up access to the main pharmacy. In the old days, the nurses would just walk into the pharmacy to get the carts the pharmacists had loaded with the medication trays for their patients. Under current standards only pharmacy staff could be given access to the pharmacy itself, and even the Dutch door to the hallway with the upper half that had always been left open had to be replaced by a solid core door. The management renovated an old broom closet that shared a wall with the pharmacy by busting through the wall and creating a door. The pharmacy staff filled the carts in the pharmacy, used an access card to open the door between the pharmacy and broom closet-cum-dispensary, and left the carts for the nurses. The nurses had access cards that allowed them to enter the dispensary from the hall side, but not from the pharmacy side. They collected their carts when it was time to take medicine to the patients and off they went to deliver medicine to the patients.

Linda entered the dispensary as usual to grab her cart and found Veronica with a pill bottle in her hand leaning over the old janitor's sink which had never been removed when management renovated the broom closet. Linda was still trying to take in the scene as Veronica bolted for the door, dropping the pill bottle into the sink and shoving Linda backwards as she ran out the door. All but about a dozen pills spilled into the sink. Linda used a paper towel to grab the bottle and thought "Jackpot" as she read the label: MS Contin 30mg. She poured the pills from the bottle into the cup of her padded bra, careful not to touch the bottle with her bare hand. As she dropped the bottle upside down in the sink, she gave a brief gluttonous thought to the pills lying in the sink, but even Linda wasn't desperate enough for pills that she would risk their being contaminated by whatever might be in the bottom of the old janitor's sink.

Then Linda headed out into the hall as quickly as her knees would carry her and started screaming for security. Security caught Veronica in the parking lot. She was interviewed, summarily fired and escorted off the premises.

Nancy interviewed all of the pharmacy staff and Linda about what had happened. Linda related that she had gone into the dispensary to retrieve her cart and was startled by the sight of Veronica. Linda slightly exaggerated the push that Veronica had given her on the way out the door, saying that she had fallen against her cart and she needed a few seconds to get back on her feet, buying herself the seconds she had used to grab the pills Veronica dropped before screaming for security.

Linda felt that she should express some curiosity about how Veronica had made it to the dispensary anyway, not expecting Nancy to be forthcoming with any details. Surprisingly, Nancy was so stunned by the incident that she lost her usual managerial reserve, "The stupid girl actually tried to tell us that she had gone into the dispensary because a patient asked her for a cough drop and she thought there might be some there. Oh please. She didn't even know enough to know that MA pass cards don't open the dispensary door."

"But, absent knowing what a patient was getting and what particular medicines look like, taking medicines from the carts was as likely to get her a stool softener as it was a painkiller, which is what I assume she was after. How stupid could she be?" Linda feigned ignorance.

Nancy shook her head in disgust, "Oh, she wasn't just in the dispensary, she had been in the pharmacy itself. When security made her empty her pockets, she had one of the pharmacy tech's badges and there was a bottle of MS Contin in the old janitor's sink. Didn't you see it?"

"It all happened so fast. She was at the sink when I walked in and now that I think about it she did have something in her hand but she was crashing past me before I could process what I was seeing," Linda said, not entirely untruthfully. "How did she get the tech's badge? Was the tech in on it?"

"I don't think so, but I'm going to be keeping my eye on her just to be sure. She states that she left her purse on the bench in the locker room when she went to the bathroom, and Veronica clipped it from there. Veronica had already told us essentially the same story when we confronted her with the badge, so if they were in on it together, they had to have agreed on a story ahead of time."

Again, at home that night, Linda convinced herself that she'd done nothing wrong taking the MS Contins. After all, Veronica had intended to steal the bottle, and Linda had helped prevent her from doing so. As no one could be sure that Veronica hadn't contaminated the pills, even the pills that remained in the bottle rather than the sink would have been discarded out of an abundance of caution. Hence the pills were headed to the incinerator anyway. Again, in the fog of the dysfunction of her addiction, Linda rationalized that she all she did was take something that was trash anyway.

She put the pills in a Ziploc and hid them in her underwear drawer. She was accustomed to taking immediate-release Percocets, not sustained-release MS Contins. She hoped that she had actually obtained enough MS Contins that she could achieve the blood levels necessary for sustained pain relief. The pain management specialists had all sorts of charts and formulae for converting a patient from immediate release to sustained release, but Linda had never done the calculations herself. The addicted part of her was eager to try them out. The nurse part of her who had seen overdosed addicts in the ER was afraid of not knowing if the dose of MS Contin would give her a sustained level higher than she could handle, not to mention the possible withdrawal that could occur when she ran out of the modest supply she had acquired.

The next day Linda came home around 4:30 in the afternoon after finishing up her shift. She called out for Matt as she entered the house. She got no response but Goldy came bounding out of the back of the house, where she stayed only when Matt was back on the converted sunporch.

Not long after Linda's Mom passed away, Jimmy had converted the screened in sunporch into an all season room. Matt was about thirteen or fourteen, and he had proudly helped Jimmy hold up the drywall pieces while Jimmy screwed them into place. As Matt was holding a piece in place, he had shouted to Linda over his shoulder, "Hey Mom, Dad says I can do the spackling and sanding all by myself."

Linda quipped back, "And hopefully you or your dad will manage to run the vacuum cleaner to sweep up all the dust afterwards all by yourself."

The sunporch did add a substantial chunk of year-round square footage to the house. The original house was small, just a former summer cottage like practically every other house in the neighborhood had been. As a screened in porch, the room hadn't seen much use because it was on the back of the house with no view of the water. Jimmy, Matt and Linda got much more use out of the room once they closed in the porch and turned it into a den.

Since Matt had moved back though, he had taken the whole sunporch over instead of moving back into his old bedroom, allowing him to watch TV that he claimed staved off the nightmares. He never even bothered to fold up the sofa bed. The shades and curtains were perpetually drawn to prevent light from glaring on the TV. He had effectively taken over sole use of the biggest TV in the house because Linda had no interest in sitting in a cave covered with her son's dirty laundry in order to watch TV.

Goldy refused to accept that Matt was not interested in playing with her; if Linda wasn't home, she parked on Matt's dirty laundry hoping futilely for a walk. Linda forbade Matt from shutting Goldy out, "You're going to bring pleasure to at least one inhabitant of this house, Matt. And it's not as if your laundry will get any smellier because of the dog."

Knowing Matt was home and wasn't going anywhere, Linda decided to take Goldy for her walk before tackling Matt. She should after all reward faithful behavior wherever it was found. Goldy was appreciative as ever, failing as always to catch any of the Canadian geese which had taken over the community field while Linda shivered in the cold January breeze that was stirring up white caps even on Lord's Creek. When they were done Linda as usual left her Crocs on the deck and went into the house in her socks, not wanting to bring in whatever the geese had left in the fields.

Matt was sitting at the card table in the corner of the sunporch. The table was covered with paperwork. Matt had his elbows resting on the table with his hands gripping the hair on either side of his head.

"What's the matter?" Linda inquired, careful to keep her voice as neutral as possible.

Matt did not answer. Instead, he shoved a pile of papers across the table at her. Linda read through the cover letter from the U.S. Department of Veterans Affairs. Most of the language in the letter was government-speak gobbledy-gook as far as Linda was concerned. All she gleaned from reading the letter was the bottom line was that they were continuing to reject his claim for benefits because his discharge was other than honorable and the VA had not received the requested paperwork to process a character of service determination.

"Matt, this is obviously a mistake. You weren't dishonorably discharged. We just need to send your discharge papers and clear this up."

Matt shook his head miserably. A suspicion crawled up Linda's spine.

"Matt," Linda probed gently. "Was there a problem with your discharge?"

He would not meet her eyes. He rummaged on the papers on the table and half-crumpling the paper as he shoved it toward her, he thrust another document into her hand. The top of the form read "DD 214" in the upper left corner, and in the upper right "Certificate of Release or Discharge from Active Duty." Beneath the basic biographical information and some information on training and education, Linda saw Box 24, Character of Service. Typed in the box was "Other than Honorable." Linda scanned further, hoping for more information. Box 28 was hardly more enlightening: "Narrative reason for separation" merely read "Unacceptable Conduct."

"What does unacceptable conduct mean? What did you do?"

Matt squinted his eyes and scowled. Instantly, Linda knew she'd lost any chance of meaningful dialog. Matt was so volatile, she couldn't accuse him of anything. She tried to backtrack, knowing it wouldn't work, but needing to try anyway.

"Matt, I didn't mean it to sound like that. This is the first I've heard of this. Tell me what happened," Linda pleaded.

Silence.

Linda gave up temporarily. She still had the VA letter and the DD 214 in her hands as she went upstairs. She turned on her computer in the bedroom. After it booted up, she connected to the Internet and started searching combinations of words such as discharge and disability. She learned rather quickly that a distinction exists between a dishonorable discharge, which requires a court martial, and an other than honorable discharge, the term on Matt's form. The options that she saw for getting disability benefits for someone like her son were to either get a discharge upgrade or get him declared insane as of the time of discharge. The web site even gave her a link to find the official definition of insane, 38 C.F.R. 3.354, whatever that means.

She clicked and read the federal government's definition of insanity: "An insane person is one who, while not mentally defective or constitutionally psychopathic, except when a psychosis has been engrafted upon such basic condition, exhibits, due to disease, a more or less prolonged deviation from his normal method of behavior; or who interferes with the peace of society; or who has so departed (become antisocial) from the accepted standards of the community to which by birth and education he belongs as to lack the adaptability to make further adjustment to the social customs of the community in which he resides."

Linda shook her head. Who wrote this garbage? Spend four months working a night shift rotation at an inner city ER, as Linda had during training, and you'd know the definition of insanity. And the feds hadn't been content to just define insanity; they made sure to further define insanity causing discharge. Linda read, "....when a rating agency is concerned with determining whether a veteran was insane at the time he committed an offense leading to his court-martial, discharge or resignation (38 U.S.C. 5303(b)), it will base its decision on all the evidence procurable relating to the period involved, and apply the definition in paragraph (a) of this section."

Linda was even more disgusted. Typical government bureaucratese. Irrespective of whatever mumbo-jumbo definitions were used, Linda had seen enough mental illness to know that Matt was mentally ill. The question though was whether mentally ill equated to this bogus lawyerly definition of insane. If so, then Matt should be able to appeal to get his benefits, which he'd been counting on so heavily. Only the federal government was insane enough to tell a mentally ill person that he or she was responsible for proving his or her own insanity in order to receive benefits.

She leaned back in the chair and stared at the computer screen until the screensaver came on. Linda's mind turned to the psychiatrist who occasionally called in to consult on patients at work, Dr. Rhee. The next time she came in, Linda was going to ask her if she knew anything about establishing insanity per the U.S. government. Psychiatrists routinely have to make assessments for courts about people's mental competence; surely the psychiatrist had some familiarity with determining if a patient fit the legalese bureaucratese definition of insanity.

Linda ordered Matt's favorite pizza for dinner. Fortunately, she was able to entice him out of the sunporch with it. She tried to put her words as gently as possible, "Hey Matt, I went upstairs and was reading about VA benefits and discharges on the computer."

Silence.

"There are ways you can still get benefits. Like if we try to get a discharge upgrade. Or if we can show that there were extenuating circumstances," Linda knew she was massaging words.

"Yeah, right. You mean write some personal statement that proves that I was fucking crazy when I told the LT he could go fuck himself if he thought I was gonna go right back out and start gunning people down two days after I get out of the hospital for going crazy over all the people I killed. I'd barely been out of the hospital for a week after they fixed me up after the bomb damned near killed me before they're sending me out into the field. The first thing I see in my sights the first time they stick me back in the field is this goddamned kid throwing a grenade, and when it went off, I just went nuts. Then they stick me back in the hospital, have me talk to some shrink-type, and before I know it throw me back out to my unit, no pills, nothing. And the LT tells me to get back out there and do my job. I shouted at him to fuck off and took off. When they discharged me they argued that the hospital wouldn't have released me if I was insane, so I couldn't have been insane when I went AWOL for two days for trying to force me into that truck. I don't know what's worse: being told there's nothing wrong with me and I just need to man up or being called a fuckin' head case."

"Matt, you had an injury to your brain. The brain is an organ like your kidneys or your liver or your stomach." Linda's brain was trying to process the info in Matt's outpouring about hospitalizations she had never heard about before at the same time she was using her calmest most unemotional voice to reach Matt. Matt at least looked up from his pizza at her words, "If you got a bullet in your gut, it would damage your organs and they'd need to heal. If a bomb damages your brain, your brain needs to heal too."

"What do you mean, damages my brain? Are you saying you don't think I'm crazy cuz that's how everyone treats me?"

"Matt, there will always be a lot of ignorant people who don't understand what you're going through. But when your brain gets hurt, it swells. The swelling hurts. C'mon, remember when Jonesy sprained his ankle on that rope swing whose location was such a big mystery." Matt smiled. "Jonesy couldn't walk because his ankle was so swollen. I'm not an expert on what happened to you, but concussions make the brain swell, and then the brain doesn't work one hundred percent. That's why all those football players are suing the NFL for their brain injuries. We just don't know nearly as much about how to fix a brain after it gets hurt as we do an ankle."

"Hmm," Matt grunted.

"I want to help you Matt. I'm not the expert, and that's why I want to get you to people who are. I don't care what label some ignorant paperwork wonk wants to put on you, not if it gets you some help."

Matt had at least calmed down. He ate more pizza before he grinned with his impish little boy face, "So, you're saying that we should fill out the VA's bullshit paperwork convincing them that I was a stark raving loony because that's what some ignoramus wants to hear."

"If I could win the lottery by pretending I was a stark raving loony, I'd do it."

Matt and Linda laughed together and finished the pizza. Linda couldn't remember the last time she and Matt had genuinely laughed and enjoyed each other's company. God, she missed it. She wanted her son back, and dammit, she was going to figure out how.

As Linda went back to bed that night, she tried to put a timeline in her head of Matt's specific injury and his hospitalizations. She was having difficulty reconciling his raging about multiple hospitalizations with any of the information that she had received at the time he had been injured. Not for the first time Linda thought that part of what made PTSD so challenging was the difficulty in getting a consistent story out of the patient.

The next time the consulting psychiatrist came to make rounds on the patients at work, Linda asked Dr. Rhee if she knew anything about documenting mental illness in order to get VA benefits. She replied that she herself did not, but that her husband's sister was a social worker at the VA in Perry Point. She promised to get the number from her husband. She noted that her sister-in-law always commented on how heavy the case load was at the VA and how understaffed they were since the discharges from the Iraq and Afghanistan wars.

Linda had to wait another two weeks until she ran into Dr. Rhee again and got the phone number, but she was happy for any help whenever it came.

Linda was a little embarrassed about calling a VA social worker out of the blue, but Virginia clearly had no problem going on and on and on about the ills of the VA system. She indicated that most of the people she helped had already been deemed eligible for VA medical care but were also seeking a VA disability rating that would provide them with a measure of monthly income. Linda's head started to whirl as Virginia rattled off federal alphabet soup.

Virginia congratulated Linda on making sure her son had a place to sleep, "You know, at least 100,000 veterans are homeless at any given point. The statistics are appalling. Most of them have mental health issues. Your son is so lucky that at least he has a place to sleep and a mom who cares enough to try to help him get the VA to do what's right."

She recommended that Linda and her son look for free clinics offered by organizations like the VFW, "These organizations get lawyers to volunteer for the day to do a walk-in clinic or to take up a veteran's case. I've had any number of them call me once they've taken a case and see my name on the medical record as a social worker for the veteran. Some of them specialize in helping vets get their discharge upgrades."

Linda mulled this over, "So you really think he needs an attorney?"

"Depends how good you are with paperwork. The thing with these vets with PTSD, and I don't know how bad your son's case is, but they get frustrated so easily with the bureaucracy and then end up giving up because they don't understand how to break through. A lot of times with these applications it's a matter of persistence, so someone like you could probably do it. But most of these attorneys do this for free, and how can that be bad?

"What you definitely could do on your own," Virginia continued, "is request your son's medical records from his time in the service. It can take two, three, four even six months to get them. There's a special federal form, the SF-180, to get them. And if he was hospitalized for his PTSD in service, you've got a much better chance of getting your son some help than these poor vets that never reported their problems while they were in the service because they were afraid of not looking macho. Then ten years later when they're homeless and on drugs and have gotten arrested a handful of times, they have a hell of a time proving that their mental health problems started in the service. Anyway, if you have your son's medical records by the time you find an attorney, you've saved months of time. And since you're a nurse you might see something in the records, like if they didn't handle his treatment properly."

"Wow, a lot to get your head around. I had no idea. But thank you so much for talking with me and making this a little clearer," Linda scratched down SF-180 while she finished up her conversation with Virginia.

"No problem at all," Virginia said. "I do this for a living and it drives me nuts. It's gotta be tough for somebody outside the system. You have any more questions, you just give me a call."

Linda searched for SF-180 on the computer and sure enough a form appeared on her screen. She browsed through the boxes on the form and concluded they looked straightforward enough. She would have to get Matt to sign the form and have them sent here. If he was in one of his difficult moods getting his signature could be more challenging than negotiating the bureaucracy. Linda, however, welcomed the idea of getting her hands on Matt's service medical records rather than trying to get an accurate story out of Matt, who in his better moments admitted that he didn't know what was real and what was the endless succession of nightmares.

Later that evening Linda found that she was down to three of the Percocets taken from Ms. Daniels, which meant that Matt had thought to look in her house sweater pockets. She cursed at him under her breath. But then, she decided to use it to her advantage. If he was under the influence, he would probably be calm enough for her to get him to sign the SF-180. Besides, she had the new MS Contins safely in her underwear drawer.

As usual when he was home, he was half-reclined on the sofa bed which was never put away.

"Hey Matt," she started. "I did a little bit of homework on the internet about getting discharge upgrades and then getting the disability benefits. One of the web sites indicated that it's crucial to get the medical records from your time in the service to prove any injuries you suffered. And that it can take months to get them. The web site recommends sending the request in right away as soon as you want to start applying for benefits." Linda did not mention that she had talked to a social worker. And she also did not mention that the medical records might be of use in establishing insanity in order to help qualify for a discharge upgrade.

Matt made no response to her little speech. When she handed him the paper attached to her kitchen clipboard and showed him where to sign, he took the pen from her and scrawled his signature.

"Great," Linda said. "Having a nurse for a mom has to help. I can at least read the medical records when they show up."

Linda made a copy of the form on her little home printer and stuffed the original in an envelope she had filled out before taking the form to Matt. Now all she had to do was make sure she got the mail when it came in to prevent Matt from hiding any embarrassing parts of it from her. Of course, these days even bringing in the mail was more than he typically managed.

CHAPTER NINE

Goldy was a blessing to Linda in many ways. The time she charged full steam into the back of Linda's left knee at the park in single-minded pursuit of a fleeing pair of mallards did not initially appear to be one of those blessings though. Linda went down face forward onto both knees, with the left knee landing on a rock to boot. Linda's hands landed squarely in a pile of goose droppings to add the cherry on top of the sundae. After the initial shock wore off, she rolled over onto her right side and got her butt under her. She wiped as much as she could of the sludge off her hands on the cleanest grass she could find near her.

The mallards having eluded Goldy, she turned back around to find Linda, ran for her and proceeded to slobber on Linda's face which was approximately level with her own.

Two of the neighbors who were arriving at the park with their labs saw the whole incident and when Linda made no move to get up, they came over to check on her, "You OK?"

"I'm not real sure. I banged my knee pretty good when I came down. Could you help me up?" Linda almost pleaded, unable to stop tears from escaping from the corners of her eyes.

The wife of the pair took both leashes allowing the husband to help Linda. He got behind her and put his arms under her armpits, assisting her to a standing position. Linda could not put any weight on the left knee.

"Dammit Goldy," Linda cursed. "I just got the right knee back in shape."

The wife questioned, "You live right there across the street, don't you? We see you come out with your golden all the time."

Linda nodded affirmatively.

"Well, let us help you back in the house. I don't think you're going to make it on your own."

Linda was grateful that she didn't have to ask for the help she knew she needed, "You're lifesavers."

While Goldy was sniffing the couple's labs, the wife quickly grabbed Goldy's collar and hooked on the leash she had picked up from the ground before Goldy knew she'd been captured. The wife took charge of all three dogs and walked them across the street, while the husband put Linda's arm around his shoulder and helped her limp home.

Linda thanked them profusely, promising them a box of dog treats the next time she saw them at the park. As Linda couldn't possibly bend over to wipe Goldy's feet off, the kitchen floor ended up with a parade of paw prints.

Linda took her purse off the kitchen door handle and dug around in her purse for her Sucrets tin. Since she had finished her Percocets yesterday, she had tucked a couple of the MS Contins in the Sucrets tin. She had done the opioid conversions as well as she could and if she had done the math correctly, the MS Contins would give her a slightly higher sustained blood level than the peak dose she had been getting with the Percocets. She took two ibuprofen as well knowing that she would not get immediate relief from the sustained-release MS Contins and that she needed the anti-inflammatory effect of the ibuprofens as well.

Since Matt, of course, wasn't home, she took off her jeans right there in the kitchen and inspected her knee. A large contusion was forming, and the knee was already at least a third bigger than her right knee. She scooted the kitchen chair across the kitchen floor until she could reach the ice dispenser on the fridge without having to stand up. She took the towel off the door handle and dispensed a large pile of ice into it. Forming in into a bundle, she hooked a second kitchen chair, put her left leg up and put the towel full of ice on top of the knee. She leaned her head back until it was resting on the fridge hoping that the ibuprofen would provide enough relief for her to get up the stairs.

Linda ate leftover spaghetti straight out of the bowl without warming it up. Then she hobbled to the stairs and sat down on the second one. One step at a time she lifted herself with her arms sliding her butt onto the next step up. After what seemed an endless amount of time, she reached the top of the stairs and painfully lifted herself to a standing position. In her bathroom, she found one of the flexible braces she had for her right knee and figured out how to invert it and work it onto the left knee. With the brace, she could almost put her whole weight on the knee.

Fortunately, Linda did not have to work the next morning. The bruise on her knee had fully formed with a beautiful display of the blue end of the rainbow. After a cursory shower, she tried to decide what to do.

Nancy would have a cow if she tried to come to work in the current condition, and Linda quite frankly wasn't sure she could do a whole day on her feet. At an ER she would be triaged to the bottom of the list behind the heart attacks and hemorrhages. She decided to take a chance and show up at her orthopedist's office to see if they could squeeze her in. She decided not to even call to give them a chance to tell her they couldn't see her. Figuring she might have a long wait, she stuffed her latest mystery novel in her bag.

The receptionist at the orthopedist's was not pleased and gave Linda little hope of being seen. Linda felt like mentioning how much her right knee had enriched the coffers of their office over the last year, but chose to abstain. The receptionist did at least go get one of the nurses to come talk to Linda.

The nurse had been with Linda's orthopedist the whole time she had been coming to this practice and gave Linda a friendly smile before looking down at the knee. When she saw the brace on the left knee, she looked up again and questioned, "Wait, we did your right knee, correct?"

"Yes," Linda confirmed. "However, Dr. Rosen said that my left knee also had wear and tear that would eventually require replacement. My golden retriever decided to help it along a little yesterday."

Even though Linda had taken two more ibuprofen that morning to reduce the swelling, with the effort of getting to her doctor's office, the knee was again so swollen that the brace was cutting into her skin.

The nurse sighed, resigned, "Well, the ER would only x-ray it, give you ibuprofen and send you over for us to figure out what to do. I'll try to get you in somewhere along the way."

Linda had to wait over two hours before Dr. Rosen could see her, during which time she ate two more ibuprofens. Thank goodness she had brought a new novel.

Dr. Rosen reminded her that in his assessment the knee was bone on bone and was going to need replacement in the not too distant future. When she told him how much ibuprofen she had already taken since she fell, without of course mentioning the MS Contin, he gave her a prescription for fourteen low-dose Percocets to avoid taking too much ibuprofen. He warned her, however, that he was only giving her enough to last until she came in for a follow-up appointment after the swelling subsided. He also gave her a note to stay out of work for two more days. She made a follow-up appointment at the desk with the still unhappy receptionist.

On the way home, Linda filled the Percocet prescription. Goldy greeted her as she came in the door. Holding the drugstore bag in her hand, Linda smiled to herself, "Well, Goldy got me more Percocets, so her bumping into me yesterday may have been another one of her blessings."

And then Matt wiped out her Percocet supply again before she even started the bottle. She had been working through the supply of the MS Contin that she had diverted from the work incinerator, and hadn't wanted to switch back and forth between immediate and sustained release. She had therefore foolishly left the new bottle of Percocets in her purse hanging on the back of the kitchen chair. When she came down from her shower to grab coffee before heading to her night shift, she figured she had probably made a mistake. In the parking lot of the facility she dug out the bottle. He hadn't even left her a single pill. Linda's next orthopedist appointment was three days away, and she figured the orthopedist wasn't going to hand out more Percocets because Linda was too chicken to have her left knee replaced.

Linda had truly convinced herself that she had not really stolen any pills in the past. However, if she couldn't get her hands on some through another 'patient mistake,' she wondered to herself if she was greedy enough for the relief the pills produced to actually take some from work.

She knew how she would do it too. She had seen the opportunity for years working at the facility. As an ortho rehab center, physicians were not present every second of the day. Residents and fellows were not constantly in on-call rooms the way they would be at a teaching hospital. Yet patients recovering from orthopedic surgery or with spine injuries or with broken limbs could be in considerable amounts of pain. Many of them experienced what the pain management folks called breakthrough pain. The strategy in dosing such patients was to give them as a regular dose the amount of sustained-release pain medicine to deal with their chronic pain and then have a standing order for additional doses of an immediate-release drug PRN, or *pro re nata*, Latin for as the circumstance arises.

In some hospitals, patients had a PRN button hooked up to IV lines. If the patient experienced breakthrough pain, the patient pushed a button and a dose of an opioid flowed down the plastic tube into the patient's vein. Linda's facility frowned heavily on such arrangements for their patients. While breakthrough pain was definitely a problem for their patients, their facility was supposed to be rehabilitating them, which included minimizing their painkiller use as they progressed. Patients who only have to squeeze a button were less inclined to make progress, at least in the opinion of her management. They also were less inclined to accurately convey the level of their pain and how often they truly experienced breakthrough pain. Finally, patients got impatient. Even with the pain medicine being delivered directly into a vein, the pain relief was not instantaneous. Patients therefore could give themselves more than they needed to control the pain because they weren't patient enough to wait for the effect of an appropriate dose.

Because her facility frowned on the PRN IV drips, the oral PRN system was where Linda's workplace was most vulnerable. The physicians and the pharmacists were not present at three in the morning. Linda, however, had had many nighttime shift experiences where a patient woke up screaming having an episode of breakthrough pain. The facility's procedure was for the nurse to document the episode, request that the patient rate the pain on a scale of one through ten, and then determine from the standing order in the patient's chart how many pills to retrieve from the dispensary. Oxycodone was one of the preferred immediate-release drugs for breakthrough pain, and over the years Linda had cared for many patients with standing PRN orders for their breakthrough pain, allowing the patient to receive one to three pills as needed based on intensity of pain and the patient's tolerance for opioids. After removing the correct number of pills from the locked cabinet in the dispensary room, the nurse would carefully document the number of pills removed and given to the patient. But at three in the morning, no one other than the patient could gainsay if the nurse's documentation overstated the pain rating in order to dispense extra pills, and patients in tremendous pain were often not accurate in their recall.

Linda's first patient that night was the perfect example, a 40-something-year-old carpenter with degeneration in his spine, the reason for which had not yet been adequately explained. The history in his chart explained that six months ago he had started complaining of severe pain in his lower back. On MRI, he was determined to have a herniated or bulging disc at T9-10, the disc being the spongy material between the vertebral bones. The vertebrae were numbered in sections; the cervical spine, the thoracic spine, and the lumbar spine. T9-10 indicated that the herniated disc was between the ninth and tenth vertebrae of the thoracic spine. The patient received epidural therapy as an outpatient, and his healthcare team had all expected that he'd be fine in six to eight weeks. Six weeks later, he showed up in the emergency room of his local hospital complaining of intolerable pain. Linda could almost sense the reluctance of the ER staff to order a repeat MRI, assuming the patient was only jonesing for more painkillers. To the surprise of absolutely everyone, the herniated disc was improved but the patient had compression fractures in four vertebrae in the thoracic spine. The patient denied any accidents or falls that could have explained the improbable amount of damage. He was referred to all sorts of specialists on an outpatient basis to determine what could be causing the spinal degeneration. Before any of the specialists could figure out what was going on, the patient did fall, ended up back at the ER, where

MRI revealed fractures in three more vertebrae. The patient was admitted and examined by every conceivable specialist. He was determined not to be a candidate for surgery. A special white plastic brace was created for the patient, making the patient's torso look something like an egg. The patient was then transferred to the orthopedic rehab unit at Linda's facility where he could hopefully be stabilized while someone figured out how to stop his spine from deteriorating further and what was causing the collapse in the first place.

When this patient rang his bell at 2:30 am declaring breakthrough back pain following a strained bowel movement, Linda followed the procedures and the standing order. Except she boosted the patient's pain rating in the chart. She doled out three tablets, instead of the two that the patient's actual response would have demanded. She took one of the three in the dispensary room using a handful of water from the sink to wash it down. Then she took the two tablets to the patient and helped him sit up enough to swallow the pills with some water.

Driving home at the end of her shift, Linda again rationalized her actions. She would never ever harm a patient. She would never take pills that a patient genuinely needed. The cost of the oxycodone she had taken was minimal, probably less than the nitrile gloves, gauze, bandages and other small items that she knew other nurses took home from the supply cabinets. She simply added one pill to the chart.

Linda also knew that the way that she had taken the pill was virtually foolproof. Over a thirty-plus-year career she had seen many staff get caught stealing pills. Most of them however were ridiculously stupid when they did so. Like the tech that they had fired last month, they brazenly walked into a dispensary and tried to take a pile of pills. Or they stole them right out of the cup in the patient's room in the patient's sight. Here, her patient received the correct dose of medicine for his pain and would under normal circumstances never have a chance to see his chart to know that Linda had written a larger dose than she gave him. And even if he did, he wasn't likely to do so anytime soon, and then the discrepancy could be explained by a faulty memory of a patient in great pain in the middle of the night.

Also Linda rationalized to herself, she had a valid prescription from a physician for Percocets, which were oxycodone combined with Tylenol. She would never have had to take a pill from the dispensary if her son wasn't stealing the Percocets she legitimately had. Her only problem now was getting through the next two days until her doctor's appointment with no Percocets. But, then Linda told herself, she could use that as a test of how hooked she was on the damned things. And once again, she convinced herself that once she got through the next handful of days, she would never need to resort to faking PRN orders for patients.

When she got home, she clipped the leash on Goldy for her walk because the neighborhood kids were still waiting on school buses. The elementary school bus stop was at the corner of her block, and as it had been when she and Laurie were going to school as well as when she had sent Matt off to school, the bus stop was a coffee social hour for the mothers of those too young to go to the bus stop alone and a mini-playground for a dozen plus kids. Many of them got to the bus stop on their scooters. When the bus arrived, the kids would carelessly throw their scooters in the tall grass at the edge of the drainage ditch and board the bus. The scooters would remain there until the bus returned them in the afternoon. One of the things Linda loved most about her neighborhood was that in all the years she lived here, including her childhood, Matt's childhood, and now the current generation's childhood she had never heard of a scooter or skateboard going missing from the drainage ditch while the kids were at school.

One of the little boys at the bus stop was wearing a Cub Scouts uniform. The sight of him reminded Linda of Matty wearing his uniform to school in the early years of elementary school. Matty had loved Cub Scouts through the early years of elementary school despite the fact that the father he idolized hadn't seen the point. Jimmy had said, "I can taking him camping and hunting with me, and he can even stay out overnight with me. He doesn't need to wear a stupid uniform for that."

"Shhhh. Don't call it stupid where he can hear you," Linda had scolded. Linda thought Matty was adorable with the neckerchief. Since she and Jimmy had decided not to have more kids after Matty, Linda wasn't going to have a little girl to dress up. Getting Matty in a Cub Scout uniform was going to have to do. "Besides, he can still go camping and hunting with you. But in Cub Scouts he'll be with other boys his age, even if it is just day camp until he gets older. It'll be good for him. And he'll be so proud to show you he learned how to use a compass and whatever else it is they do."

Matty loved the day camps, but had little use for the regular meetings. He fidgeted and squirmed with the uniform on, and ultimately he refused to keep going to the meetings if he had to wear the uniform. Linda had even tried to persuade Jimmy to be one of the parents on the camping trips, "Matty would be thrilled to have you showing off to the other boys how much his father knows about hunting and fishing." Jimmy would have none of it, and Linda knew she had lost the Cub Scouts battle. "My boy is never happy unless he's outdoors getting dirty," Linda had remarked to her mother when she finally had to give up on seeing her boy in a darling uniform.

"He's a boy. That's what they do. I was so happy I had girls. Never had to do any of that stuff. Your father would have loved to have a boy to take hunting."

"Well, the way he taught us about guns, Dad was obviously trying his hardest to pretend that Laurie and I were boys."

Linda's father had died while she and Laurie were in nursing school. He was almost twenty years older than their mother, and he firmly believed that bacon and eggs for breakfast followed by a ham sandwich with mayo for lunch and steak and potatoes for dinner were the only food a man needed. No one was terribly shocked when his heart gave out early. He never got to meet Matt, but he would have loved the fact that, if he had to have daughters, at least one of them found a hunter for a husband and produced a grandson who loved the outdoors as much as he had.

* * * * *

Linda had initially been thrilled when Matt announced he was going hunting with his high school friends Alan and Jonesy on the upcoming weekend. She wasn't sure that carrying a gun was the best thing for someone as mentally unstable as Matt currently was. However, the hunting trip was the first sign Matt had shown in months of having a social life. When he asked her to open the safe to get the guns out, she hadn't even blinked.

Linda was dog-sitting Siobhan's two chocolate labs over that same weekend, and she was just as happy to have Matt out of the house. Although she had worried about whether she could handle having three full-size dogs to walk and clean up after given the state of her knee, she decided that having three full-size dogs plus Matt in her house all at once for an entire weekend was probably worse. After all, she could take the dogs out one at a time.

Linda had just come in the house with all three dogs as Matt was getting ready to leave on Friday evening. Matt raised his eyebrows when three dogs sniffed at his camping gear. He then stated that he was crashing at Alan's for the night, and then they were getting up at the "butt crack of dawn" to get into the deer stands early. Linda didn't start to worry until Monday evening after she had returned the chocolate labs to Siobhan. A weekend-long hunting trip was fairly standard. By Tuesday, Linda was biting her nails and trying to reassure herself that if he had blown his foot off while hunting, she would have been called from the emergency room.

On Wednesday, she called up Alan's mother to see if she would give Linda his number, "Hey Alice, it's Linda MacDermott, it's been a while. How are you?"

Alice took a second to respond but was warm in her response, "Just fine. Wow, haven't heard from you since the boys stopped hanging out all the time."

"I know, I know," Linda acknowledged. "But that's actually why I was calling. Matt was headed out with Alan a few days ago, and I need to get hold of Matt."

"Really, Matt went out to Oregon? I didn't know that," Alice sounded surprised.

Now Linda was confused, "Alan's in Oregon?"

Alice replied, "Yes, he's been there for over a year."

Linda was too worried to try to cover for Matt, "I don't think I misunderstood Matt. Honestly, I expected Matt back two days ago from a hunting trip, and I'm worried as a mother hen. But hell, if Matt did decide to visit Alan all the way out in Oregon, there's no way he could be back yet."

Alice's voice now sounded concerned, "Let me call Alan and see what the scoop is, Linda."

Linda would have preferred to have tried Alan herself rather than leave Alice in the middle of one of Matt's crazy disappearances. But she could see why Alice wouldn't want to hand out her son's number.

When Alice called back less than an hour later, Alice's tone clearly indicated her overall disapproval, "I hadn't wanted to say so earlier without confirming with Alan, but Alan stopped having anything to do with Matt over a year ago. Alan didn't even give Matt his new number out in Oregon, and I'm afraid I won't give it to you because I can't risk Matt getting it from you." As if Linda could not be trusted to keep a phone number confidential if asked.

"Alan said that Matt is completely out of control with his drinking and all he can talk about is how horrible he had it over in Iraq. You know, it's not my place to say," Alice continued, Linda knowing that wasn't going to stop Alice from saying. "If you didn't let him stay at home, he'd have to get a job and then maybe he'd move on."

Linda was overjoyed that Alice had the problem of Matt all solved for her. Still, there was no reason to make the situation worse. "Thank you for checking with Alan for me, Alice, and for taking the time to call me back. I really appreciate it." She didn't appreciate all of Alice's lance-like thrusts at her parenting skills. But she did appreciate the phone calls.

Linda didn't have a number for Jonesy, but his parents still lived a few blocks over. Although she wasn't up for a second "you're a bad mother" lecture in one day, with Matt gone longer than ever and on a story that was clearly a lie, her worry overrode her pride. She hooked Goldy to a leash and headed over to the Jones'. Maybe she could sic Goldy on them if they started lecturing.

Pete Jones opened the door at Linda's knock. "Hey Pete," Linda started. "Sorry to just show up. I'm a little embarrassed to have to admit this, but I'm looking for Matt. He's been gone for a few days, and right before he left he fed me some cock-and-bull story about how he was going hunting with Alan and Ben." Before knocking on the door, Linda had struggled to remember Jonesy's Christian name, since Matt hadn't referred to him as Ben in at least a decade.

Pete answered, "Oh, Linda, don't worry too much. Ben won't tell us where he's going or what he's doing 99% of the time. He's got a new girlfriend now and the only time we see him is when they've had a fight. I'll get you his cell, and you can see if he's seen Matt. He might answer if he doesn't recognize your number. If he sees my number, he'll ignore it for sure." Pete took a pair of reading glasses out of his shirt pocket, pulled a flip phone which probably qualified as an antique out of his back pocket, grunted a bit as he pushed buttons, and then smiled after about thirty seconds, "Here it is."

Linda pulled her phone out of her pocket, tucking Goldy's leash between her thighs and typed Ben's number into her contact list under "Jonesy." Goldy butted her head up against Pete repeatedly while Linda was trying to do this. Fortunately, Pete was overtly a dog lover and scratched under her ears affectionately.

Linda called Jonesy when she got home. He hadn't heard from Matt in weeks. Linda's next step was a visit to the county park where Matt had set up his pup tent during prior disappearances. She had no luck there either.

The next day, Linda was worried enough that she even called and explained Matt's disappearance to the police operator, who told her with a heavy weight of disapproval that she could feel coming through the phone that for a young man in his twenties with a history of disappearing for days at a time, Linda couldn't expect much action on their part if she filed a missing person report. She didn't bother filing the report.

After she got home from her shift at the end of the eleventh day of Matt being gone, she found Matt curled on the sofa bed so soundly asleep he didn't even hear her come in.

Even with only the light of the kitchen filtering into the sunporch, Linda could tell that Matt looked like hell. She doubted that he had shaved the entire time he had been gone, and his sandy-brown beard had come in rather scraggly. Even through the facial hair and baggy clothes she could see that he had lost weight.

She ate leftovers at the kitchen table, making as much noise as she could in order to see if he would wake up. As she was doing the dishes, he made a trip to the bathroom and immediately returned to the sofa bed without saying a word to Linda.

Linda went into the sunporch and leaned against the arm of the sofa bed, "I love you, and I'm glad you're alive, but I gotta tell you these disappearing acts don't work for me. I made an ass out of myself calling Alan's mother and showing up at the Joneses to see if they had heard from you."

"Oh, for Christ's sake," Matt exclaimed.

"Oh, don't you oh-for-Christ's-sake me Matthew MacDermott! You feed me some BS story about how you're going hunting with your buddies and then you show up eleven days later looking and smelling like a dead rockfish carcass Goldy dragged up from the beach."

"It's been eleven days?" Matt asked her with a spacey expression and eyes widened from disbelief.

"'Fraid so, son," Linda answered. "So are the guns in some nearby pawn shop or did you give them directly to your dealer to buy whatever it is you're snorting or smoking or shooting up?"

"They were practically my guns anyway. The only reason Dad left them was for me to hunt. Otherwise he would have taken them."

"No, let's stick to real facts, son. Those guns were your grandfather's, my father's. And yes, your father was planning to take them but I pointed out to him that he, first of all, had no right to my father's guns and second, that the least he could do was leave his son the hunting rifles." Linda could not prevent the anger from surging into her voice. She had tried not to involve Matt in her and Jimmy's disputes, but she was not going to stand for Matt inventing his version of the truth to her detriment.

The fog cleared a bit from Matt's face as he realized the depths of his mother's anger.

"So Matt, I love you. You have a problem though. I did more than enough time in an ER trying to save overdosers who got dumped at the ER door by their friends who were afraid they'd get arrested if they walked in the place. You're robbing me blind. The guns are gone. The tools in the shed are gone. My diamond engagement ring is gone. And Lord knows what else I haven't discovered is gone. So here's the deal, under this brilliant new Obamacare, you should be Medicaid eligible. We're going to get you signed up, and then we're getting you into the finest treatment program that Medicaid will buy. Then we get you working with a doctor who can treat people with PTSD, 'cuz that's what you have son. You do all that, you can stay. Because as much as I love you, I am not going to come home from work every shift wondering what the hell I'll find on my sofa bed."

Linda's words had roused Matt out of the last of his fog and he was angry too, not that Linda cared at this point. "Oh, you're a fine one to talk. Your knee surgery was months ago, you don't even limp anymore but you're still poppin' those Percocets you manage to get hold of all the goddamned time. You think I've got a problem, you need to look in the mirror."

Linda sucked in her breath, her anger having taken the elevator up to furious. "You have no idea what the hell you're talking about. I get my pills from a doctor who prescribes them because I need them because now my left knee is shot too. I go to work every shift even when I can barely walk by the time I get home, and I pay all the bills around here."

While Linda was speaking, Matt had leaped up from the sofa bed and grabbed his rucksack. He shoved a random pile of clothes in it and pushed past her, almost knocking her off the arm of the sofa bed onto the mattress.

"Go to hell, Mom. I'm sick of you judging me. You have no idea what I went through, and if you did, you'd know the only thing that will shut the nightmares up are the pills." He strode out of the house.

Linda wept.

After her nose was so stuffed she couldn't breathe through it anymore, she pulled herself together, washed her face in the kitchen sink and dug out a Sudafed from her purse to clear her sinuses.

She called Laurie, "I threw him out, Laur. He was gone eleven days. He's pawned everything he can get his hands on in the house. And all he wants is his next fix. Christ, if he can't sleep here, the next call I get is probably going to be from some ER telling me the naloxone was too late to save him."

Laurie used her best calm, firm charge nurse voice when she responded, "Tell me what happened."

"So wait," Laurie interjected as Linda was winding up her story, "you told him he needed to get on Medicaid and get help to stay in the house, and he told you to piss off and ran out?"

Linda affirmed this sequence of events.

"Lin, you did not throw him out. He walked out. Every place anyone lives has conditions. If he chose not to live with yours, you did not throw him out. You cannot destroy yourself for your son. If he'll accept the right sort of help, then you can help him. But you cannot keep giving him the means to spiral down further. Get yourself a glass of wine and go to sleep. Then call me back in the morning if you have any more misplaced feelings of guilt."

The twins talked a little longer, largely repeating Linda's expressions of guilt and Laurie's no-nonsense, protect-yourself-then-help-him stance.

Linda locked up the house and went upstairs. She pulled out the high dose OxyContin pill that she'd hidden in her underwear drawer all those months ago. When she had looked up the dose of the pill from Mr. Johnson's chart, she had almost thrown the pill out because the dose was so high that she was afraid she'd kill herself. But that was months ago, and her tolerance had increased. Besides, if she ever deserved a good chill pill, tonight was it. She didn't have another shift for two more days.

After ten or twenty pages of the latest Danielle Steele, she could feel her respiration slowing down and her frayed nerves calming.

When she woke up twenty-two hours later; it was already dark. She'd missed the whole day. She felt sick. "Oh, crap," she thought to herself. "Matt was right. I have as big a problem as he does. I probably damned near killed myself with that dose."

Her worries shifted back and forth between herself and Matt. In the middle of a second beer she realized that she had not told Jimmy anything about what was going on. Linda could claim no serious faults with Jimmy as a father whatever her own issues with him were. Matt's problems were serious enough that Linda had no right to withhold the information from Jimmy. If something lugubrious ended up happening with Matt, and she had never let Jimmy know, he would have every right to be furious.

Last she had heard Jimmy was out in Colorado. After Linda and Jimmy split up, Jimmy had rented rooms out of people's houses for cash from people who weren't reporting the extra income. He kept a post office box for mail, but left his physical address as Linda's house. She gave him credit for finding ways to hang around close enough that he could retain a relationship with Matt through the end of high school, mostly by camping and hunting together. Only after Matt had enlisted in the Army did Jimmy finally give up the pretense of keeping a business open and living near Maryland. Linda didn't know if he ever got square with the IRS or Maryland tax authorities, but since he never rolled through Maryland, she suspected not. His cell phone number still had a 443 area code though.

Jimmy had grown up a couple creeks further down the South River, closer to the Chesapeake than her family home. Jimmy's family, however, had lived in one of the tiniest, most ramshackle homes inside the boundaries of a water-privileged neighborhood, such that if his family had had the money to pay for the community amenities, they could have had access to a community beach and boat ramp. Jimmy's parents were both alcoholics though and were probably lucky they had held onto the house. Jimmy had kept silent about his home life with her and everyone else during middle and high school.

Jimmy had been much more popular than Linda in high school. When Linda had run into him in a bar one night right after she got her nursing license and her first job, she couldn't believe he was paying attention to her. He was a smooth talker, and damn he was good looking. He was ambitious too. Linda had been impressed when Jimmy had talked about how his uncle had already taken him into his contracting business and set him up in the carpenters' union apprenticeship program.

Linda did not find out until they had been dating for several months what a disaster his home life had been. Jimmy's father worked episodically for Jimmy's uncle when he could stay sober for long enough. His mother had never worked. His parents fought and screamed at each other and at Jimmy constantly. Jimmy never admitted to being physically abused, but Linda wouldn't have been surprised given what she heard about his parents' violent tendencies.

To Linda, Jimmy's determination to get out of his bad home life and make something of himself was exotically attractive. Linda's Mom had seen the situation differently, not believing that Jimmy was good enough for her college-educated daughter. She had come around slightly only after she saw how determined Jimmy was to be a better dad to Matt than he had had.

Small wonder though that, with such a difficult upbringing, Jimmy had no problem after Matt enlisted with packing up his life in Maryland and heading out to Colorado with barely a glance backward.

To Linda's surprise, Jimmy picked up on the second ring. "Linda," Jimmy answered. Not a hello, not how's it going, just Linda.

"Hey Jimmy," Linda returned. "I thought you should know that I had to throw Matt out of the house." Linda knew that if Laurie heard her accepting blame for throwing Matt out of the house she would be subject to another Laurie tongue-lashing, but she couldn't help believing that if she hadn't given Matt an ultimatum, he would still be safe at home.

"What the hell did you do that for?" Jimmy demanded. Perhaps she should have prefaced her remark with something about Matt's drug problems. Too late now.

"Matt is abusing painkillers and God knows what other drugs, Jimmy," Linda plowed ahead.

"Huh?"

"I can't be sure how long he's been using them, but after my knee surgery I noticed that my Percocets were disappearing way too fast. Then I started noticing things missing from the house."

"What do you mean 'things'?" Jimmy quizzed skeptically.

"He's pawning anything he can get his hands on. He stole my engagement ring from you out of my jewelry box. He fed me some BS story about a hunting trip with Alan and Jonesy, and the entire collection of rifles and shotguns has been gone ever since. He disappears for days at a time. When he came home after being gone for eleven frickin' days, I told him he needed to get help or he couldn't stay, and he walked out."

"Why the hell didn't you clue me in before this?" Jimmy's tone had changed. He was angry, but a trace of alarm was also there.

"You're absolutely right. I should have let you know before it got this bad. I kept hoping I was wrong, that I'd find the ring, that I was wrong about the Percocet count. But Christ, he was gone eleven days this last time. I was so crazy with worry my brain wasn't working well enough to call you," Linda decided to eat crow on her timing.

Jimmy harrumphed but didn't say anything. Linda kept gushing, "Last night I finally lost it. I promised I would help him get signed up with Obamacare and help find him a treatment program, but that he couldn't stay in the house robbing me blind getting worse and worse. He told me to go to hell, grabbed his backpack and took off. I was so upset I took a sleeping pill. I'd never taken one before, zonked the crap out of me. When I woke up, the first thing I thought of was that I needed to tell you."

"Damned right. Damn, I wish you hadn't sent him packing before you called me. Maybe I could've got him to come out here. He would love Colorado. He'd forget all about using some stupid pills once he saw the racks on the deer out here."

Linda doubted this. Jimmy had many fine qualities, but his understanding of opioid addiction and how intractable a problem it could be was zero. People with addictions and PTSD as severe as Matt's didn't quit using just because they could hunt big game.

"Did he take his cell phone with him?" Jimmy asked.

"Yes, he did. I haven't tried to call him. I know if he saw my number he'd ignore me anyway."

"Right. Well, I'll try to call him. I'm sure he'll talk to me. I'll try to calm things down, maybe invite him out here."

"OK, well let me know if you find out anything."

Jimmy hung up without promising much of anything. Linda knew that she didn't have much right to demand that Jimmy keep her in the loop when she had brought him up to speed this late in the game. Also, Linda tried to tell herself, she had thrown Matt out of the house in order to get a respite from dealing with him. Why was she so eager to hear from him? "Because he's your kid, he's in trouble, and you can't turn off loving him," she answered herself.

Ten days later when Linda returned home from work, Matt was sleeping on the sunporch. To avoid waking him, Linda went upstairs and called Jimmy. "Well, thank God. Next time you're thinking of doing something stupid like throwing him out again, give me a call first please." Linda hung up. Jimmy wasn't here getting robbed by her son, he was doing absolutely nothing to help, but he had no problem judging her failures. Asshole.

Linda forced herself to wait until after she'd called Laurie to take more Percocets. Laurie of course had the opposite reaction to Jimmy, "Well, is he getting help?"

"I don't know. He was sound asleep when I got home, and I was so relieved to see him alive, I didn't wake him."

"Then, nothing's changed," Laurie sounded exasperated.

"Give me a break, Laur. My son was gone for ten days, and no one on the planet knew where he was. Aren't I allowed to feel better for an hour or two before I go back to trying to fix him?" Linda would never tell Laurie, but she sometimes felt that because Laurie had never had children, her twin found it too easy to be dispassionate. But, of course, over the upcoming months, Laurie was proven correct: Matt would promise to go to a doctor, but never go, and Linda did nothing but allow him to sleep on the sunporch, and then she would take too many Percocets when he pulled a disappearing act to avoid worrying.

Laurie backed down, recognizing that she'd pushed her twin too far, "I know, I was worried about him too. But he's got to get some real psychiatric help. How about if you just drive him up to the VA yourself? I mean, how can they turn away a veteran with a Purple Heart who shows up at their door."

"What do you mean, Purple Heart? Matt's never said anything about a Purple Heart," Linda responded quizzically.

"You told me he was hospitalized while he was over there. How can he not have a Purple Heart if he was injured badly enough to be hospitalized on site? And how can they give a veteran with a Purple Heart anything less than an honorable discharge? You're outta this man's Army because you went AWOL for a night or whatever he did to get booted out, and don't forget to take your Purple Heart that we gave you for getting blown up for your country with you."

"You know, you're right, Laurie. Something isn't right about this story. I'm gonna dig through Matt's paperwork and do some homework on the internet."

When Linda got off the phone with Laurie, she searched the internet for criteria for being awarded a Purple Heart. She wanted to have some background on the award before she tried to tackle a conversation with Matt. The first link after the paid ads on the results screen was a 2011 article about the Army issuing clarifications of the rules for Purple Heart eligibility. She clicked, and her heart sank as she read. Apparently the Army's official clarification had become necessary because commanding officers had been refusing to issue Purple Hearts to soldiers whose only physical injury was a concussion. Linda thought bitterly that in the macho world of military service a concussion wasn't considered a manly enough injury to warrant an award. Matt's hospitalization was pre-2011, so dollars to donuts, Matt's commanding officer had probably done nothing when Matt was hospitalized for his concussion. And of course, if Matt had no Purple Heart, then discharging him with an other than honorable was that much easier. Linda vowed she would ask Matt at the first opportunity that wouldn't have him go off in a rage, but she was sure that Matt would confirm her suspicions.

CHAPTER TEN

Linda had angrily cursed the happenstance that the next several new patients who were admitted arrived on other nurses' shifts or other nurses' wards. Dr. Rosen had sworn that the cortisone shot he had just ordered was the last he would order before surgery, and she was once again running low on her pain medicine supply. She had therefore been hoping to once again use her trick of taking some of the patients' stock of pain medicine which they brought with them on admission. Although the first time that she took pills from Ms. Daniels' stash she had convinced herself that she would never resort to that route to obtain Percocets for herself again, in the ensuing months, as Matt had become more erratic, she had helped herself to incoming patients' home supplies on a number of occasions. She didn't let herself count how many times. While she cursed the luck that she wasn't the admitting nurse, she didn't know that it would turn out to be a career-saving blessing. As it turns out the next two patients from whom she would have purloined pills would have been the incidents revealing her thefts to her management because the nurse who admitted those new patients got caught doing exactly what Linda had intended to do.

Like every other nurse in their facility, Linda had received the recent blast e-mail from management with the article describing a recent study documenting how many ways the chain of custody for opioid prescriptions between a hospital and a nursing home were being broken. Unbeknownst to Linda though, based on that study her facility had instituted stricter paperwork controls on the medicines that patients brought on their person when admitted or were brought by a well-meaning family member at a later time. Linda couldn't count the number of times she heard, "Oh, but Brian needs his back pills, so I brought those for him." Linda couldn't fault the family member; if the patient had already paid for the medication, the last thing a patient with marginal insurance needed was to have to pay her facility for another supply. Patients also got justifiably frustrated if their particular medication was not in stock at the facility, and they either had to substitute or wait for the pharmacy to get it in stock. To them and their family, the idea of waiting for medicine they already had in order to follow the facility's rules instead of just calling up Aunt Susie and asking her to bring the pills on the next visit was nonsensical.

The front desk staff, however, had now been instructed to specifically ask family members when they checked in to visit if they had brought any prescriptions with them for the patient. The front desk staff then explained to the relative that in order to prevent medication interactions the medicine would be held by the pharmacy only until the attending physician reviewed it in light of the patient's other prescriptions. What Linda didn't know was that an auditor, probably Siobhan, had suggested that the family members be required to count the pills at the front desk and sign off on an inventory. Whoever checked in the family member then handed the pills to the nurse who was in charge of the patient. The nurse was responsible for documenting the existence of the prescription in the patient's chart and then transporting any pill bottles in a labeled clear plastic container to the pharmacy for safekeeping during the patient's stay or until a physician had cleared their use.

The nurses, however, were deliberately not informed that the pills were inventoried before being handed over to the nurses for documentation in the chart. And apparently Linda wasn't the only nurse who had ever conceived of taking pills out of the stock temporarily confiscated from the patients on admission. Corrine was a heavyset LPN in her late fifties with teased blond hair straight from the 1980s, who wasn't the smartest nurse Linda had ever seen but whose patients instantly loved her for the way she had of treating them like her best friend rather than a patient. No sooner had Corrine checked in the second of the two new patients then she was caught with a dozen Vicodins in the deep pockets of her nursing smock after the pharmacist found that the container brought to the pharmacy contained fewer pills than the inventory signed by the patient's husband. As Corrine was still in her probation period, she was summarily fired.

Nancy alternated between grumbling at the poor quality of candidates sent by human resources: "I can't believe that a health care company as big as ours cannot find nurses who aren't all drug addicts. I mean I laughed as hard as anyone when the VP sent us all that drug diversion article from Mayo Clinic describing all the different ways health care workers had been caught stealing opioids, like that nurse who had gone so far as to sew a special compartment into her scrubs to hide the fentanyl syringes she was stealing, but I thought those must have just been flukes. We've had two employees in one year caught stealing, and we are a tiny little place." And her glee about the report that she was writing to the Board of Nursing: "I'll make sure she can't get a job anywhere in the state of Maryland no matter how many patients ask me what happened to Miss Corrine."

Linda was privately certain that the reason their little rehab and nursing home facility got such lousy candidates was that they paid much less than hospitals paid. Linda escaped from Nancy's kvetching as soon as she could and headed to the break room.

Linda ate her ham sandwich in the break room where at first she started shaking with relief. She had been envious that Corrine was assigned to check in those two patients, and she had been planning to do the exact same thing Corrine did. Thank God that Corrine had been stupid before she had been. After the fear of her close call wore off, Linda grumbled angrily to herself that a route of obtaining additional pills had apparently been closed off, unless she found a way to finesse the new inventory controls. For now, she'd have to resort to taking pills off the PRN patients or exploiting a hole she had found when the patient's medication list was transferred from one month's paperwork to the next. Those routes, however, were good for only one or two pills at a time, whereas taking from the stock the patients brought in from home was usually good for a dozen or so pills at one shot.

A tiny voice in the back of Linda's mind was telling her she should be appalled at herself, that if she was plotting different ways to obtain pills she might have a problem. She had, however, done such a thorough job of convincing herself that she hadn't actually stolen from the patients, and that the patients were not being harmed by anything she did that she was able to shutter that voice off.

What Linda found herself obsessing over was, with that avenue of obtaining reasonable quantities of pills in a single shot cut off, how could she obtain more pills? And then the next day, she was talking to one of her patients who gave her the perfect avenue. "I did not want this surgery," the patient griped. Linda was only half listening as she checked out where the patient's orthopedic brace had rubbed the patient's skin raw. "I must have gone to ten different orthopedists hoping one of them would tell me there was anything other than surgery. But when that many people tell you that physical therapy isn't going to fix the issue, you gotta give in."

Linda lifted her head as the patient talked about the number of physicians she had seen and looked the patient straight in the eyes, finally realizing she needed to say something, "Well, I'm glad you finally came to the right decision. I've been putting off a second knee surgery myself."

That night, Linda searched on the internet for the names of local orthopedists. How could getting a second opinion not have occurred to her before this? After three decades as a nurse, she should have thought of this sooner. When her conscience niggled at her about the heresy of making appointments if she was only doing so to obtain more pills, she argued back with herself that she truly didn't want to have a second knee surgery. Therefore she was consulting other physicians to find out if there was any way she could get by without the surgery.

Linda decided to make appointments with two orthopedists in case one of them turned out to be a dud. When she made the appointments, cheeks burning with worry that they could sense her intentions through the phone, she told the receptionists in each case that she was looking for a second opinion about whether her left knee required surgery imminently or whether she could see improvement with cortisone shots, physical therapy and anti-inflammatories until she retired in three or four years. She didn't count on how long it would take to get appointments with these specialists as a new patient; she was accustomed to her doctor's office working her in in short order. However, she went ahead with scheduling them, but then fretted for half the night about how she would get hold of enough painkillers to last until the appointments.

The next day she complained about it to Renee in the break room, "I've been trying to tell my orthopedist that I cannot afford to take off for a second surgery yet. I need another cortisone shot or more physical therapy or just more ibuprofen."

"Linda," Renee started in scolding tone. "I can tell it's you from the far end of the hall even if I don't see your head, you're limping so bad. Are you honestly just taking ibuprofens with your knee in such bad shape?"

"Well, my doc won't give me any more painkillers. He doesn't want me to use the pills to delay the surgery he knows I need."

"Oh Christ, what crap, it's not like you're addicted to the damned things. Did you ask Dan for a few to get you through until your next appointment?" Dr. Dan Weiss was one of the consulting orthopedists for their facility.

"I can't ask him. I haven't ever been seen by him as a patient."

"He gave me a week's worth when my back went out. He's doing rounds right now. Go grab him."

"I can't do that. I don't want half the facility thinking I'm some dope seeker, when all I am is a big fat chicken who's putting off a knee surgery I definitely need."

"Oh stuff it. C'mon," Renee grabbed Linda by the elbow and pulled her down the orthopedic ward hallway. Dr. Weiss was coming out of a patient's room.

"Dan," Renee called. "Have you seen how Linda here is limping?"

"Yeah, I've noticed. I heard you were out for knee surgery a few months ago though. And you're still having problems?"

Renee jumped right in, "It's the other knee now, but she needs a little more rehab time on the right knee before she can handle surgery on her left knee. But anyway, her orthopedist didn't do her Percocet refill before he went on vacation Friday afternoon. Can you fix her up so she doesn't drop one of your patients?"

Dr. Weiss shrugged, "I don't see why not. Even if she didn't pick me as her surgeon. And, really, your ortho guy should have you working with a pain management specialist, ideally one who works with your physical therapist. You won't heal right if you're in too much pain." Dr. Weiss smiled, pulled out his prescription pad, double checked the spelling of Linda's last name on her ID badge, and scribbled out a scrip which he handed to Linda.

"Thanks, Dr. Weiss. And it's nothing about you as a surgeon. Going to the orthopod I work with is a little too close to home though....."

"I was just teasing about being your surgeon. I'm a back guy, not a knee guy." Dr. Weiss went into the next patient's room.

Linda was astonished at how easy that had been. She would never have had Renee's nerve and said as much to Renee.

"You're too worried. It's nothing, it's just a few days of pills. Besides, he's right, you should have a pain management specialist. If you're doing the second knee, you won't be through all this mess for months. Nancy sees you limping around here, she'll send you home."

Linda put the scrip in her locker in the break room and then went back to work. On the way home, she dropped the prescription off at the pharmacy. She didn't even notice until she pulled the prescription slip out of her purse that Dr. Weiss had written her a thirty-day supply. She was expecting a scrip for a week's worth to tide her over. She sighed with relief and went in the store. She told the pharmacy tech who took her order that she wanted to wait.

Linda wandered through the store browsing the aisles until she heard her name over the PA system. She went up expecting to pay for the prescription. Instead, the pharmacist was waiting for her at the consultation counter, "I wanted to check on this because it's a different doctor. Your prior doctor had denied a refill on the same thing."

Linda's heart jumped a little bit, but she recovered quickly, hoping he hadn't noticed any change of expression on her face, "Well, Dr. Rosen is pushing me hard for a second surgery, and I had such a hard time with the first one and I was out of work for way longer than I could afford. So, I decided to get a second opinion from Dr. Weiss. I'm still definitely going to have to get the left knee replaced at some point, but I was hoping Dr. Weiss would tell me I could let the right knee and my bank account recover a little bit longer before a second time under the knife."

"OK," the pharmacist said, apparently reassured. "Sorry to be a pest, but pharmacies these days are getting pushed hard by the state because of all the prescription drug abuse. I'll have this ready for you in five more minutes."

"Sure, no problem. I understand." Linda twisted and untwisted her hands around the strap of her purse for the next five minutes while sitting in the chairs for waiting customers. She popped two of the Percocets as soon as she got in the car. She made a mental note to be careful about any prescriptions she got from her upcoming appointments. She'd have to go to a different pharmacy. She'd probably have to pay out of pocket, because if she gave them her insurance card, her insurance company might start flagging her for filling prescriptions too soon. Well, she'd worry about that when the time came. For now, she had a supply.

* * * * *

Linda had almost forgotten about the request for Matt's service and medical records. When she opened the mailbox one day more than six months after the initial request, she found a large signature U.S. government brown envelope. As the envelope was addressed to Matt she felt she should at least inform him it had arrived.

"Hey Matt," Linda called to the sunporch. "Guess what finally showed up."

As far as Linda could tell from the kitchen, he didn't even move his head from its TV-watching position.

"Your service records that we ordered months ago have arrived."

No response.

"Do you mind if I open them? I want to see the medical records to see what we can do to get your benefits going."

Still no response.

Linda decided to accept silence as affirmative permission.

Once Linda had changed out of her scrubs and taken Goldy for her walk, she sat down at the kitchen table and started looking at the papers. The first several pages were filled with training completion certificates, uniformly positive ratings on Matt's teamwork and leadership signed by his superior officer, and copies of a plethora of awards for superior marksmanship.

Matt's service medical records consisted of a fairly sparse set of pages considering that by his admittedly confused stories he'd been hospitalized twice. His intake physical and subsequent routine exams showed only that Matt was a supremely healthy young specimen of a man. The records then jumped to his first hospitalization after the bomb went off. The records detail his squad mates reporting that Matt had been unconscious but that by the time he reached the field hospital, he had started to groggily come to. The physical exam showed minor lacerations none of which even required stitches. He had been given analgesics for what he called a blinding headache, observed overnight, and then released. Linda had first learned about this hospitalization from the middle-of-the-night call in early 2009 from Matt's platoon leader in Iraq, but she remembered that she didn't learn much more from his call than she was learning from looking at the hospitalization record.

Linda struggled to recall as much detail as she could about the call from Matt's teammate and friend, the husky Latino grenadier Rico. Rico had called the day after the explosion from his own phone card to tell her as much as he could about what had happened, "I can't tell you much about what we were doing or where we were. But, we were in this abandoned building, and Matt was at the edge of the doorway looking through the scope of his rifle. I was in the room behind him squatting on the floor. All of a sudden Matt says, 'Hey, there's a kid out there, there's not supposed to be any kids, oh God no....' And next thing you know there's this explosion, and I'm on my butt watching Matt flying backwards from the doorway hitting his head against the back wall. I crawled over to him. He was unconscious. I dragged him out the back of the building, and we got him to the field hospital."

Linda had thanked Rico for calling and had been about to hang up when he asked, "Would you please let Casey know what's going on?" Linda then realized that as merely his girlfriend Casey would not even have received the fairly uninformative call that Linda had received.

"Do you have her number?" Linda requested.

"Of course, and thanks for doing this. I'd do it myself, but I'm running out of calling card minutes."

Linda called Casey immediately after hanging up with Rico. Casey started sobbing as soon as Linda had the words out of her mouth. "Casey, pull it together. He has a concussion. He's in a field hospital getting treated. He's not going to die. I'm sure you'll be able to talk to him soon."

On the way home from work the next day, she bought several prepaid international calling cards and sent some to Matt and some to Rico to make up for the minutes he had used up making calls for Matt.

When Matt called her after being discharged from the field hospital, he told Linda that Rico was receiving some sort of well-deserved decoration for pulling Matt back to safety. Matt was still complaining of a bad headache but said that otherwise he had been lucky not to be more severely injured.

The next set of medical records were dated starting two weeks after the first hospitalization. All of the parts of the record describing the circumstances leading to the hospitalization had been blacked out with a thick magic marker before being copied. Linda had to assume that whatever Matt and his team had been doing was classified. The records showed severely elevated respiration, heart rate and blood pressure at admission; Linda therefore had to assume that based on the period of time that must have elapsed between whatever happened in the field and the taking of the first set of vital signs that Matt must have experienced some sort of severe panic attack. The physical exam was otherwise normal with no trauma or injury noted.

Linda had not learned about the second hospitalization until Matt inadvertently mentioned it while raving at her one night about the unfairness of some lieutenant's behavior. Presumably Matt had been ashamed to tell Linda that he had a nervous breakdown in the field. At least now she knew he hadn't been hallucinating a second hospitalization. Linda skimmed through the pages covered with the typically illegible scrawl of various physicians looking for the diagnosis, which was listed as panic disorder and PTSD. In today's current scramble for maximum reimbursement rates, the tersely scribbled hospital discharge note she found at the end of the records would never have made it out of a private hospital as it wouldn't have garnered a high enough claim rate, but a single line item on the discharge slip caught her attention. "D/c all meds." Linda paged back through looking for the documentation of the meds her son had been on.

Alprazolam, the generic name for Xanax. A benzodiazepine, the family of drugs in which Valium also resided. The only psychiatric agent her son had received had been Xanax.

Linda took the papers upstairs with her to the computer and searched on Xanax and PTSD. To her surprise, her search revealed numerous links to sound peer-reviewed work finding that benzodiazepines such as Xanax were contraindicated for PTSD due to withdrawal symptoms and ineffectiveness against the principal symptoms of PTSD. In fact the Army Surgeon General's Office had even recommended against Xanax's use in an official report dated April 10, 2012, more than three years after Matt's discharge from the Army.

Linda leaned back against the chair sure she had just hit the jackpot. Her son, who was diagnosed with PTSD in an Army hospital, was given Xanax, the use of which is now contraindicated for her son's condition in part due to withdrawal symptoms. Then upon hospital discharge, the attending physician discontinued the Xanax. Less than a week later according to the heavily redacted report of Matt's commanding officer, Matt is refusing to obey orders in the field and going AWOL. The end result is an other than honorable discharge. And now, the VA had the nerve to deny her son benefits because of his discharge status.

Linda was furious. Linda was so furious she was ready to take on the entire federal government to get her son the benefits he had earned. She dug around through her desk drawer until she found the VA social worker's name and phone number. She dialed.

"Hi, Virginia, it's Linda MacDermott," Linda started when the social worker answered. "I don't know if you recall, but we spoke a number of months ago about my son and his need for a discharge upgrade. I truly appreciated the advice you gave me."

The voice on the other end gradually clarified, "Oh yes, yes, yes, I remember. Well, I hope the advice helped."

"Well, actually it has. As you suggested, I ordered his service medical records. After almost six months, I just got them and found something not quite kosher. Would you happen to have time for a couple quick questions?" Linda asked hopefully.

"Well, sure," Virginia sounded a little hesitant.

Linda charged forward quickly before she had a chance to change her mind, "What I found was that he was given Xanax for his PTSD in the Army hospital, which I've read is contraindicated for PTSD in part because of withdrawal problems."

"You betcha," Virginia sounded more interested.

"And, they discontinued the Xanax the day they discharged him and sent him back to his unit to gun people down. Why would they do that?"

"You mean, why give it to him in the first place? Or why discontinue it on discharge?"

"Well, both, I guess."

"My best guess for why they started is that's the drug the hospital had available to it. Also, depending on when he was hospitalized, all the reports about Xanax withdrawal and PTSD may not have come out yet. My next best guess for why they discontinued it is that there's probably an Army regulation about not giving a guy who's on Xanax a .50 caliber machine gun and telling him to go out and shoot people."

"You're probably right," Linda acknowledged. "But I guess my main question to you is whether I can argue that he's eligible for a discharge upgrade because he was insane when he refused a superior officer's orders because he was first inappropriately treated for his condition and then discontinued from the inappropriate medication known to cause withdrawal symptoms?"

Virginia said, "It's a start, but...."

"Well, hallelujah," Linda started talking before Virginia finished whatever she'd been planning to say. "That's the first good news I've had on this front in a long time. Thank you soo sooo much for talking to me again. I won't take any more of your time, but thank you, thank you, thank you."

Linda was searching on "how to apply for a discharge upgrade" even as she was hanging up. She hit the print button and decided to go try to share the news with Matt.

Matt was still sitting in the same position on the sofa bed, remote in hand. Linda sat down on the arm of the sofa bed, "Hey, Matt, I think I found something good in your service records we can use to get you upgraded."

Without looking at her, Matt replied, "What, you found a note from a doctor saying I'm totally fucking insane."

"No, not that. But it turns out you were given Xanax for PTSD while you were in the hospital. And even the Army as of 2012 has acknowledged that Xanax is not an appropriate treatment for PTSD."

She had finally said something that caused Matt to look at her. "And that means?" he asked.

"Well, part of the reason that class of drugs is not appropriate for PTSD is that it causes withdrawal problems. And they discontinued your Xanax just before they discharged you and sent you back to your unit."

"Fuckers."

Linda decided to ignore the eloquent response and went ahead, "So, when we put in for a discharge upgrade for you, we argue that you were given the wrong treatment for your disease and then it was discontinued, and that the withdrawal symptoms plus your PTSD meant that at the time your officer claimed you disobeyed a direct order, you were temporarily insane. Hell, if murderers can get off for temporary insanity, we should at least be able to get you up to a general discharge, which would get you your benefits."

"General discharge, my ass. I did everything they fuckin' told me to do until that bomb put me in the hospital. Now you tell me the fuckers gave me the wrong meds, cut me off them, and I should be happy with a general discharge. I wanna ask for an honorable."

Matt finally had a little spark to him. Linda was thrilled to see that back.

Linda went back to her computer and found magic form DD 293, allegedly the start to the whole process of getting a discharge upgrade. She started typing in info into the PDF online, but hesitated on Boxes 5 and 9. In Box 5 she was supposed to choose which level of discharge Matt was seeking. Matt had told her he wanted an honorable, but he didn't need that much of an upgrade to get benefits. If he checked the box for honorable and the Army decided he didn't deserve it, would they upgrade him to a general discharge without his having asked for it? Or would Matt have to start all over again to request a general? She also didn't know what to do with Box 9 where Matt had to indicate whether he wanted a record review or whether he wanted a hearing "at no cost to the government." Linda's fear on the one hand was that if she requested a record review, some mindless government bureaucrat with no medical background might not understand the medical mistake that was made or not want to own up to the mistake. On the other hand, Matt was so unpredictable these days that she was afraid of his behavior at a hearing. If he became angry at the hearing and started mouthing off, he would spoil his own chances for an upgrade. And these days, Matt would disappear at the drop of a hat. Linda could only imagine setting her alarm for the day of the hearing only to find that Matt had vanished in the middle of the night.

When she had been searching the internet for info on discharge upgrades, Linda had been bombarded by ads from attorneys promising to help vets get their benefits, which triggered her memory of the VA social worker's describing how veterans' organizations like the VFW ran free legal clinics. Deciding she should find one of those clinics to see if she could inveigle a lawyer to answer her questions before she finalized the paperwork, Linda returned to her searching. She found a hotline number for a Maryland legal aid service which provided free brief advice to veterans. She printed out the number to call during business hours. She hoped that they would take her call even though she was only the mother of a vet. In his current state, Linda did not want to try to get Matt to sit civilly through a phone call.

* * * * *

Linda's second opinion orthopedic visits went off without a hitch. A friendly young physician's assistant at the first place triaged her, "So, tell me why you're here today?"

"Well, I had a right knee replacement about a year and a half ago. While I have to admit that the knee is a lot better, better than it's been in years, recovery from the surgery was awful. I'm a nurse, which as I'm sure you know, means I am up on my feet all the time. After the surgery, I wasn't able to work my regular shifts for over two months. And now, the orthopedist who did my right knee is telling me that I need to have to have my left one done too. I can't afford to be off work for two more months so soon after the last surgery. Don't get me wrong, I like my orthopedist, I worked with him a million years ago when I was at the hospital, but I figured I should get a second opinion on whether I have any options. Can I wear a brace, get more cortisone shots, take more anti-inflammatories, or do more physical therapy? At least maybe put this surgery off for a few years. After all, I'm about four years out from retirement; I'll have all the time in the world then."

An x-ray and a short visit with the actual orthopedist later, she walked out with an order for an MRI and a prescription for thirty Percocets which she filled at a new pharmacy paying in cash.

The next visit went similarly.

The bad news was that both of these other orthopedists also ultimately advised her that she was bone on bone based on her scans. While Dr. Rosen placed more emphasis on the need for surgery in the near future, Linda suspected that because these other orthopedists didn't know her the way Dr. Rosen did, they were just more cautious in pushing a major surgery on a new patient. They both obliquely hinted that based on the number of cortisone shots she had already had and the degree of pain and discomfort she was experiencing that surgery was the only next step. Linda knew that, irrespective of how they delivered their advice, none of these orthopedists was going to keep filling opioid prescriptions while she tried to remain a chicken.

PART THREE

CLIMBING BACK

CHAPTER ELEVEN

Linda was going to die of shame. Siobhan had figured out that she had been stealing opioids from work. Linda's heart raced the whole time it took her to get back to the house, toweled off Goldy's feet and let herself back into the house. Her heart rate was still well above normal even now, and she couldn't guess how long she had leaned against the front door sobbing, trying to understand how the gravitational force of the pills and the stress in her life had sucked her so near a black hole.

Irrespective of how she had started downward, she had to keep herself from crossing the final point of no return. But where to start? Start with saving her job and saving her nursing license. Losing her nursing license was tantamount to be excommunicated from the entirety of her professional career. How had she led herself to the heretical belief that she wasn't really stealing? How had she become so short-sighted as not to appreciate the consequences of getting caught? How had she become so arrogant as to believe that she wouldn't get caught when over the course of her career she had watched dozens of other people get caught? How had she become so indolent that she determined that the best way to cope with her life was to escape into the pills rather than cope with Matt's issues as directly as possible?

Linda tried to think carefully through exactly what Siobhan could have determined and how much could be directly attributed to Linda. Linda knew that she was safe as far as the OxyContin that landed in her bra went. She knew that the facility had instituted new procedures for checking in a patient's home supply of medicine a few months ago. Siobhan was smart enough to figure out that the staff could have been diverting pills by not having strict enough controls on the pills patients brought in with them. But, if Siobhan could have pinned those thefts directly on Linda, then Nancy would have been all over Linda back then. Since Corrine had been fired after being caught in that snare, the only pills she had been daring to take had been via her overstating her patients' PRN needs or "correcting" mistakes she found on some of the patient charts. But how could Siobhan have figured those out? She would practically have had to interview patients and the other nurses, and then compare their comments against what Linda had recorded in the chart. Linda had thought her methods were pretty foolproof, but obviously Siobhan had figured something out somehow.

The good news, if there were any at all, was that Siobhan had as much as told her that she couldn't definitively prove that Linda was the thief, just that there was a thief. But how had Siobhan even gotten onto her trail? Linda had trouble not focusing on her belief that she had been so careful.

And besides, all this time Linda assumed Siobhan had only been auditing the clinical trial being done at the facility. Although, as she reflected, Nancy would be the sort to order regular pharmacy audits at the same time as research audits if she could squeeze them in.

And Linda knew Siobhan was an exceptional auditor. Any auditor would have discovered the nitwit pharmacy tech who merged the prednisone supply from the regular pharmacy with the supply from a clinical trial. But Siobhan hadn't stopped at discovering the mistake, she had doggedly tracked down each and every last pill. She found out which trial patients got the regular supply and which regular patients had gotten clinical trial supply, using the lot numbers in the patient charts, pulling the charts of every patient in the facility until she had them all. Linda had been the designated research nurse for that particular trial, so her presence at the audit close-out was required.

The poor pharmacy tech hadn't even been smart enough to realize that she'd done something wrong, "But it's all prednisone, all the same dose, all within expiration date. What does it matter which bottle I used?"

Siobhan's exasperation was palpable, "That's like saying it doesn't matter whether I took the money out of my bank account or my boyfriend's, it's all money. Bet your boyfriend would care. Clinical trials require perfect drug dispensing, and the source of supply matters."

As the pharmacy tech had still been within her six-month probation period she was dismissed. In Linda's opinion the pharmacist should also have taken a bit of heat for not overseeing the tech better.

Linda realized she had allowed her mind to wander. The gist of her ruminations was that Siobhan was meticulous to a point that would drive many people to insanity. If anyone could have figured out what Linda had done, Siobhan would be the person.

Linda had convinced herself that she had been incredibly clever. As a senior R.N. in a facility perpetually short of senior nursing staff, Linda was floated to all the different wards in the facility: the long term nursing home residents, the special orthopedic recovery ward, the intermediate care ward, and more rarely to the assisted living building on the other side of the parking lot. Most nurses who stole worked one ward, and if the nurse had any sort of opioid habit whatsoever, the volume of pills missing from his or her ward quickly became unmistakable, whereas Linda could spread her thefts out over the whole facility.

Of course, now that the management knew a thief was out there, Linda had to figure out what to do. She had watched too many employees over the course of a career try to deny or bluff their way out of a situation. This tactic never worked. Linda knew that Siobhan would not turn over her findings to the management if she wasn't absolutely certain. However, Siobhan had indicated that she couldn't prove who the thief was; Siobhan was an evidenced-based person, and her report would contain only provable facts. Siobhan would leave it to the management to interview staff and try to determine the identity of the thief, meaning that Linda had to be very careful about what she was going to say.

She decided to call in sick in the morning to buy herself a little time. She called right before the shift change, knowing the night nurse would leave the message for Nancy, but that Nancy wouldn't get in until 8:30 or 9 at which point the night nurse would be gone; then Nancy would have no chance to question the night nurse about what exactly Linda had said. Linda also called Renee at home, pleaded bad Mexican food and clued her in that she might be able to grab Linda's shift. Renee's daughter had started college this semester, and Renee begged for any extra shifts she could get.

Linda's initial plan had been to hold out on the second surgery for as long as possible. However, as she considered how to handle the current situation with the opioids and work, she worried about getting herself completely clean only to have to go through surgery six months later. Linda had tried hard not to use opioid painkillers with the first surgery, but she simply hadn't been able to handle the pain.

Why get clean now and then fail with a second surgery? Why not call up the orthopedist and schedule the surgery now? She was going to need the surgery. She could get the surgery over with, have Laurie help her through the pain medicine dosing following the surgery, clean herself up as she recovered from the second surgery, and then not have to worry about getting off the pain meds twice.

If Linda called up today while she was off and scheduled the surgery, she could call Nancy this afternoon and tell her she was set for the surgery. If the orthopedist was able to schedule the surgery fairly quickly, she might even be able to use sick leave up to the surgery. Linda knew how these opioid disciplinary proceedings work. They would have to meet with her. She would be given a chance to do a treatment program. But, if she preempted the whole issue by signing up for the surgery, they might not even be able to hold the personnel meetings until after her surgery. At which point she would be clean.

She called Laurie, "You up for taking care of a crip again for a little while?"

"Huh? What for?"

"Orthopod's insisting that I shouldn't wait any longer to get the second knee done, and the guy I got a second opinion from was even more insistent." Linda did not tell her sister that she had gone to two other physicians and gotten pills from both of them.

"You've done a good job stalling for as long as possible."

"As long as possible may have arrived. I'm going to see what dates are possible. Are there any dates I should avoid?"

"Nope, I'll make things work. The hospital can't deny FMLA leave, and you'll have no problem getting a note from your orthopod indicating you won't be able to care for yourself." The Family Medical Leave Act, the first law that Bill Clinton signed, guaranteed employees the right to take sick time to care for family members.

Linda then called her orthopedist's office. She was transferred to the scheduling clerk who put her on hold while pulling her chart.

"Dr. Rosen made a note about your reluctance to proceed, but he feels you would genuinely benefit from the surgery. Glad to see you changed your mind. Did you have any particular dates in mind?"

"Unfortunately, the sooner the better. Gives me less time to chicken out and I'm pretty uncomfortable after a day at work. I don't know why I've been stalling."

"Let me give you a call back. Our OR time has been shuffled lately, and I want to make sure I have it straight. You have the pre-op exercise sheets, right?"

Linda confirmed that she did.

"Once I get you a date, we'll need to get you the prescriptions for your pre-op meds as well."

Linda called Nancy while she was waiting for the scheduling clerk to call back.

"Hey Nancy, it's Linda. Sorry about the short notice today but we went out to dinner last night and the Mexican on top of the worry over my knee just didn't work for me."

Nancy grunted.

"Anyway, at my orthopedist's yesterday, he strongly urged me to go ahead and get the second knee replaced. He tells me it's bad enough that he wouldn't sign off on my fitness for duty at this point." The orthopedist had only hinted that he wouldn't sign any more work papers for her if she needed them to return. When Linda had fallen in Mrs. Nelson's room back before her first surgery though, Nancy had been almost apoplectic that Linda was working without a specific sign off from her orthopedist. Linda therefore knew that Nancy wouldn't argue about the timing of any second surgery if the orthopedist was refusing to sign off, irrespective of how unhappy she might be about having to find coverage for Linda's shifts. "I've been pretty chicken about doing it because the first one knocked me down for the count, but I've been putting off the inevitable. The scheduling clerk is supposed to call me back by the end of the day, but I wanted to give you a heads up."

Nancy thanked her with a tone suggesting she was anything but thankful.

Linda stuffed her cell phone in her jeans and took Goldy across to the park. With any luck she could get the surgery over with before the best part of the summer arrived. She would hate to miss an entire boating season. And, swimming in the river was great physical therapy without much strain on the knee.

Linda did not touch another pill from her facility for the entire time between when Siobhan confronted her and the surgery. Her cheeks grew hot every time she remembered Siobhan's words at the park, and her shame helped her keep under control. Linda had a low dose prescription of Percocets from the orthopedist to get her through to the surgery plus what she had gotten from her second opinions. Linda counted the pills, divided by the number of days until the surgery, and forced herself to take only the pills allotted for each day so that she could make it to the surgery without needing any more. She only allowed herself to have only one pill at a time in her purse. She kept the rest of the pills in the gun safe upstairs, forcing herself to climb the stairs on her backside pulling herself up each step with her arms to get another pill and insuring that if Matt showed up he couldn't get hold of them. Whenever she felt herself weakening, she envisioned Siobhan telling Nancy about finding a pill thief, and somehow the shame was a more powerful inhibitor of her cravings than anything else had been.

Nevertheless, Linda knew she would be in a tremendous amount of true pain following the surgery, and she wouldn't be able to labor up and down stairs to regiment her supply of pills. She knew she would need help keeping the monster at bay, and she knew that the best and only help was her best friend and twin sister.

Linda therefore confided in Laurie two nights before the surgery. She had to work herself up for it, and swallowing her pride to confide even in the person closest to her in the world was almost more than she could do, "I couldn't get myself off the Percs after the first surgery, Laur. I've never stopped taking them. I kept lying to the orthopedist to get him to prescribe me more of them. I want to stop taking them. I need to stop taking them, but I'm terrified that I'll need them so bad after this knee that I'll be in even worse shape, that I'll have even more of a problem after this second surgery."

Laurie took a long sip off her martini, "I wondered because I saw you taking pills here and there along the way. But you were so uptight about taking pills before the surgery I figured I was mistaken. Of course, I suppose you're going to blame me for stealing your license and filling your Percocet prescription the first time." The twins both tried to smile at the weak joke, but it failed.

"It gets worse," Linda continued. "Matt's using them too. Once I figured out he was stealing my pills, I started hiding them. In my underwear drawer for heaven's sake."

"Matt's pill problem has nothing to do with your pill problem or your needing the surgery," Laurie said.

"I know, but it does relate to why I need you to help me. You keep the pill bottle, and give me just what I need. Then wean me off them. And then Matt can't get hold of pills he doesn't need from me."

"Consider me recruited."

Linda just hugged her sister, took the prescribed one Percocet for the evening, and then handed her sister every last Percocet she had in her possession. "I'm counting on you," she said as she got up to leave.

"You're sleeping here tomorrow night, right? We'll have to get up early enough as it is without my coming to pick you up at the crack of dawn."

"Of course, but tonight I've got to get all the bills paid, do laundry, et cetera. Also, I'm hoping Matt will be home so I can read him the riot act about taking the garbage out while I'm gone."

Laurie offered no comment about Matt, and Linda knew what she thought anyway. Linda, however, had decided that she needed to fix her knee and her own problems first before she tried to tackle Matt.

Back at home, Linda sat down at the kitchen table with all of the bills that would be coming due soon, making sure she didn't need to worry about checks to write during the first part of her recovery. She tucked the electric bill payment stub and her check in the envelope, and wrote $223.56 in the check register next to check number 2498. Then she flipped back to the checks and found only deposit slips. Where were 2499 and 2500? She went back to the register and made sure she hadn't accidentally pulled checks in the wrong order.

Racking her brain, she went upstairs to log in to her bank account. To her horror, the transaction history showed that 2500 had cleared two days ago for a thousand bucks, and 2499 last week for $500. If it had been during business hours, Linda would have called the bank immediately to demand answers for their clearing checks she hadn't written. But then she clicked on the hyperlink for 2500 and leaned heavily against her chair back. The check had been written to Matt MacDermott, unmistakably in Matt's handwriting. Even on the digital image, the signature looked like it had been etched into the paper, as if Matt had been tracing her signature.

For a solid two minutes, all Linda could do was exhaust her expletive vocabulary. She'd be lucky if Matt didn't pawn the light fixtures in the house by the time she came home from the surgery. She thought about calling Laurie for advice, but she decided to sleep on it.

In the morning, she called a locksmith and requested an emergency visit to change the locks. They promised to arrive between noon and four. Linda printed out the images of the fronts and backs of the two forged checks and drove to her bank as soon as it opened, where she asked to speak to a manager.

"I don't know what the rules or the law on this is, but these checks are forgeries," Linda proffered the printouts of the checks. "I can tell that my signature has been traced even on the scanned image. Anyone who works in a bank should have been able to see that on the actual document."

The bank manager kept a poker face, but pulled a form out of the file cabinet. She completed most of the form and asked Linda to fill out the boxes she'd marked with an "X" and to sign the form. On the form entitled "Inquiry" that the manager placed in front of her, Linda wrote that the checks were forgeries and her signature had obviously been traced. She signed the form. The bank manager informed her that they would investigate her claim and have an answer within ten business days. If the bank found her claim to be correct, her money would be refunded provided she cooperated with the bank in any attempt to recover the funds.

Linda got fried chicken from the drive through on her way home where she waited for the locksmith. After eating, she wrote a letter to Matt. She shredded at least ten drafts before deciding on the simplest text possible:

Dear Matt,

I'm sorry that I can't tell you this in person, but my surgery is tomorrow and I will be at Aunt Laurie's until I can move on my own. Since you just cashed a forged check for $1000 from my bank account two days ago, I don't know how long it will be before you come home. I have changed the locks on the house, and you cannot stay here anymore. I love you and I want to help you but I cannot let you bankrupt me or I won't be able to help you. I hope when you get this that you come to see me at Aunt Laurie's. I want to get you the help you need.

Love, Mom

She left the letter in an envelope in the shed where they had always kept the spare key to the house.

When the locksmith showed up, she had him change the locks on the front door, the door between the kitchen and the sunporch which had originally been an exterior door, and the exterior door on the sunporch. She put all three copies of each of the three keys in her purse to take over to Laurie's.

Her last action before packing herself and Goldy into the car was to call Jimmy. She was relieved to get his voice mail as she didn't want to argue with him.

"Jimmy, this is Linda. I'm having my second knee surgery first thing tomorrow morning, so I'll be hard to catch up with for the next couple days, but I found out yesterday that Matt forged my signature on two checks and stole $1500 from my bank account. I changed the locks on the house today so that he can't steal anything else while I'm recovering from surgery."

When she got to Laurie's, she asked, "Am I allowed to have a drink tonight? I'd love to get drunk, but I know better."

Laurie squinted at her, "What's up?"

Linda related the story of the forged checks and the locksmith.

Laurie sighed, "I'm sorry my nephew is so screwed up, Linda, but you did the right thing. I know you'll be worried about him while you're over here, but he's been surviving just fine when he disappears."

Linda made one very strong vodka martini to eat with the Chinese food they ordered for dinner. Laurie sensed that Linda didn't want to talk so they ordered a movie on demand and watched it quietly.

* * * * *

The second surgery was every bit as debilitating as the first one. Except for her physical therapy sessions and while doing her at-home exercises, she spent the first several days after she was released on her sister's couch with her leg up and the excruciatingly uncomfortable compression sock on. Laurie had relented once again and allowed Goldy to come with Linda, primarily because she knew Matt was no longer at the house. Linda had had to promise to pay for Laurie's next four housekeeping visits to deal with the pet fur. "I found Goldy fur everywhere for at least two months after I finally kicked you out after the first surgery," Laurie had mockingly complained. Goldy curled at the base of Linda's couch for hours at a time. As if she knew something was wrong, she would periodically sniff the bandages on Linda's knee.

As the sisters had agreed, Laurie doled out the Percocets strictly. On the first day Laurie went back to work, Linda hauled herself with her walker to the bathroom and started going through the medicine cabinets hoping Laurie had left the bottle somewhere obvious. Although Linda had been far too ashamed to admit to Laurie the lengths she had gone to obtain more pills, Laurie had been a nurse long enough to know how desperate a pill addict could be and obviously hid the pills accordingly.

While Linda sat on her sister's couch recovering, she tried to decide on a course of action when she was interviewed about the thefts Siobhan had uncovered at the facility. She was so anxious though that she found thinking logically and linearly to be extremely difficult. Her first thought was that if she believed Siobhan's statement that Siobhan's evidence could not prove the identity of the thief, she should flatly deny everything and force them to prove it was her. However, if Nancy could combine her shift schedules or other personnel records with Siobhan's evidence to prove Linda was the thief then Linda was done for if she denied everything. Also, what if Siobhan wasn't being entirely truthful when she said that she couldn't prove who the thief was. Linda wasn't sure she had the nerve to gamble her career on the weakness of the evidence.

Linda decided she wasn't worried about the management ordering drug testing of the employees because her surgery was a legitimate reason to have been taking painkillers. On the other hand, the employee handbook said that she had to admit to a problem and request counseling before they drug tested her in order to avoid suspension or termination.

Linda therefore wondered if there was any value in admitting she had some level of problem before they even interviewed her, feigning ignorance of Nancy's investigation. Before she even went back to work, she could tell Nancy that she was going to counseling on her own dime, explaining that after the first surgery weaning herself off the pills had been so difficult that she wanted to make sure she had no problems after the second surgery. Of course, if she admitted to any level of problem, Nancy would probably assume she had been the thief all along and had found out about Nancy's investigations from a co-worker; then Linda could end up demoted or have a stain placed on her nursing license when she was only four years away from early retirement.

The final option would be to fess up only once she had been interviewed. Given her long-standing stellar record with the corporation, Linda was unlikely to be fired as long as she immediately accepted counseling. She couldn't remember whether the employee handbook distinguished between just being caught using or in possession versus taking pills from the facility. However, she had sat on the other side of disciplinary hearings, and she knew that if the employee had a medical problem and agreed to seek treatment, the employee could hire a good lawyer and make life difficult for the management if they precipitously dismissed the employee. Linda had always been a little jealous of the employees who appeared to get off scot-free from stealing from the facility by claiming that they had gone to counseling and now they were a changed person. Sitting on the other side of an addiction problem, Linda now knew that she had been wrong to envy such people. Getting off the pills was nothing about which to be envious.

Fate stepped in to save her from the need to decide among her options though. Her eyes sticky from the sleep of the afternoon naps she took against the advice of her post-op instructions, Linda was awoken by a call from one of her company's vice presidents. Linda was terrified when the VP identified himself, worried that he was calling to say they had proof positive that she was a thief and her final paycheck was in the mail. Amazingly, he had what Linda considered great news, "Linda, we realize you still have two to three weeks before you're back at work, but we wanted to inform you that Nancy Grogan has resigned as the manager of your facility."

"What? Nancy's leaving. Where's she going?"

"You'll have to ask her yourself if you have a chance. She only gave us permission to say that she has taken a position which is better suited to her personal life at this point. We wanted to tell you before you came back so you would know who to contact for your schedule. Renee Amato will be covering interim management duties at the moment. Based on your seniority, we would have also asked you to take over certain tasks while we identify either a temporary or permanent replacement, but your medical leave made that problematic. Do you have a fixed return date yet?"

"Originally, my return was two weeks from now, and as far as I know I'm on track for that. However, I see my orthopedist tomorrow, so we'll see what he says."

"Well, the sooner the better from our point of view as we'll be very shorthanded until we fill the vacancy. For now, contact Renee to set up any shift schedules. If we have any changes to the chain of command, we'll let you know who to contact."

Wrapped in a blanket gray with too many washings on Laurie's coach, Linda called Renee on her cell phone that evening, guessing that she would have worked until seven. Renee picked up.

"Hey Renee, I hear Nancy's leaving."

"Ding dong, the wicked witch is dead."

"Oh, she wasn't that bad."

"Ha," Renee contradicted. "She and I never got along, and boy if you could hear what she's been insinuating about you since you went out for your surgery, you'd be singing with me."

"Really, what's she been saying?" Linda could only surmise that Nancy had been clever enough to guess that Siobhan's evidence of theft pointed at Linda.

"Oh, she's been sighing about how you can't take action against an employee when they're out on medical leave and suggesting the timing of your surgery was a little too convenient given that she's investigating a theft."

"What!" Linda feigned shock. "What theft? And how the heck does she get off implying I invented knee surgery to avoid an investigation. Most of you gave me hell about how long I put off these surgeries."

"And I was one of those people. But you must have heard how Nancy's been interviewing everyone in the place."

"No, what for, theft? Theft of what?"

"Pills of course. I guess you did go out on leave not long before this all blew up. Were you there when that redheaded auditor with the funny name was here last?"

"Who, Siobhan? No, I haven't seen her at work in months. She lives in my neighborhood though. Our dogs play together."

"Yes, that's the one. Didn't know you knew her. Anyway, she found several things on her last audit. You'd think someone just announced Santa Claus was coming twice this year. Nancy started hauling everyone into her office the second the auditor left."

"I'm surprised she gave her notice then. Why leave when she's having so much fun?"

"Oh, the rumor is one of her kids is out in New Mexico and is having a major life problem. Just like Nancy to move out there to fix her kid's life. And anyway, the way Nancy's been interviewing employees, she's probably certain she'll have the thief hanging from a tree in the courtyard before she's done."

"Ugggh. When's her last day? I'll make sure my orthopedist doesn't write me back in until afterwards."

"Smart move."

"Mr. VP said that you're in charge of shift schedules until they come up with a replacement."

"Yeah, they stuck me with scheduling. I suppose it's not such a bad thing. I can give myself the good shifts. I have no interest in being a manager though. I hope they get somebody decent in fairly quickly. I hate doing all this extra crap."

The two nurses talked for a little while longer about inconsequentials before hanging up.

Nancy's departure could only be a blessing to Linda. Since the first surgery Nancy had done no more than tolerate Linda because of her R.N., her seniority and her willingness to take crazy shift schedules. Hell, if Nancy couldn't finger the thief before she left, the new manager wouldn't be able to start re-investigating the second he or she walked in the door. He or she would be too busy with learning all the new responsibilities. By the time the new person got around to investigating, the evidence trail would have gotten colder, more employees who could have been the culprit would have left as nurses came and went like the place had revolving doors.

Linda began to feel a little glimmer of hope. Now she had to make sure that Laurie helped her off the damned pills. And she was going to go to one of those counselors to make sure that she was strong enough to try to help Matt instead of just being angry with him for stealing all of her valuables.

CHAPTER TWELVE

Wrapped up in her own alarm about the potential discovery of her thefts at work, Linda had never followed up on the discharge upgrade paperwork for Matt. Then she had scheduled the surgery and had been staying at Laurie's for weeks. And then after she was able to move back to her house, Matt had been so angry with her for changing the locks on the house that she wrathfully refused to put forth effort to help someone who wouldn't help himself. She focused instead on establishing a good relationship with the new supervisor at work, thus dispelling any suspicions Nancy may have left behind about the identity of the thief.

Hence, the pile of Matt's medical records had lain fallow on her desk for almost a year until the visit from Jimmy's nephew Tim. Matt had been staying in the basement of Tim's house since she changed the locks. Matt was three years younger than Tim, but they had played together at family gatherings as children. Linda was sure that Matt fed Tim some cock-and-bull story about how horribly Linda was treating Matt when he went to live with him. Linda had therefore been surprised to find Tim smoking on her deck one afternoon when she got back from work.

"Hey Tim, how's it going?" Linda said for lack of anything better. She let Goldy out onto the deck. "Goldy's been in the house all day. Mind if we walk over to the park for a second."

"Nope, that's fine," Tim replied, scratching Goldy's head as Goldy burst past him on her way to the park. Tim remained silent, and Linda could read the embarrassment on the young man's face.

"Tell me what's going on, Tim."

"I don't know what to do with Matt, Aunt Linda."

"Keep going."

Tim relentlessly smoked two cigarettes in a row while Goldy chased ducks, and Linda wondered if he was ever going to tell her. Finally, he started, "All he does is stay on the sofa bed and watch TV. He barely ever showers. I never see him eat. My wife is about to have a fit. Thank God we have a separate basement entrance because she made me lock the door between the basement and the upstairs so he couldn't come up. He scared the kids too much. When I told him I locked the door, he got so mad at me, I was afraid of him. I couldn't tell my wife how he reacted because she'd make me throw him out."

"Tim, I don't know what Matt told you when he moved in with you, but he is suffering from post-traumatic stress disorder. Worse still, instead of getting proper medical treatment, he is self-medicating with anything he can get hold of. I had two knee surgeries in the last three years, and he kept stealing all my pain meds. And then, when he couldn't steal those anymore, he started pawning things from the house. I finally changed the locks after he forged my name on some checks and stole $1500 from my bank account."

Tim's expression had grown ever more startled as Linda proceeded, and Linda didn't need Tim to tell her that Matt had given him a very different story.

"Tim," Linda continued. "I love Matt, and I would love to help him, but he doesn't want the right kind of help. I could not let him continue to rob me blind. I'm sorry he landed on your door step, and I'm grateful to you for giving him a place to stay. If you can't continue to let him stay, I will not hold it against you. In fact, I completely understand. You should not feel guilty. Matt needs professional psychiatric help, and nothing you do is going to take the place of that. To be clear, I will continue to try to get Matt the help he needs, but until he accepts the right kind of help, he's not going to live with me again."

Tim and Linda exchanged a few more words, mostly Linda reassuring Tim that she understood if he needed to throw Matt out.

That evening Linda saw the pile of Matt's discharge upgrade and paperwork and knew she needed to get back on track. She was a year past her second surgery, she was off the Percocets herself, and now it was time to put some effort toward her son. She had to keep her anger at Matt at bay and try to get him help for his mental illness, if for no other reason than that her son in his current condition was a menace to his family and friends.

As a first step atoning for slacking off on Matt's discharge paperwork, Linda stayed up well past midnight going back over all the paperwork she had assembled and researching discharge upgrades on the web. Barely able to contain herself until business hours began, she dialed the number for a legal aid group helping veterans first thing the next morning. The group apparently employed a triage system, and the young woman who answered the call took down Linda's name and the fact that she was seeking advice about a discharge upgrade and veteran's benefit application for her son. Then she was placed on hold.

After about 15 minutes of waiting, a different voice came on the line, "Hi, my name is Heather. I'm an attorney volunteering for this legal aid group. Before we discuss any details of your issue, I have to make sure you understand that our service offers brief legal information and advice to veterans. We do not become your attorney because of this phone call, and although any information you may share with us is confidential, we are not creating an attorney-client relationship. Do you understand this?"

Linda affirmed her understanding.

"OK, how can I help you today, Linda? I understand you are calling about veteran's benefits."

Linda started, "I'm trying to help my son with a discharge upgrade in order to be eligible for benefits."

Heather asked, "Is your son with you, Linda?"

Linda replied, "No, my son suffers from severe PTSD, and he can't handle this paperwork. That's why I'm involved."

"Well, I'm supposed to work directly with the veteran."

Before Heather could summarily hang up on her, Linda jumped in, "I just need a couple questions about the process answered. I don't need to discuss his details."

Heather paused but then said, "OK. What are your questions?"

"On the DD 293 form, the one that's the application for discharge upgrade, for question 9, where it asks whether you want a hearing or a record review," Linda paused until the attorney threw in an "Uh huh."

"My son would not hold up well at a hearing, but I'm worried that if we request a record review we don't have any way of being sure a properly trained medical professional reviews the paperwork. See, I'm a nurse, and I've reviewed my son's medical records from his accident onward. The military doctor improperly discontinued a psychiatric medication, and I believe that the withdrawal from the drug caused the behavior that got my son discharged."

Heather responded, "Oh wow." Linda found herself picturing a 24-year-old blonde who still lived with her parents on the other end of the phone and wondered when Valley Girl talk came back in style. "Usually discharge upgrades are more successful if the veteran's behavior has been exemplary since discharge, but if there was a genuine medical error just before his discharge, you might be able to make a case for it."

Linda was a little impatient, "So, should I request the records review? What if whoever reads the records doesn't understand what happens when you take someone with PTSD off Xanax cold turkey?"

Heather finally focused on her question, "Oh, well, if the result of the record review is negative, the veteran can always request a hearing afterwards. So, a request for record review isn't the end of the line if it's not successful."

Linda exhaled, "Oh, that's a relief. I guess it will add time to the process, but I'm glad to hear it's not final. I'll definitely start with the record review then."

Heather continued, "Also, there are special rules about how the military has to handle discharge upgrade applications from veterans with PTSD, particularly if the veteran served in Iraq or Afghanistan."

Linda jumped in, "My son served in both Iraq and Afghanistan."

"Oh good," Heather went on, still sounding like a Valley Girl teenager to Linda, "because if you end up having to appeal the record review decision, they have to include medical and psychiatric personnel in the review board. And, last November or December, there was a Congressional inquiry about the number of soldiers with PTSD or TBI who might have been inappropriately discharged, and the Army told Congress they would conduct an investigation. I'm not sure what that will mean for cases like you son's, but it can't be bad."

"No, it can't be."

"OK, well was that it?"

Linda responded quickly, "No, I had one other question. If my son asks for an upgrade to honorable, but they decide he doesn't deserve honorable, can they give him a general discharge instead? Since we're only trying to get VA benefits, all he needs is a general. Is it better to just go for as little of an upgrade as he needs?"

"I would put in for an honorable. The only thing the board can't do is make the discharge worse. They can leave it the same or they can upgrade it to whatever level they see fit. I don't see how it hurts you to go for the honorable."

"OK, great."

"Oh, and Linda," Heather continued, "if your son only needs VA benefits, the VA does have a way to offer benefits without the actual discharge upgrade. It's called a character of service determination or CSD."

"Is it better or faster to do this CSD thing?"

"Well, the bad discharge can hurt your son for future jobs as well as VA benefits. If you can help him get a discharge upgrade, he'll be better off all around. But, I wanted to make sure you knew about the VA process so you can explore all your options."

"How do you apply for this character of service thing?"

"Take a look at your son's denial letter for VA benefits. An application for any type of VA benefits triggers a CSD, and they probably requested additional information. The letter he got should mention something about a CSD and what you would need to send in to get one."

Linda shuffled the papers she had in front of her, but couldn't find the original denial letter. She thanked Heather, deciding it wasn't fair to make the woman wait on line and preparing to hang up even as she still shuffled through all of the papers, looking for an initial denial letter.

"Oh, and Linda," Heather interjected, as Linda snorted to herself over another sentence starting with "Oh and." "Do you live near Baltimore?"

"I'm closer to Annapolis."

"Well, the VFW in Baltimore County is holding a free clinic with volunteer attorneys in two weeks. Your son would probably have to be with you, but you could bring the paperwork to the clinic to have a volunteer attorney review it before you submit it."

"Wow, that's terrific. Can you give me the details please?" Linda took down the date, time and location for the clinic. Heather might sound half Linda's age, but she had been helpful.

Linda looked through more than a dozen web sites purporting to help people with the discharge upgrade process, describing various strategies. Linda struggled to understand what they meant by an equity argument, but just found herself frustrated by the fact that most of the sites just repeated the same quote from the same government regulation about how the discharge review boards could "grant an upgrade if the current discharge policies and procedures are materially different than those that led to the applicant's discharge." Equally unhelpful and as often repeated was the quote that a discharge may be deemed inequitable if "[t]here is substantial doubt that the applicant would have received the same discharge if relevant current policies and procedures had been available to the applicant at the time of the discharge proceedings under consideration."

After tossing the language around in her head, Linda came up with a spin for her argument which she liked. Matt had been treated with Xanax for his PTSD. Linda had a document released by the Army in 2012, after Matt's treatment, that the Army no longer recommended the use of Xanax for PTSD. Therefore, by the relevant current procedures of the Army, Matt would not have received the same treatment. He also would not have been put at risk of withdrawal when the Xanax was discontinued. Therefore, he should be eligible for a discharge upgrade.

Having figured that since Matt should be eligible for a discharge upgrade, she put the sticky note with the term Character of Service Determination on one of the stacks of papers she didn't deem as important.

CHAPTER THIRTEEN

"Nothing to complain about here," Linda observed to Laurie as they looked out the bungalow windows at Orient Bay on the French side of the Caribbean island of St. Martin.

The sisters had hopped on the first flight out of Baltimore to Charlotte in the morning, and then when a light drizzle produced ground delays at Charlotte, had had to run their best sprint to the international terminal to catch their flight to St. Martin. Fortunately, for a four-day trip, Laurie and she had each packed lightly enough to do carry-ons as checked luggage would never have made the connection.

In St. Martin, the rental car booth inside the airport was sketchy, and the counter at the rental car pick up lot was even sketchier. Linda took pictures of the big dent in the rear of the miserable little hatchback and made sure that the rental paperwork noted the dent's presence.

Once they started driving, the condition of the roads made the condition of the rental cars quite explainable. Linda navigated while Laurie negotiated around the worst of the potholes. And then miraculously, they saw the French flag as they crossed from the

Dutch territory to the French side of the island, and the driving conditions improved dramatically. Not long after crossing the border, they passed an immaculately uniformed, groomed and coiffed line of young schoolgirls, consistent with the overall improvement in cleanliness and orderliness of the buildings and parked cars on the French side.

When Linda had mentioned that she wanted to find a way to celebrate the one-year anniversary of being off the Percocets, Laurie had immediately hopped online to book a two-bedroom bungalow in Orient Bay with a decent ocean view only steps from the beach.

"I'm up for leaving our stuff packed and heading straight for some lunch, more importantly an alcoholic beverage and then vegging out on the beach. How 'bout you?" Laurie called from her bedrooms.

"Works for me," Linda responded, already rifling in her bag for a swimsuit.

A few minutes later they were walking into the first bar and restaurant combo on the beach they saw, a two-story wooden affair with a thatched roof. They took a table up on the top level on the water side with direct views of Orient Bay. The menu emphasized fried. Fried shrimp, fried calamari, fried fries. With lots of mayonnaise-based sauces for dipping.

"Guess I need a fairly significant concentration of alcohol to dissolve all this fat," Linda remarked. She order a fruity rum drink along with the cholesterol special. Two drinks and some tasty but overly heavy food later she told Laurie, "I need to roll out to the nearest clear patch of sand and let all the blood flow to my stomach."

"Oh no you don't," Laurie contradicted. "The best part of the beach is about a ten-minute walk south of here, and that's where we're headed."

"Uggh," Linda groaned but followed Laurie anyway.

After about ten minutes of walking, Linda noted a line of people standing with their backs to the approaching women atop a jetty which interrupted the clean white sand of the beach.

"What are they all standing there for?" Linda inquired.

"Oh, you'll see," Laurie replied. She nudged her way in amongst the onlookers and kept walking. As Linda followed, she realized why they were staring.

All of the people on this part of the beach were nude. As far down the beach as Linda could see, yellow umbrellas with two matching yellow plastic beach chairs under each one were filled with pair after pair of nude men and women. Mostly in the fifty-plus age group. Mostly hetero couples with occasional exceptions to both characterizations dotted in.

Laurie kept marching southward, Linda a few paces behind. Linda asked, "You're not serious, are you?"

Laurie turned only her head back and quipped, "As a myocardial infarction!"

Laurie identified a deeply tanned young man standing guard over stacks of unused beach chairs and handed him some cash to set them up with an umbrella and chairs. Laurie dropped her beach bag on one of the chairs and proceeded to pull her cover-up off and then undid her bikini top.

Linda stared. Laurie gave her a look of disdain, "You're a nurse, and you've been skinny-dipping in the Chesapeake your whole life. Don't tell me you're going to make a big deal about sitting on a nude beach."

"Well, no, I guess not," Linda gave in, "but I hope they sell booze around here. I need to get properly sloshed if I'm going to be naked before God and everyone."

Laurie laughed and pointed a dozen yards down the beach at a small hut boasted a short line of people and a couple exiting with promising plastic cups in hand. "There," she pointed. "Go get us some drinks and then take your bathing suit off, you prude."

Linda complied. In fact, she was the only clothed person in line at the bar and she felt overtly conspicuous. The fiftyish bartender with peroxide blond hair was admirably keeping up with all the calls for attention from the obvious regulars seated around the bar, while simultaneously serving the line of walk-ups. Linda grabbed two rum punches with pineapple slices and maraschino cherries and headed back to her sister. She nuzzled the drinks in the sand between the two beach chairs to prevent spilling, dropped her bag on the empty chair, thought "What the heck," and pulled off her cover-up and her one piece bathing suit. Spreading her towel over the chair, she parked and looked out at the water. Sipping on her drink she looked over at her twin and remarked, "Good idea."

And she meant it. She had never particularly contemplated going to a nude beach before, but Laurie was correct that skinny-dipping in the Chesapeake was all too common when anchoring in isolated creeks and coves. Without staring at anyone in particular, Linda looked around. Most of the folks stretched out on the beach chairs were similar in age to her. No one was engaging in any raucous activity. A few folks were talking in small groups. For the most part, people were quietly reclined with their e-readers or books.

She pulled her own e-reader out of her beach bag, adjusted herself under the umbrella to have the right amount of light and started one of the new mystery novels she had downloaded right before the trip. Periodically, she leaned to the side and sipped the rum punch through the neon green straw, trying not to get sand from the bottom of the plastic cup on herself.

When the first round of drinks were done, Laurie suggested, "Wanna go swimming?"

"Sounds great," Linda replied, noting that the late afternoon sun behind their backs was still intensely warm.

The water was almost flat, particularly considering how it came straight off the Atlantic. In the middle of the mouth of the bay

Linda noted a small island with breakers running in a line from the island to the arms of the bay. Linda guessed that a formidable rock barrier continued under the surface, protecting the bay from wave action. Must have been a nightmare for early sailors to figure out how to get their boats to shore without reaming the keels of the boats.

The water was cool, probably in the high seventies, but eminently swimmable. About fifty or sixty yards out from shore a floating wooden raft with a stainless steel ladder was anchored as a platform for swimmers. Laurie glanced over at Linda, nodded meaningfully and then launched herself with a small dive into a full crawl stroke. Linda snorted and followed suit. The two women raced out to the platform with their strong crawls. Linda had always been faster in long races. She knew she would catch Laurie, which is why Laurie had taken off first. Linda grabbed the rung of the ladder a half stroke before Laurie did. They hauled themselves up on the platform.

"Hope this thing's so waterlogged we don't get splinters anywhere embarrassing," Linda joked once she had enough breath back.

"I'm glad you decided not be a prude," Laurie teased.

"I take it you've been here before," Linda asked with a raised eyebrow.

"Yeah. Remember four or five years ago, I went on a Caribbean cruise with a handful of ER and ICU nurses, the cruise you couldn't get off work for? Well, we decided that each day one person got to pick the activity off of the boat. That plan worked until about day two. But anyway, my co-worker Joan declared that she wanted a relaxing beach day and so she picked this great beach she had heard about on the French side of St. Martin. So, four of us got in a tiny taxi with our beach bags and our matching beach towels from the ship. I wondered what was up when the taxi driver grinned at us after Joan requested that he take us to Orient Beach.

We get out of the taxi and walk out to the beach and lo and behold naked bodies everywhere.

"My colleague Deanie just about had a total hissy fit. What kind of godless slut did Joan think she was?

"Joan laughed at her. She said, 'Deanie, between the four of us we've been nursing for over a century. We wipe more butts in beds in a month than there are on this beach.' That about shut Deanie up, that and Joan buying her her first Hurricane of the day. She never did take her bikini bottom off, but then not all women do."

"Well, as you rightly pointed out, I've never had a problem skinny-dipping. I guess somehow I thought nude beaches were probably pick-up joints. But this place is about as tame as a nursing home," Linda commented.

"Call me greedy for wanting to enjoy myself for a change, but it certainly beats being back home at Lord's Creek trying to get a discharge upgrade for my son who barely acknowledges I exist," Linda exhaled resignedly. Since Linda had changed the locks just before her second surgery, her relationship with Matt was frosty at best. "Jimmy's cousin Tim sent me a text the other day to let me know he'd thrown Matt out."

Both women were lying on their backs on the floating raft. Laurie rolled her head toward Linda and commented with a sad look, "Good move for Tim."

Back on the beach, Linda fell asleep prone on her lounger, not even pretending to read, for part of the afternoon. The beach began to empty out in the late afternoon. The warmth of the day created the false expectation of a long day for beach dwelling, but the fall days were shortening even twenty degrees latitude closer to the equator than home.

The twins packed up their beach bags and put on clothes to head back to their rental unit. Linda found herself strangely resentful of the need to pull the bathing suit back up thighs sticky with the salt water residue.

That evening, the twins took a taxi to dinner in Grande Case, the home of the island's gourmet cuisine. They strolled up and down the main road trying to decide where to go. The lobsters sat in their tanks at the front of the restaurants waiting to be selected by the customers. Maître d's stood outside the restaurant hoping customers would be enticed by their menus.

"You'll kill me, but I feel a little guilty sitting here stuffing butter-soaked lobster down my craw while my son is homeless yet again," Linda couldn't help saying after they had selected a restaurant and been served their French-Caribbean fusion style dinners.

Laurie finished chewing her piece of lobster while staring balefully at her twin, "Do you need me to go through all the reasons why that's bullshit?"

Linda didn't answer.

"OK, you do. You gave him a free place to live for almost five years up until he forged checks from your bank account. The bank even admitted they could tell that the checks were forged and was going to return your money, but only if you pressed charges which you refused to do. You offered to pay for him to see private doctors and he refused. You've been trying to help get his discharge fixed or whatever you call it so that he gets his free VA medical care. You didn't turn him into the police when he pawned your diamond ring. He's lucky he had a roof over his head for as long as he did, and Tim was a saint to put up for him once you threw him out.

"I love him too. He's my only nephew. But he's mentally ill and if there's any help out there for him, it's not anything you have to give. C'mon, if he had cancer and all the chemo had failed, you wouldn't feel like it was your fault that there wasn't a better chemo out there. As a country, we suck at treating mental illness and on top of it we try to make the patients and their families feel like failures when they can't fix it themselves."

Linda swallowed her current bite of lobster, "You're right, as usual. And you're definitely right that even some physicians don't understand mental illness. I convinced Matt to go see Dr. Samuelsson, our old family doctor. Since I had completely failed at getting Matt to see a psychiatrist, I convinced him that maybe Dr. Samuelsson could help him with some sleeping pills so he wouldn't wake up with the nightmares. Obviously sleeping pills aren't the correct treatment for PTSD, and I knew that Dr. Samuelsson wouldn't fall for that. But I was hoping that if I could get Matt to see any sort of health professional, particularly one he trusted from childhood, they might be able to get him on the right path. But no. I was home when Matt got back from his appointment. He went straight to the fridge to grab a beer.

"I asked, 'How'd it go?'

"'Fuckin' waste of time, that's how it went. Waste of your money too.'

"'What do you mean? What did Dr. Samuelsson say?' I could tell Matt was pissed off, he was snorting through his nostrils. He was so mad I wasn't sure he was going to answer me at first, and then I almost wished he hadn't.

"'Fucker said it was all in my head. I was home from the war, and I just needed to get over it. Said sleeping pills were for people with real problems. I just needed to move on with my life. Like it's that easy to shoot some kid pointing a grenade launcher at you only to have their fuckin' dad blow up a bomb at your position and you wake up in the hospital. Somebody should blow up one of Samuelsson's grandkids right in front of his face, see if he can just get over it.' Matt stood in the door of the fridge and poured the entire beer down his throat without pausing. He crumpled the can up and threw it at the trash can, grabbed another beer, slammed the fridge door and threw himself on the sofa bed.

"I couldn't believe it myself," Linda remarked when she finished relating Matt's reaction to Laurie. "Even someone as old school as Dr. Samuelsson should know that PTSD is not something you can just wish away. I mean, I've pulled up a handful of articles on PTSD and TBI to try and get my head around what's going on with Matt. You only have to do the most cursory searches to find dozens of new articles where researchers are finding actual evidence of the permanent damage blast forces do to the brain. Of course, they find it at autopsy."

"Right, which doesn't do Matt a hell of a lot of good," Laurie agreed. The lobster was all gone and the twins finished the bottle of white wine the sommelier had recommended. "Think there's a bar around here where we might get lucky?"

Linda was taken aback, "Here you convince me that going to a nude beach doesn't make you a sex-starved pervert, and then you tell me you want to pick up some guy at a bar."

Laurie responded coolly, "We are no longer on the nude beach, and I did not try to pick up a single man while we were there. I'm talking about picking up men fully clothed. Seeing them naked before you pick them up takes all the fun out of it. And don't act like we've never gone barhopping in search of men before."

"Yes, but that was when we were in nursing school, not a couple of old cougars."

"Prude," her twin retorted. They paid their check and headed out into the Caribbean night with the fragrance of mango trees wafting about their heads as they walked in search of a bar. Ultimately, they found a bar featuring a flaming volcano punch a block down from the restaurant where they had dined, but the other patrons were all married couples, not single men with lusty intentions.

They took a cab back to their place and headed off to bed. Perhaps because of the nap on the beach, Linda had difficulty falling asleep despite the heavy dinner. She had told herself hundreds of times the very things Laurie detailed about Matt's condition, but somehow hearing her twin enumerate them did help assuage her guilt. She had almost ruined her career and therefore her life as she knew it with her inability to cope with Matt's illness. She had to first save herself, in fact not merely save herself, but also take steps to care for herself first. Then, if she was able to do anything practical to genuinely help her son, she would do so, but not at the expense of herself. She was of no help to Matt if she lost herself. And she realized that she was having a good time on this vacation. She enjoyed their time on the boat at home, but Linda could not remember the last time she had gone on a vacation, certainly not since Matt had come home. As her guilt faded, she drifted off to sleep.

PART FOUR

SOLDIERING ON

CHAPTER FOURTEEN

Before Linda even swung her carry-on bag through the front door, she knew Matt was in the house. First, Goldy came rushing from the sunporch, not a preferred sleeping spot unless Matt was there. Also, the back of the house was pitch dark. Linda enjoyed the light from the porch, but Matt turned the sunporch into a cave when he crashed there. Although Linda was used to seeing Matt reclining when he was there, Linda was alarmed to see him curled in a fetal position on the pulled-out bed, the credits of a movie rolling by on the screen. Ignoring for the moment what he must have done to get in the house without the keys, she sat on the edge of the bed, feeling the iron support of the sofa bed press uncomfortably into the backs of her thighs, "Matt, what's wrong?"

No answer. "Matt, what's wrong?"

Still no answer. "Matt, Matt, what's wrong?"

He was rocking himself in a way alarming to Linda after having seen many psychiatric patients in her ER days. She pushed her face up near his and tried to force him to look at her. His eyes were rolled to the side and he seemed to have no idea she was there. He just kept rocking.

She lifted herself painfully off the bed with its support having dug into her flesh in the brief time she sat there. She took her purse up to her room and used her cell phone to call 911.

"911, what's your emergency?" The toneless operator answered.

"I need medical assistance." She gave the operator her address.

"OK, ma'am. Can you explain the nature of the emergency?"

"It's my son. I think he might have OD'd. He's thirty-two, he's curled up in a fetal position and he just rocks himself. He's not speaking. His eyes are kind of glazed." Now Linda knew damned well that what she was looking at was not the result of an OD, but rather some sort of mental breakdown, which of course didn't preclude his having prescription or illegal drugs on board. However, Linda was enough of a veteran of the health system to use the buzz word OD which would trigger a more urgent response.

"OK, ma'am, we have an ambulance on the way."

To 911's credit, the ambulance arrived fairly quickly. The EMTs were unable to get any response from Matt either. One of them observed, "His respiration is a little shallow."

Linda piped in, "He's got a painkiller problem. No surprise if his respiration is down."

The EMTs looked at her, and then one of them pulled a Narcan injection out of his bag. They carried in a gurney with collapsible legs with wheels on the bottom. The two EMTs lifted him onto the gurney. Even after the injection, Matt never moved voluntarily. In fact, it was almost as if some of his muscles were in a sort of rigor.

Linda knew from experience that it would take time to get Matt checked in at the ER. Before leaving the house therefore she took the time to call Jimmy. His phone went straight to voice mail, but she left him a message that Matt was going to the ER, that it didn't appear life-threatening but he definitely needed help. To be sure he got the message, she also texted him with a "Matt going to ER, not imminently life threatening, but serious." Then she called Laurie.

"Want me to meet you there?" Laurie offered.

"God no, no reason for both of us to be bored out of our minds in a waiting room. I'll let you know what's up," Linda responded.

Linda took a new romance novel off the stack and stuffed it in her purse. She found Matt's backpack on the floor of the sunporch and rummaged through it until she found his driver's license. She rolled a slice of ham and a slice of cheese together and munched on them on the way out.

At the ER, she informed the desk staff that her son was being brought in by ambulance. Despite Linda's dawdling to reach the ER, at least twenty minutes passed before a young woman in scrubs brought her a clipboard with various forms.

"Are you responsible for Matt MacDermott?" the young woman inquired.

"I'm his mother."

"Oh good, well I need you to fill out these forms," The young woman put the clipboard down on the table next to Linda and walked away without another word.

Linda filled out the top form which requested basic demographic information. She filled out as much of the health history as she knew. One of the forms was a financial responsibility form asking for insurance information. She wrote Matt's name, DOB and social on the form, filled in none for insurance and added it back to the pile on the clipboard unsigned.

She took the clipboard to the desk and informed the young woman, "I've filled out as much as I can."

In about fifteen minutes, the young woman was back. The only form on the clipboard was the incompletely filled-out financial responsibility form. "You didn't finish this one, ma'am."

Linda replied, "I told you I don't have some of the information. I've done what I can."

"But you have to sign this," the young woman persisted.

"No, I don't. I am not financially responsible for my son. He is thirty-two years old. He doesn't live with me. All I can tell you is that he does not have insurance."

"But we can't treat him if someone doesn't sign this," the young woman protested.

"Nonsense," Linda responded. "I was an ER nurse for over a decade. And I know under federal law the ER has to at minimum stabilize the patient. I also know I am not financially responsible for my adult son. I will not sign that paper. And this ER will give my son the care the law requires."

The young woman stared at Linda in mild shock, then took her clipboard and returned to the back, probably to talk to a supervisor who had at least attained puberty.

An older woman sitting with her husband made a comment which she probably believed was under her breath, but like many hard-of-hearing people, she obviously had no idea how far her voice carried, "Sure, stick the taxpayers with her son's medical bills while she carries Vera Bradley bags."

Linda sucked in her breath through her nose. At first she was going to leave the comment alone, but then she decided there was no particular reason to do so.

"Actually, ma'am," Linda started in a voice loud enough for the hearing impaired. "My son is a veteran of the U.S. Army, did two tours in Iraq, one tour in Afghanistan, suffered a serious concussion when a bomb went off near him, was hospitalized with his head injury and post-traumatic stress disorder, was given inappropriate medication for his condition, and then got sent home a broken wreck of the young man I raised. And now, the U.S. Army doesn't want to give him his veteran benefits. Well, you know what, if the U.S. government won't pay for his medical care through the VA like they should, then you're damned right, I'm going to let him go on Medicaid and the taxpayers can pay for him that way."

Both members of the older couple were staring at Linda, obviously scared at her reaction. On the far side of the room, two bikers started cheering. "Damned straight Momma. They sent us to Vietnam, let us get fucked up with Agent Orange, and then sent us home without so much as a thank you."

Fifty pages into her new paperback, she was called back to Matt's cubicle. The hospitalist who had examined Matt informed her that his vital signs were stable and there was no evidence of acute distress, "I'm not sure why he's not responding but I don't see anything particularly wrong with him physically. Unless the tox screen unexpectedly comes back positive for something problematic, we'll just observe him here for a few hours. Then once he shows some sign of response, you can take him home."

Linda was infuriated, "I'm not taking him home. All you've done is take his vitals and not made the slightest attempt to figure out why a 32-year-old man is curled in a fetal position. If it's whatever junk he took, fine. But I can also tell you this young man has PTSD, and you aren't just foisting him back off one me without making sure there isn't something more serious going on, whether it's physical or psychiatric."

"Ma'am, I understand most people find it alarming to find their child like this. But I can assure you that my exam…."

Linda cut him off, "Don't give me that nonsense. I was an ER nurse before you were potty-trained. He doesn't have insurance, and your hospital doesn't want to be bothered with getting him set up with Medicaid and getting approvals for psychiatric care. Now let me be clear. I am leaving this hospital. I will leave a cell phone number at the desk. You may call me if he has a significant change in status, good or bad. But I will not be here for you to decide that the second he's conscious, you're going to load him in my car and wash your hands of him. And if you call me and tell me he needs to be picked up, he damned well better be capable of having a coherent conversation. Having been an ER nurse, I am well aware of what the law requires you to do. If I find out that you dump him on the sidewalk the second he blinks at you and you've called that stable, I will make your life miserable."

Linda picked her purse off the chair and walked out of the cubicle. She wrote her cell phone number down on a piece of paper and left it at the desk.

Linda drove home and took Goldy for an epic walk through the neighborhood. She felt a little soreness in her knee after the exercise and unconsciously went looking for the Percocet bottle which had been a regular inhabitant of the bottom of her purse.

When she realized what she was doing, she berated herself. She had gotten herself off those damned things over a year ago and she wasn't going to ever have another bottle of Percocets in her purse as long as she lived. She dug around in the purse until she found her ancient Sucrets tin with its motherlode of common medicines and found an ibuprofen. She made a ham and cheese sandwich and ate at the kitchen table.

She kept picturing how her son had been lying on his side with the thin cheap hospital blanket covering him, reminding her of how he used to sleep in the fetal position when he was sick as a little boy. During one fever in particular where he couldn't stop shivering, Jimmy had brought in one of his extra warm camouflage blankets he took hunting with him. Jimmy had wrapped Matt up in the blanket which was big enough to go around his body at least twice. The Tylenol kicked in not long afterwards, evidenced by the beads of sweat which broke out on Matt's forehead. When he woke the next morning in Jimmy's blanket, he had refused to let go of it even though it was soaked in his sweat. Jimmy had had to buy a new blanket for his hunting trips because Matt insisted on using it every night on his bed and would drag it down to the couch for movie night. Jimmy grumbled a bit but Linda could tell from the smug little upturn at the corner of Jimmy's mouth that he was thrilled that his son had become so attached.

Linda wished that her son's problems were as easy to solve now as giving him a children's Tylenol and wrapping him up in a warm camouflage blanket.

After eating, she walked over to the DVD player in the sunporch and ejected the disc, looking for the jacket, which when she found it had a team of men in desert camouflage. Linda wasn't much of a war movie person so had never heard of it. She placed the disc on the plastic ring in the center and closed the jacket. She took the movie up to the bedroom with her and placed it in her own DVD. She piled the pillows high against the headboard and sat on the bed to watch.

During the endless previews she went downstairs, where she put a mug of water in the microwave and dropped a chamomile and peppermint tea bag in the mug. She headed back upstairs where the previews were finally ending.

Linda wasn't sure what she was expecting from the movie, perhaps a generic war movie where the good guys win, the bad guys are destroyed and all the patriotic people cheer. She was not expecting a story that so powerfully showed the effect of these tours of duty not only on the soldiers but on their families. Although Linda knew the basics of Matt's time in the service and his hospitalizations, she had never been able to visualize what his time overseas had been like. She wondered if the movie was realistic enough that it had somehow pushed Matt back into that time in his life and sent him into his catatonic state. She searched on the internet trying to get a handle on how true to life the movie was.

Having satisfied her curiosity, she put the computer to sleep and turned off the TV and DVD player, turned out the lights, and curled up to sleep. She lay awake for a while, anxious. A vision of swallowing a small white Percocet started to invade her mind, and she cursed herself yet again for having allowed it to become a crutch. She forced herself to lie in bed without recourse to even another ibuprofen. Although it felt like forever, she eventually fell asleep.

In the morning before work she inspected the windows and doors of the sunporch suspecting they were the easiest routes for Matt to have entered the house. The latch on the window at the corner opposite the door had obviously been forced. As she moved the latch back and forth trying to get the window to lock again, she could see that the latch was so loose that a man as strong as Matt would have had no trouble forcing it, and he could force it again anytime she wanted. If she didn't want to invest in all new windows for the sunporch, she supposed that she could always start locking the door between the kitchen and the sunporch; prior to closing in the sunporch that door had been the original exterior door so it was good and sturdy.

Linda ate a cereal bar and headed off to work with no word from the hospital. She checked her cell phone on her lunch break. She had a voice mail from a psychiatrist affiliated with the hospital. All he left on the voice mail was that he had been called on to consult on her son, and he was hoping to speak to her.

Going out the back door of her facility because she did not want any of her co-workers to know about this current issue with Matt until she had more information, Linda called the psychiatrist back. She had expected to play voice mail tag so was pleasantly surprised when he picked up on the second ring, "Dr. Raj"

"Hi, Dr. Raj, this is Linda MacDermott. You had called me regarding my son Matt who was in the ER last night."

"Yes, thank you for calling. The hospitalist on duty filled me in on your comments to him." Carefully phrased code words for the hospitalist told the psychiatrist that Linda had thrown a temper tantrum in the ER. "The hospitalist mentioned that you believe your son has PTSD. Can you tell me more about his background?"

"Yes, but can you tell me what condition my son is in? And I am a nurse by the way, so please don't dumb things down."

"Of course. He's still pretty much as you left him. His vital signs are stable, but he shows no sign of responsiveness, essentially catatonic. His respiration is normal, and the tox screen from the ER sample was negative for opioids or other drugs so something more than drugs is going on. But without more info on his medical history, I don't know what. That's why I was hoping to get a bit more info from you."

"Thank you. My son did a tour in Iraq, a tour in Afghanistan, and then another tour in Iraq. He served as a marksman on his team, and was hospitalized after a bomb went off near him on his final tour. He had a severe concussion and some minor scratches. The first time he was in the field after he recovered from his physical injuries, he had some sort of mental breakdown and was hospitalized with PTSD. He was ultimately discharged from the Army because he couldn't handle gunning people down anymore, and he and I have been fighting the VA over his benefits ever since. They claim when he was discharged from the hospital he was fixed of his PTSD, and he was therefore derelict in his duty. As his mother, I can tell you he's not the same young man he was before his hospitalization. His drinking has been epic since he was discharged. And then over the last couple years or maybe more, he's been self-medicating with opioids. I had two knee surgeries, and I figured out he was stealing my Percocets. Then he started stealing from the house, presumably pawning things to buy more drugs. I had to change the locks on the house to keep him from bankrupting me. I came home yesterday, and he had broken a window latch to climb into the porch.

"He was curled on the sofa bed in a fetal position much like you're describing. Last night when I got home from the ER, I found a war movie in the DVD player. I watched it and some of the scenes seemed pretty similar to what he described doing. Maybe watching it triggered something, but I'm not expert on PTSD," Linda finished.

The psychiatrist was silent for a few seconds, "Well, your background info is very helpful. I will be honest and tell you that I'm no PTSD expert, if there is such a thing. Catatonia is a relatively rare occurrence with PTSD, therefore I can't yet rule out the possibility that there's another problem. But I am going to try to get your son admitted where they can try to figure out what's going on with him. As I'm sure you know, inpatient beds are hard to come by for psych issues especially for Medicaid patients; it may take me a while. We'll call you back when we have some options."

Linda thanked him, hung up and went back inside. She wolfed down her lunch and went back to work.

A nurse called Linda the following evening. She and the psychiatrist had finally located an inpatient bed for Matt. The only hitch was that the facility was an hour and a half away, and for some bizarre bureaucratic reason Medicaid would not pay for the transport. "Are you willing to help with this?"

"You mean, drive him there?" Linda asked.

"No, no, no, we wouldn't recommend that," the nurse quickly responded.

"Well, why not? and what's the alternative?" Linda continued.

"We wouldn't recommend it because your son is still very unstable and we don't know how he would react with you. The alternative is for you to pay out-of-pocket for the transport," the nurse answered.

"Unstable how? Is he still catatonic?"

"He's regained consciousness. But ma'am, you have to understand that we haven't fully explored with your son how much he wants revealed to family members. I heard that you're a nurse, so I'm sure you realize that especially when dealing with psychiatric issues we have to be careful about what we say to whom. The transport van will be about $800."

Linda cogitated silently for a minute.

"Ma'am, are you still there?"

"Yes, I'm here," Linda acknowledged. As long as Matt had been unresponsive, they could assume his consent to talk to his mother. Once Matt had regained consciousness they would have to get his permission to talk to her. Linda decided that as long as Matt was getting help, the exact particulars were none of her business. And if the alternative to paying $800 was that they would release Matt back onto the street, then $800 was a bargain.

"I'll pay for the transport. Just tell me what I need to do," Linda replied.

"Oh, excellent. I haven't worked with your son for long, but getting him into treatment is the best option. You'll need to give the transport company a credit card number, and we'll arrange the details."

"Can you at least give me the name, address and phone number of the facility you're sending my son to?" Linda questioned.

"Well, yes, get a pen and paper and I'll give you all the information."

Linda took down all the details. She called the transport company and gave them a credit card number to pay for Matt's transfer.

She called Jimmy next. During the whole two days since she had sent Matt to the ER she had not heard from him, but fortunately he picked up quickly this time, "Hey, Linda, sorry I was out hunting in the back country and we had no cell service. I got home less than an hour ago and I was just going through all the voice mails and texts. What the hell's up with Matt?"

Linda described finding Matt unresponsive on the sofa bed. Jimmy uttered the occasional "Holy Shit" while she was telling him the story but other than that was silent. She finished up by telling Jimmy that the psychiatrist at the hospital had gotten him a bed in an inpatient facility, but now that Matt was conscious they had clammed up about telling her anything about Matt's condition. She gave Jimmy the contact details for the facility and suggested,

"Maybe if they let him have visitors, you can figure out a way to go see him."

"Yeah, yeah, I didn't realize how bad things were getting for him. Maybe when they're ready to release him he can spend some time out here. A change of scenery can be good for people. The hunting is great out here. I can take him camping."

Even though Linda had grown up with an avid hunter for a father and had been taught gun safety at an early age, Linda had serious reservations about Jimmy's idea to put a gun in the hands of their mentally unbalanced son. She knew that saying this to Jimmy was pointless, worse than pointless as Jimmy would accuse her of having joined the liberal assholes who didn't understand the difference between a hunter and a street thug. As she also knew that hunting was how Jimmy and Matt related to each other, instead of voicing her concerns, she said, "I think it's a great idea if his health care folks do, if for no other reason than that he's obviously figured out how to get hold of pills around here. At least if he went out to Colorado he wouldn't have all the connections."

Jimmy didn't respond. Linda wasn't sure that Jimmy had accepted Matt's drug problem. Linda had had a hard time accepting that her son was stealing from her in order to get pills, and she was here experiencing it. Jimmy had only Linda's word that Matt was so desperate for the pills that he would steal for them. Not that the pills were Matt's only problem either, but Jimmy, who wouldn't even take an aspirin if he hurt himself on the job, would have a hard time relating. He thanked her for the contact info and the update and promised to do whatever Matt and the treatment center would allow.

* * * * *

Linda hesitated before driving to the VFW for the volunteer attorney clinic. She hated to waste hours of her time if they refused to see her without Matt. She decided she could try for the sympathy card: while my poor veteran son is in the hospital with his PTSD, I came to try to get him help. She hoped by showing up first thing when the clinic opened, she might have a better chance of getting in before they got busy. At least a dozen veterans were already sitting in the waiting area when she got there fifteen minutes before the clinic opened though. She added her name to the sign-in sheet and sat down at a small round table at which only one other veteran was already seated.

Linda pulled her latest mystery novel out of her purse. The veteran at her table had two huge, black three-ring binders spread out on the table. He was an older black man, significantly overweight, with bloodshot eyes. When he first started speaking, Linda thought he was talking to himself. Only when he repeated himself did she realize he was asking her a question, "Would you look at my table of contents, ma'am?"

"I'm sorry, look at your what?" Linda tried not to appear too baffled by this request out of left field..

"My table of contents, ma'am. You see I've got all these service records and treatment records here. I got kicked out of the service in 1986 when they found out I had AIDS. I've been trying to get my benefits for years." While he was talking, he was pushing four sheets of paper across the table at her. When Linda continued to just look at the man, he said, "No, please ma'am, look at these. I'll take any advice I can get."

Linda looked down. On the table in front of her were four separate tables of contents. All were in the same font. All of them looked substantially the same. "Now take your time please ma'am, but I'd sure appreciate any advice you might give. You see, I'm sure that if I have the material organized right, that I'll finally get my benefits. You see, I figure this much paper," and he pointed to the two large binders in front of him, "is enough to confuse anyone, so I've got to get it organized."

Linda nodded, "I'm afraid I don't have any expertise in this myself. I wouldn't even know where to start."

Evidently believing this was an invitation to explain further, he pulled back the tables of contents, opened one of the binders, turned it to face her and pushed it across the table. A rainbow of colored tabs stuck out from the edges of the papers with labels neatly printed in childish capital letters. "You see, I think I should start with my service record, because I had a good clean record in the service. But then you see, when my sergeant found out I had AIDS, he told everyone in my unit. And back then, everybody thought the only way you got AIDS was taking it up the you-know-what, and I couldn't get a moment's peace. And that's when my service went downhill, and not to mention what some of those men did to me." While he was going on shamelessly about exactly what some of the servicemen did to him, he was flipping pages of the binder and pointing at papers at the same time.

After all her time as a nurse, Linda recognized mental illness when she saw it even if she couldn't give it an exact diagnosis, and she knew that only a person with some form of mental illness would have spent dozens of hours compulsively organizing this binder. "So, how long have you been trying to get benefits, sir?" Linda wasn't sure what else to say.

"Oh, ever since I got out really. I used to have this attorney, and my case went all the way up to the big appeals court in Washington, DC, but that didn't work. That attorney, he told me there was nothing more he could do for me, but you see, I didn't have the binders organized like I do now. That's why I think it's time to try again. See here, I've got the letter from the last court." The man flipped to a bright yellow tab where he'd even bracketed the word "APPEAL" with six-pointed stars. "You see, the court wrote that their decision didn't have anything to do with my being bad or anything. That's why I think it's got to be because they couldn't get their head around the paperwork."

With the man thumping enthusiastically on the piece of paper in the binder, Linda had no choice but to politely bend her head to skim the document. She saw the phrase the man had highlighted where the court had written that they did not believe Mr. Tucker's continued appeals over the course of more than a decade were the result of any bad faith on his part, but a product of his mental illness. Nevertheless, the court found no evidence that any of Mr. Tucker's medical conditions met the criteria for service connection and his appeal for benefits was therefore denied.

Linda figured that if multiple attorneys and courts over the course of a decade had not convinced the poor man that his case was hopeless, nothing she could contribute would change his mind. Rather she simply said, "Well, I think you've done a marvelous job organizing the binder, but you obviously have much more experience with what the courts want to see than I do. I hope that the volunteers here can give you good advice about which table of contents to use."

Linda picked her book back up before the man could say anything else and buried her face in it. The man was called back to meet with one of the volunteers about five minutes later; Linda wondered if the man had camped out here the night before to be at the top of the waiting list. Linda herself had to read a good hundred pages of her book before her name was called.

Although the volunteer attorney did frown at her at first when she stated she was there on behalf of her son, her sympathy ploy worked because he agreed to look at the discharge upgrade application once she had explained that her son was hospitalized for his PTSD a few days ago.

Linda had been pleased at herself for having almost completely filled out the form. She hadn't been as elaborate as her fellow tablemate in tabbing her documents, but she had highlighted the physician's note indicating that all his medications were discontinued on discharge. She had also printed out the 2012 U.S.

Army document indicating that Xanax was an inappropriate treatment for PTSD.

The attorney looked up at her after skimming through her documents and asked, "Do you have the character references you're planning to submit?"

Linda was baffled, "What character references?"

"I'm not sure a discharge upgrade has any chance of success without character references."

"I don't understand. My son received medically inappropriate treatment. His behavior was affected by the withdrawal symptoms. I don't see why it's any more complicated than that. What do character references have to do with his upgrade?"

The attorney sighed, "Mrs. MacDermott, I should probably start at the beginning. Are you aware that only a vanishingly small number of the discharge upgrade applications which are submitted are successful?"

Linda responded, "No, but when there's such an obvious medical mistake, I still don't see…"

The attorney cut her off, gently touching her hand as he did so, "The mistake many veterans make is assuming the discharge upgrade process is easy, and that it will be obvious to the DRB that they're eligible. They think all they have to do is scribble a few words on the DD 293 and twelve months later they'll hear that they've been upgraded to honorable."

"What's a DRB?" Linda interjected.

"Sorry, a Discharge Review Board. As I was saying, these DRBs are required to start with the presumption that everyone involved in your son's discharge acted correctly. In order for your son to get an upgrade, your son has to prove that they were wrong. This isn't like a criminal court, there's no presumption of innocence for your son.

"It's definitely true that a lot of medical mistakes were made with diagnosing military personnel as having a personality disorder when in fact what they have is PTSD, but you're not arguing that your son was misdiagnosed."

"No, he wasn't misdiagnosed, but he was mistreated."

"Well, that would be up to medical experts to determine."

"Sir, with all due respect for your legal expertise, I've been a nurse for thirty years, and as soon as I read his service medical records, I knew my son had been mistreated," Linda used her sharpest get-back-in-line nurse manager tone.

The attorney did blink at her, "OK, I'm not meaning to question your medical expertise. Again, I'm here to help you put the best case together. And I'm sure you are qualified to judge that your son was mistreated, but we have to put on our skeptical hats here. The DRB must presume the Army did everything right. All you've written in this application is that they should look at this piece of paper indicating Xanax isn't the right treatment. If this is your best argument for your son to get his discharge upgrade, I would have your son's medical records reviewed by a psychiatrist who specializes in PTSD and have him or her examine your son. Also, have him or her offer an expert medical opinion as to how withdrawal from Xanax would have caused your son's behavior to change. Even if you are an expert, the Army isn't likely to take a family member's word that the Army got it wrong."

Linda started to cool down, "I see what you're saying. This DRB thing is going to see me as biased, and I can't assume they'll get it. Well, the good news I guess is that Matt is in a hospital being treated by people who are supposed to be experienced with PTSD. Maybe one of the psychiatrists can provide a statement."

The attorney nodded, "Great idea. The worst mistake you can make here is throwing an application together not understanding what the DRB is looking for. You won't want to hear this, but character references are really really important. People who are successful at getting upgrades tend to be the ones living like model citizens after they get out of the service. They've gotten married, they coach their kid's little league team, they work sixty hours a week. The priest, the president of the PTA and their boss all write letters about how fabulous John is, and gee, if only he didn't have this pesky discharge problem, he'd surely have been promoted to a big management position by now."

Linda nodded, "I get that that's what the Army would be looking for, but for a kid with PTSD, it's a bit of a catch 22 isn't it. I mean, my son received the wrong treatment. He gets discharged for behavior resulting from his withdrawal symptoms. He can't get VA benefits because of his discharge, so he can't get the proper treatment for his PTSD, so he can't act like a model citizen because he's not getting medical help he needs, but yet, to fix this discharge that's preventing him from getting treatment by the VA, he has to be the model citizen he can't be without treatment."

The attorney chuckled ruefully, "I get it, I hear you. If this were my kid, I'd be flaming mad. But again, I'm here to help you see how to work the system. Your son has fifteen years from his discharge to get an upgrade. If he's only now getting the treatment he needs, he might be better off waiting until he has a solid year plus of good conduct under his belt before putting the application in. It's true that the DRB has to include a mental health professional if the veteran has PTSD, and they are supposed to be liberal in finding a connection between the veteran's service and the PTSD. Nevertheless, the presumption is that the Army acted correctly, and DRBs like to see good conduct after discharge."

"Problem is," Linda noted, "he's getting treatment on Medicaid but with all the noise about Trump wanting to repeal Obamacare, I don't know how long Matt will be eligible for Medicaid. Without proper treatment Matt's conduct is not going to get any better than he is right now."

The attorney sighed, "I understand your concern. My job though is to give you the best shot I can. Has your son submitted any paperwork for a Character of Service Determination yet?"

Linda replied, "I vaguely remember the hotline attorney talking about something like that, but the discharge upgrade sounded like a better deal, and since the Army obviously made a mistake...." Linda trailed off, realizing that the attorney had just counseled her on not assuming that anything was obvious to the Army. "OK, would you please remind me what this character of service thing is?"

"The VA can still give your son certain benefits following a character of service determination or CSD even if his discharge doesn't get upgraded."

"I'm confused."

"You should be. And to be even more confusing, there's a difference between character of service and characterization of service. We're talking about the first one here. Basically, if a veteran had a good record throughout his or her service, but made one mistake which got them discharged, the VA can determine that that one mistake shouldn't preclude the veteran from benefits."

"What kind of a mistake?"

The attorney considered for a few seconds, "Well, for instance, if a veteran had a great service record for seven or eight years, but then finds out while he's in Germany that his mom had a heart attack and died completely unexpectedly. The guy loses it, goes out on a five-day bender not reporting for duty and receives an other than honorable discharge for being AWOL. The guy applies for VA benefits, and the VA asks for info to do a CSD. In this case, the vet would want to write a letter talking about how, if true, mom was his only living relative who raised him on her own while working three jobs, and when he found out his mom was gone without having had a chance to say good-bye, he lost it. There are some catch phrases to use in such a letter.

"The VA is not supposed to grant benefits if the misconduct was willful or persistent. The VA should grant benefits if it finds that the veteran's service was otherwise honest, faithful, and meritorious. So, you want to feed those words right back at the VA. I made one mistake, my misconduct was not willful or persistent. You get the picture...."

Linda nodded.

"Also," the attorney continued, "character reference letters can be helpful. And these are easier to get than for a discharge upgrade because if you're talking about one bad episode or misconduct which only started after someone is diagnosed with PTSD, the letters need to talk about how the bad episode or the PTSD changed the behavior. 'My buddy was a perfect soldier. He wrote to his mom every night unless we were out on ops. He called her whenever we were allowed to call. I was there when the sarge gave him the news about his mom, and he completely lost it, he couldn't stop crying. He was crazy, swore he could never forget he didn't get to tell her good-bye.'"

"I get it. This CSD thing sounds a little easier to prove than the discharge upgrade. And if I can make sure he can continue to get treatment, he'll be much better off. I hadn't ever looked for any sort of CSD request in his papers before, but I'll go home and see what's there. Then I guess I'll work on that too."

"Sounds like a plan. Once you've had a chance to go through the papers, if you have any questions, call the hotline again. Or if you happen to catch one of these clinics, you could come in."

Linda gathered her papers and got up to leave. "And Mrs. MacDermott, I hope you realize how incredibly lucky your son is to have you." Linda looked back at him, remembering that the VA social worker had made a similar comment. "I'll be here all day with these vets, and I'll be amazed if even one of them has a relative or friend available to help them. These clinics are all most of these guys have in the way of help. They know they need help, but they don't have the first idea how to make a case for themselves. From what you've told me, it sounds like you can make some sort of case for your son."

Linda reached over and shook his hand, "Well, thank you for caring enough to try to help both me and all these folks here."

Linda piled Matt's papers on her desk when she got home, with Goldy bursting with impatience at having to wait until Linda put her things away to get her walk. While she was watching Goldy hopelessly chase ducks, Linda decided she had mixed feelings about the day. On the one hand, the attorney had talked to her even without Matt present and had given her genuinely helpful tips for assembling Matt's paperwork. On the other hand, Linda found it immensely frustrating that getting the Army or the VA to see that her son deserved VA assistance was going to be a long process with a lot of work on her part.

Linda had intended to dive right into the papers when she got back in the house, but her head hurt. She found the vision of a Percocet creeping into the back of her head almost as if an alien were planting the idea. When she realized what she was thinking, she yelled out loud, "No, dammit, no." Goldy lifted her head off the dog bed. In a quieter voice, but still out loud, she chanted to herself, "I am not going to take a Percocet for a headache. I will not go back down that road." Instead, she grabbed a beer, which she would have been lucky to find had Matt been around, made a turkey sandwich, and found a good CSI re-run to watch on the sunporch. She fell asleep on the sofa bed with Goldy curled on the rug on the floor next to her.

* * * * *

Matt did not accept or wasn't allowed any visitors for the first two weeks he was inpatient, Linda wasn't really sure which. Linda was shocked therefore when she got a call from the facility indicating that Matt wanted her to come for visiting hours on Sunday. Linda quickly agreed. Then she made phone calls until she found a nurse willing to exchange shifts with her.

The long drive to the only psychiatric facility in Maryland with an open bed willing to take Medicaid patients did nothing to quell the butterflies in her stomach. She found herself thinking that if only she had a Percocet, she would be calmer. Fortunately she had none with her and when she realized where her anxiety was leading her, she mentally berated herself, "This is how you got yourself into your Percocet mess in the first place. Taking a pill rather than dealing with the problem. Go see your kid and do what you can."

The facility was a plain brick building in between a rather run-down strip mall and a small industrial park. Linda checked in at the desk and was pointed in the direction of Matt's room. Matt was lying in bed watching TV with a remote in his hand.

"Hey, Matt," Linda started, bending down to kiss him on the forehead. He didn't shirk away, which Linda took as a positive sign.

"I figured the food in here had to suck so I snuck in a cold cut sub," Linda extracted a sandwich wrapped in wax paper from her dump bag and handed it to him. "I'll block the view from the hallway while you eat."

Matt grinned at her. Linda was inwardly surprised to note how much joy one little grin from her kid could elicit.

"Has your father been here yet?"

Matt nodded. Still Mr. Loquacious, Linda thought.

Linda had decided before she came up that she was not going to question him about how he was or how the treatment of whatever sort was going. She was simply going to hang out with Matt and take whatever he volunteered.

Matt flicked through the channels before speaking again, "Dad says I can go out to Colorado and stay with him for a while."

"Do you want to?" Linda asked.

"Maybe," Matt answered. "I've never been there. Dad was raving about the unbelievable hunting."

"I've never been there either. I hear it's beautiful, but I can't add anything else."

They sat silently for a little longer. Matt continued to flip through the channels. Instinctively Linda reached over and tousled his dirty blond hair. Surprisingly, Matt allowed this without complaint, as he had so seldom accepted any of Linda's attempts at affection over the last few months. She realized he was drifting off to sleep when the remote started to slide to the floor, and she grabbed it a second before it fell off the bed. She saw the salt of dried-up tears at the corner of one eye and held her own back through force of will.

The PA system announced that visiting hours were ending in 15 minutes. With the noise from the speakers Matt came back out of his drowse.

"Do you need anything, Matt? I'm not sure if I'm allowed to send anything by mail, but I can try."

Matt joked, "You could see if they'll let you ship a bunch of those sandwiches in. The food here is crap, almost worse than an MRE."

"Well, if you think of anything, let me know. I imagine the Nazis will be coming to throw me out soon," Linda stood up. She kissed him on the forehead one more time and started to leave.

"Hey Mom," Matt said and Linda turned around.

"Throw that damned movie out," Matt continued.

"Huh?"

"The one in the machine in my room. Don't ever wanna see that thing again, don't need any reminders of what it was like."

"OK, will do. Luv ya."

Linda knew absolutely nothing about how her son was doing, had learned nothing about how long he would be there, but still she was happy. She had sat with Matt for almost two hours without any confrontation whatsoever. For now, that was enough. The attorney had urged her to get support letters for Matt's discharge upgrade application and his character of service determination from his psychiatrist and other medical professionals on his team, but she knew if she brought up the discharge upgrade with Matt on her first visit to see him she would be doing more harm than good.

She dug around under the seat of the car before getting in and found an audiobook of a Danielle Steele on CD. Anything was better than being stuck worrying about Matt for the whole car ride home.

After Linda got home and took Goldy out for her walk, she scooped out a bowl of leftover spaghetti and meatballs from the Italian takeout and microwaved it. She poured a glass of milk, put the food, drink, a napkin, cutlery and the movie on a cheap plastic tray Matt had stolen from a fast food joint as a teenager. Then she went up to her bedroom wanting only to veg. She hit the DVD button on the remote by mistake, and the menu for a movie appeared. She simultaneously remembered that she had watched the movie the night she found Matt catatonic and that she had promised Matt this afternoon that she would destroy the DVD.

Linda watched part of the movie while she at her spaghetti, reflecting on Matt's statement that he didn't need reminders of what his experience had been like. After she finished eating and had as much war movie as she could take, she ejected the disc and took it down to the trash. After she put the dishes in the dishwasher, Linda decided to call Jimmy. He picked up on the second ring, "Hey Linda."

"Hey Jimmy. I went up to see Matt today and thought I should let you know."

"How's he doing?"

"Better than the last time I saw him, but I decided before I went that I wasn't going to ask him anything. I figured the two of us had argued too much lately, and I was going to try to have a positive time with him."

Jimmy didn't respond.

"He seemed interested in coming out to Colorado with you, or at least as interested as he's been in anything these days."

"Good. I was there last week and we talked about it. I'm sure good Colorado fresh air and getting a trophy buck or two will snap him back out of it."

Linda bit her tongue. Jimmy was naïve if he believed that a little bit of hunting would fix everything, but she decided she would stick with pleasant and non-confrontational for the whole day. "Did he say anything to you about how long he would be there?" Linda queried.

"He didn't know. He's supposed to call when they tell him so I can make a flight for him."

"Will you let me know if you get a date from him? I don't want to mother hen, but I'd like to be sure he's out there safely."

Jimmy said, "Sure. I'll call you once we've got dates set."

They hung up.

Two weeks later Jimmy called to tell her that Matt was all set with a flight two days later, "But, hey, Lin, the flight to Colorado turned out to be way more than I expected, what with it being one way, and being such short notice. Any chance you can split it with me?"

Linda furrowed her eyebrows in annoyance. Matt had been robbing her blind for months. She'd lost way more than the cost of a flight to Colorado with just the wedding ring he hocked, not to mention the guns, the door locks, the forged checks and God knew what else. But rather than express her annoyance, she asked, "How much?"

"Oh, 500 bucks would do it. It was a little over a thousand, but that's close enough."

"Sure, OK if I mail you a check?" Linda figured to herself that $500 was a hell of a lot cheaper than re-doing all the locks and adding security to the sunporch windows.

"Yeah, great, thanks. Oh, and hey Lin, I got him a parrot," Jimmy announced proudly.

"A what?" Linda wasn't sure she had heard correctly.

"A parrot. Anyhow, at the clinic when I went out to visit him, I was talking to one of the nurses there. She said people with PTSD do great with parrots. There's even a place out in L.A. where vets with PTSD take care of hundreds of parrots. Apparently it helps them. Anyway, there's a pet store downtown where I did some shelving work a few years back. The guy there gets all kinds of parrots once people realize the birds live 80, 90 years, they outlive their owners, and people bring the birds to him. I figure, parrots help vets, I'll get him a parrot."

Linda shook her head, grateful Jimmy couldn't see her reaction through the phone. She knew she'd search the internet for parrots and vets with PTSD when she got off the phone, and she'd probably find some article demonstrating how taking care of a bird lowers the incidence of hospitalization rates for vets with PTSD. But Jesus, for Jimmy to believe that just because he was going to take Matt hunting and get him a talking bird, Matt would wake up the next day and wouldn't have PTSD anymore and wouldn't have a pill problem anymore. For Chrissake. She knew Jimmy didn't have medical training but she didn't think he could be that naïve.

But again, she didn't express herself. She just said, "Well, that's great Jimmy. Anything that helps is good."

She called Laurie later that night to bitch about Jimmy asking for $500, "Can you believe the SOB? Matt's ripped me off for thousands of bucks with his little problem, but the boy's father needs me to share the flight cost."

Linda could practically see Laurie scowling through the phone, "You aren't giving it to him, are you?"

"Oh yes I am. I don't want Jimmy to have any excuse not to have Matt come out there. I've finally been able to sleep decently now that Matt's been in the clinic, and I don't have to worry that an ER is going to call me with the news that they couldn't save him. My sanity's worth the $500 to send Matt out to Colorado and let Jimmy take the stress for a while. And anyway, it's all going to be great for Matt out there, Laur. Jimmy bought him a parrot to calm him down."

"A what?" The exact same reaction as Linda had had.

Linda related her conversation with Jimmy. Before she had called Laurie, she had in fact looked up parrots and PTSD, and yes, indeed, she found a newspaper article about PTSD vets working with parrots. But the article didn't suggest that a damned parrot was going to cure them.

"I mean, I know Jimmy isn't a nurse, but he thinks all Matt's problems are going to poof into thin air if they go out and shoot a big buck with a huge rack. Then once they get home from the butcher and the taxidermist, Matt's going to head over to the corner and coo 'Polly want a cracker' over and over again until he's not a pillhead anymore." Linda was working herself up into a snit.

Laurie played the straight man, "Does it have to be a macaw? What about a cockatoo? Was there any evidence base for which type of parrot has the best effect on mental illness?"

Linda was going to reply, "Of course not," when she realized that her sister was teasing her. She decided to play along, "Nope, but the color of the tail feathers is absolutely key."

Laurie came back with, "Hope the parrot doesn't have too much red. You know how you can't have red in a hospital because it makes patients angry. Red tail feathers might make someone with PTSD angry."

The sisters reached new heights of hysteria making joke after joke about Matt's new parrot until Linda's side hurt from laughing so hard.

"Thanks for getting me off the pissed off roller coaster. I needed a laugh."

CHAPTER FIFTEEN

CHRISTMAS AND NEW YEAR'S EVE 2016

Linda called Matt's cell phone on Christmas Day. The phone went straight to voice mail several times. By midafternoon, unable to restrain her worry, she called Jimmy.

"Merry Christmas, Jimmy," she started.

"And to you," he replied.

"I've been trying to call Matt all day to wish him a Merry Christmas but he's not answering his cell. Is everything OK?"

Jimmy hesitated long enough for Linda to be suspicious of his answer, "Yeh, he's fine. He and I probably had a few too many brews last night. He's been on the couch watching ESPN all day. I'll get him."

Linda waited until Matt came on the phone, and then they exchanged brief holiday greetings. Matt confirmed that he had received Linda's check. Linda didn't like the idea of giving her son a check as a Christmas present, but he had told her that extra cash would help more than anything else.

Linda spent the evening at Laurie's watching *Christmas Vacation* over and over again eating ham and boxed potatoes au gratin on trays in front of the TV.

She told Laurie that she was a little worried about how Matt had sounded and how Jimmy had hesitated.

"Oh, come on. Neither one of them will put ten words together unless you force them. You probably interrupted their watching a WWF marathon or a NASCAR race."

Linda allowed herself to believe this.

Then, on the morning of New Year's Eve, Jimmy called. From the first hello, she could hear a slightly panicky note in his voice. Even though they'd been apart for years, she guessed if you'd known someone since middle school, you knew them pretty well.

"Matt's been arrested," Jimmy got to the point.

"What? What happened?"

"He called me with his one phone call and asked me to get him a lawyer, said there was a bogus assault charge, and he had a bail hearing when the court re-opened after the holiday."

"What? That makes no sense."

"I didn't think so either. But I called one of my buddies who has a brother on the local force. His brother didn't want to give him a whole bunch of detail, but apparently Matt broke into a veterinary clinic."

"A what? What would he do that for?" Linda interrupted, and before she could finish her sentence, she knew why he'd broken into a vet clinic. Opioids.

Jimmy continued as if Linda hadn't even spoken, "There was a tech staying in the clinic overnight because they had a sick dog who was recovering from surgery. I guess when that happens a tech or one of the vets has to stay. Anyway, Matt apparently knocked the kid's lights out, but he didn't realize the kid had tripped the alarm before he hit him. The police got there before Matt could leave and threw Matt in the clink."

"Jimmy, you know Matt was probably looking for pills, don't you?"

Jimmy didn't respond.

"Jimmy, has Matt been clean since he's been with you?"

She could hear Jimmy breathing heavily before he answered, "Things really did go well at first, Linda, just like I told you. We went out hunting a few times. I brought him to some of my jobs with me and he did pretty decent drywall work. Then he stays out one night and when he shows up at the job site three hours late tells me he got lucky at a bar. I thought he meant a girl."

Linda knew that Jimmy would have assumed a girl, but Linda suspected that lately Matt's definition of getting lucky meant he had scored some pills.

"I make him work that day for no pay. And I think again we're OK, and what young guy hasn't been late to work after getting some."

Linda hated it when Jimmy forgot he was talking to his ex-wife, not one of his hunting buddies.

"Then a week or so before Christmas, Matt's gone for days. I almost called you then, but Matt keeps telling me how you worried over him like a mother hen, treated him like a four-year-old boy, so I tried to play it cool. He feeds me the same crap about getting lucky with this girl, but he stinks to high heaven, hasn't shaved and his clothes are so disgusting that no girl could have been excited about spending the last three days with his rank ass. He had been sleeping all day when you called on Christmas."

"So then he just up and tries to break into a vet's office after that?" Even Linda is incredulous over this escalation. She wasn't surprised to hear that Matt was trying to get his hands on drugs, and she knew that people would resort to fairly desperate means to do so, but she was surprised that Matt couldn't find someone somewhere in driving radius of Jimmy's house from whom he could have bought them.

Jimmy kept going with his recounting, "So New Year's Eve, we have a little whiskey, we're watching the games, everything was cool, but then Matt starts going crazy. Honestly, Lin, he was bat shit crazy. I sat there listening to this alien who's taken over my son. He went off about how now that Trump has won the election, Trump's going to get rid of Obamacare and he's not gonna be able to get Medicaid anymore, and the medicine they gave him at the clinic's run out. He starts raving about how he might as well just bash his head against a wall, the election has screwed him so badly, and he wishes someone would knock Trump off because then his life wouldn't be so screwed up. Real paranoid crap, Lin, I swear, I didn't know what to say."

Linda didn't either.

Jimmy called again two days later, more panicky than before, "The public defender got Matt out on bail. Well, the public defender went to his bail hearing. I put up the bail money. I bring him home. He passes out on the couch. I go to work this morning thinking he'll sleep all damned day. And I get home and goddammit he's gone again. And he may be our son, but I'm gonna beat his ass when I see him. My table saw is gone and there may be other stuff too. I haven't gone through all the toolboxes. I can't take this. Our son has turned into a crazy drug happy thief. He's not staying here. I can't afford to have my tools sold out from under me. I've gotta work for a living. If he comes back, I'm gonna tell him I got him a one-way ticket back to Maryland."

Linda had been listening to the diatribe in silence. Part of her felt like coming back with an "I told you so." Hadn't she warned Jimmy that Matt was robbing her blind? Hadn't she informed Jimmy that their son was a drug addict? But good old Jimmy, he figures all he has to do is get Matt out to Colorado and take him hunting and buy him a parrot. Problem solved. Wisely, Linda said none of this. What she did say, however, was, "Well, Jimmy, didn't you put up his bail for him? He probably isn't allowed to leave the state. And you vouched for him putting up the bail. I'm no expert but if the court finds out you paid for an airplane ticket after you got him out on bail, you could be in trouble too."

"Fuck," Jimmy exclaimed. "Fuck, fuck, fuck. What am I supposed to do? Go to every pawn shop in town looking to see if he dropped my tools off there. And how can I let him live here if he's gonna rip me off?"

"I don't know Jimmy, I really don't. I was at my wits end, which is why I threw him out. I was truly hoping that spending time with you would help." This was a true statement. Linda had hoped that being with Jimmy would help Matt. The nurse in her had realized that it wouldn't but knowledge and hope are two different things.

"Jimmy, was Matt taking any medicines when he came out to you?"

"Huh?"

"When they released Matt from the clinic, did they release him with any pills?" Linda repeated her question.

"He had some pill bottles, yeah, but what the hell does that have to do with anything? I gotta get my tools back. Now you tell me by vouching for him I'm in trouble if he jumps states."

"Jimmy, you said Matt was OK at first when you got there. He may have been OK because he was still taking whatever medicines they gave him at the clinic. If he ran out of those medicines, or didn't have any refills left, or stopped taking them, that may be why he started having problems. Maybe you could look around wherever he was keeping his stuff, see if there's any empty or full pill bottles. See if he has any refills left on any medicine."

"I already told you he was going off about how he wasn't going to be able to get his medicines with Trump as president. But, how's him having pills gonna help me get my tools back?" Part of Linda understood how much it hurt to be robbed by your own son, but Linda was going to scream if he mentioned the tools one more time. Their son was so screwed up that he would break into a vet's office and beat up a kid trying to get pills, and all Jimmy could worry about was a few hundred or even a few thousand dollars' worth of tools.

"It's not, but if he's not taking medicine he needs, he's going to be unstable. If he has refills left, get him his refills and try to get him to start taking the medicine again. If you need me to send money for the medicines, call me." Linda looked at her watch, "Hey Jimmy, I'm sorry but I've got night shift tonight. I gotta get ready for work and get out the door." This was an outright lie, but she couldn't take any more. She'd been dealing with Matt's problems ever since his girlfriend kicked him out over five years ago. Jimmy was having a meltdown after less than two months. It wasn't Linda's job to help Jimmy cope with his son, and she thought that offering to send Jimmy money for Matt's prescriptions was more than generous considering that she'd been completely supporting their son since he got fired from his last part-time job.

When Linda went up to bed, she saw the pile of paperwork she had been assembling for Matt's discharge upgrade application. "Might as well throw all that in the trash," she grumbled to herself. The attorney at the VFW had emphasized how much the discharge review boards wanted to see evidence of good conduct and a life well lived. He'd even recommended that since a veteran had fifteen years to request an upgrade, her son might even be better off waiting to submit the application until he had something positive to include. Somehow Linda doubted that attempting to rob a vet's office for the pain pills and knocking the vet tech's lights out in the process was the sort of conduct the Army had in mind as evidence of a life well lived.

Then she saw her sticky notes about character of service determinations and remembered that the attorney had indicated that based on Matt's PTSD and its probable effect on his behavior that he at least might be able to start getting his health benefits from the VA even if he wasn't eligible for a discharge upgrade. Jimmy didn't seem to be on top of Matt's medications the way she would have been, but Linda was convinced that Matt must have run out of the psych meds with which he was discharged and returned to his old ways. In fact, if he was having withdrawal symptoms from whatever medicines he was on, he might even be more unstable than previously. If Linda could get him VA health benefits and maybe a monthly stipend, she could help get him a stable supply of meds and he'd do better.

Linda sighed and started sifting through the piles of paper looking for any requests from the VA for information to use in their CSD. By this point, she had a couple reams worth of paper but she couldn't find Matt's original application for benefits or any original denial. She knew there had to be an earlier denial because on the two she had in her pile, the letters blandly stated that Matt's claims for benefits remained denied because his discharge was other than honorable and notably that they still had not received the requested paperwork to consider his character of service determination. Linda knew that she had seen at least one of these later denials, but not appreciating what a character of service determination was, the words had obviously slid right past her.

She went down to the sunporch and surveyed the room, wondering if there was any place he might have stashed his paperwork. She took the broom and moved it around under the sofa bed. A few dirty socks and a crusty pair of jeans emerged, but no paperwork. She opened the doors of the entertainment center but found nothing but DVDs and old VHS tapes. Goldy came in the room and helpfully stuck her wet nose in each of the cabinets Linda opened. Linda ruffled the fur on her head absentmindedly.

Next Linda wondered if he might have dumped anything in his old bedroom upstairs. He'd been sleeping on the sofa bed so long that Linda had almost forgotten that it wasn't his original room. Goldy followed her upstairs, clearly hoping that if she stuck by Linda's side she'd eventually be taken for a walk. Linda opened the closet door first and shook her head. Clothes were piled to the height of her head with not a single thing on a hangar. If Matt's papers were in there, she wasn't sure anyone but an archaeologist would ever find them. The top of Matt's desk was spilling over with old issues of hunting magazines and *Sports Illustrated* issues. Linda decided at some point she needed to restore this part of her house from the modern dumpster look to a clean spare bedroom, but that was not the focus of today's activities. She almost dismissed the idea of even opening the desk drawers as it was obvious that he'd been piling crap on top of the desk for so long that the drawers must be overstuffed. To her great surprise though, Linda had success in the bottom drawer of his schoolboy desk. Two brown government-issue envelopes had been jammed into the small drawer. Linda had to stick her hand partially in the drawer to push the papers flatter in order to get the drawer open.

Linda sat down on the bed, opened the first envelope and found a pile of Matt's medical records that she had already seen and a postcard from Rico. The front of the postcard showed a prototypically glorious Monterey, California sunset. On the back, Rico had written, "Dear Matt, Man, I was sorry to hear you're out. You were the best teammate I ever had, and nobody can shoot better than you. Lovin' it here in California, and I get to see Mom more often. Let me know if you're ever out on the West Coast. Rico" Linda started to stuff the postcard back in the envelope, but then she thought she might be able to submit it as a character reference. Or if the Army wouldn't take the postcard, maybe she could find Rico and get him to write a fresh letter.

Linda moved on to the next envelope. The first page had a VA seal in the top center of the page, so she scanned the text until she found the magic words character of service determination. "Woohoo," she exclaimed. The VA letter indicated that in order to conduct the character of service determination they needed his military service records as well as a statement on the circumstances surrounding the discharge. Linda already had his service records, and she could help Matt draft a statement of why his one episode of being AWOL after years of exemplary service was not willful or persistent misconduct, hopefully without stressing him out. She felt hopeful that even if Matt wasn't likely to get a discharge upgrade yet, she could at least get the VA to provide him with health benefits. Helping Matt get stable access to mental health care was the most important thing she could do for him. She gathered the papers to take to the computer. Goldy stood up at this and put her head hopefully on Linda's lap.

Linda looked into the shiny brown eyes and said, "You're right, sweetie. I've made progress. I found the stuff, and I know what I need to do next. We deserve a walk."

* * * * *

Ever since Linda realized that Siobhan had figured out about her thefts of pills, Linda had felt awkward whenever she saw Siobhan at the park. She had gone so far as to scan out her front windows before heading out to make sure Siobhan wasn't there, and if she was, Linda huddled in the house until she saw Siobhan head back toward her house. Linda however realized that it was Siobhan's wakeup call that had finally arrested Linda's slide into addiction and unemployment; she should be thanking Siobhan not hiding behind the tacky flowered living room curtains left over from her mother. Linda decided she needed to be brave, and on a sunny but cool Friday afternoon when she saw Siobhan unleash her two chocolate labs at the far end of the park, she opened the front door and released Goldy directly from the house to run into the park.

The two women approached each other. Siobhan greeted Linda, "Hi Linda, How's it going?"

"Well, I've finally got two good knees."

"That's terrific."

The dogs were cavorting, and the women were silent.

Linda forced herself to start, "You know, I had no idea how much knee surgery hurt. And I've been a nurse for almost thirty years now, but I never had to go through anything like that before. I mean, I was an ER nurse back when I first started. I've seen hundreds of people come in hurt. And likewise I've seen hundreds of 'em come in hooked on pain pills. Since I'd never taken them myself until the knee surgery, I didn't have a whole lot of sympathy for people who came through the orthopedic ward and would tell me that they didn't start out intending to get hooked on them."

Linda was having a hard time looking up at Siobhan.

"I guess I've got a much better understanding of what my patients have been through. Thank God I had my sister who happens to be a nurse. She took care of me after both surgeries, and for the second one, she hid my pills in her house. She doled them out like they were gold doubloons. Not one minute before I was due for the next one. And she tapered me right off them."

She finally met Siobhan's gaze. Siobhan said, "Well, I'm glad to see you back out here at the park, and I'm sure you're glad to have all that behind you. And really, I get it. I know you had some issues with your son as well as your own surgeries. After my brother died, my mom spent the next thirty years sneaking back into her bedroom to take Valium; they became her coping mechanism lickety-split."

"Well, I've got two brand new knees. I better not ever have any need for pain pills again."

Siobhan suddenly cried out, "No, no" and started running toward the pile of dogs. Goldy was in the middle of the tangle, with the two chocolate labs on either side rolling in the one mud puddle left in the park after the rains of the previous week, looking a bit like a canine sandwich cookie with Goldy as the icing in between.

Linda offered, "I've got a hose on my deck if you want to rinse them off before you walk home." As the dogs stood up, they shook muddy water off themselves.

Siobhan replied, "I'll take you up on that offer. Otherwise I'll be soaked with mud by the time I get home."

The two women brought the dogs over to Linda's deck. They worked as a team to hose the worst of the mud off the three dogs. The first of Siobhan's to be done found a sunny patch of the deck to sprawl on.

"Well, Godiva looks right at home," Linda observed. "Now that I'm done with all these problems with my knees, I'll be happy to watch the dogs for you whenever you need a sitter. It's the least I could do for you," Linda looked up at Siobhan.

"You don't owe me anything, but I'll definitely take you up on the dog-sitting anyway."

Siobhan was finally able to coax her two back on their leashes to leave their friend. Linda reach out and touched Siobhan's arm, "Really, thank you."

Siobhan looked embarrassed and mumbled, "No, just glad it's all over."

Siobhan headed off. Linda exhaled heavily and leaned against the deck rail. She had come so close to ruining everything important in her life. She was glad to see that she'd managed not to ruin the relationship with Siobhan. Siobhan had known but never outright stated that she knew Linda was the thief, and Linda had not ever outright admitted her opioid problem, and the conversation they just had was as far as they needed to go.

Linda stared out at Lord's Creek while Goldy dried in the last of the afternoon sunlight, and then returned inside to work on Matt's paperwork. After about two hours of paperwork, Linda went out on her deck with a bottle of beer looking out at the fireworks from further down the river. Every year on this date, a family across the river lit fireworks on the anniversary of their daughter Beatrice's death. The cloudy evening made the fireworks indistinct, hazy smudges of reds and greens over top of the smoky smudges of the low-lying clouds, looking for all the world like a battle off in the distance. She had won her battle with the pain pills. Sadly, her battles were not over. The battles can never be over when it's for your kid.

ABOUT THE AUTHOR

Ms. Sausville earned her B.A. from Cornell University, her M.P.H. from the Johns Hopkins University School of Hygiene and Public Health, and her J.D. from the University of Maryland School of Law. She lives near fictional Lord's Creek with her husband and two cats.

Ms. Sausville was inspired to write this novel by her pro bono work with veterans and their families seeking benefits from the VA. A portion of any profits from the sale of this book will be donated to charities assisting veterans.

61068915R00158

Made in the USA
Middletown, DE
17 August 2019